Everything in my life l
left with this big chunk c
thought should be a certain
easy as I'd thought it was going to be. And that realization left me unsteady and unsure.

I settled back in the seat and studied Noah. The knowledge of what could happen when I was alone with him hung unspoken between us. The hole inside me began to disappear. I could forget about all the things that weren't going the way I wanted them to. So long as I was with him.

Kissing Noah had made it easy to forget who I was. There was something in the way he never seemed to give a damn and yet always showed up when I needed him.

If I closed my eyes I could see him with the barrel of the gun pressed against his forehead, daring the redneck to pull the trigger. The reckless insanity of it was one of the sexiest things I'd ever seen. Sharper, roughened edges hadn't attracted me until now. Noah had the sort that cut deep.

He was the escape I craved, no matter how infuriating he was. But what could I do about it?

As the needle on the speedometer crept farther from the one-hundred-mark, I made a decision. The car wasn't the only thing that could move fast.

Full Tilt Boogie

by

Leslie Scott

Arkadia Fast, Book 3

This is a work of fiction. Names, characters, places, and incidents are either the product of the author's imagination or are used fictitiously, and any resemblance to actual persons living or dead, business establishments, events, or locales, is entirely coincidental.

Full Tilt Boogie

Contact Information: info@thewildrosepress.com

Cover Art by *Jennifer Greeff*

The Wild Rose Press, Inc.
PO Box 708
Adams Basin, NY 14410-0708
Visit us at www.thewildrosepress.com

Publishing History
First Champagne Rose Edition, 2020
Trade Paperback ISBN 978-1-5092-3159-1
Digital ISBN 978-1-5092-3160-7

Arkadia Fast, Book 3
Published in the United States of America

Dedication

To Shiloh, for seeing the best in me and my characters and for loving us as much as I love her.

Chapter One

I lived my life six-hundred-sixty-feet at a time. A full-on baptism of speed and adrenaline. Racing was in my blood, the definition of who I was, and the reason I shoved my ass into a pair of men's skinny jeans, tucked my hair beneath an obnoxious yellow helmet, and climbed into the most ridiculous excuse for a race car I'd ever seen.

I couldn't breathe without the surge of exhilaration that tingled across my chest and outward to my extremities.

"Hurry, go, get out of here before someone sees you!" I snapped before flicking down the helmet's visor.

My less talented racer bestie, Isaac, was wearing an almost identical outfit to the one I'd put on when I left my house.

There was no way I was the only person who thought these tight ass pants were ridiculous. But right now, Isaac's piss poor fashion choice worked in my favor. Dig night spectators crowded around the start line. Each one of them assumed that the driver of this buzzing, bastard love child of the transformer Bumblebee was Isaac Morales.

Rick Casey's youngest child—Breanna—was the one on her way to the end of the track in a black hoodie. Where she'd be sitting pretty on a golf-cart waiting to pull Isaac back around to the pits when the race was over.

Spoiler alert—and I didn't mean the atrocity bolted to the back of Isaac's Honda. Turns out, the stupid ricer was a quick little race car—with the right driver behind the wheel. And my genius best friend had gotten pissed, bet a thousand bucks he didn't have on a race he couldn't win, and well…for me, I'd take any excuse to drive.

Isaac's crew rolled me through my burnout and pulled me up to the start line—none the wiser to our deception. To be fair, the two gearheads were probably too hyped up on exhaust fumes to pay much attention to the driver.

No, this was all about the race and the pride on the line. Sure, the money was nice. The extra cushion to my bank account would get me one step closer to ditching Arkadia, Texas. But no—this was pride. Isaac and his crew could puff their chests out and swing their dicks around. But at least Isaac would know I was a badass driver.

Better still, when I could rub his nose in it.

Grudge Night was its own breed of racing awesomeness. A few times a month, after the test and tune guys rolled out—track racers who pay a small fee to make test runs on the track—Vic Morales rented out the local drag strip. Any yahoo with a signed waiver and a set of steel balls could race his car for the buy-in. That is, if you could find someone to roll to the line against you.

Isaac had found one, all right. Some kid in a murdered out little Chevy truck. See, he'd probably beat Isaac off the start line, never giving Skinny Jeans a chance to ride it out. At the big end, Isaac would start to catch him, but there wouldn't be enough racetrack left.

Not me.

I've ate, drank, and slept street racing since I was twelve years old and sneaked out with my big brother. Vic was always the flagger in Arkadia and Grudge Night was all his—his way. Arm drop starts, not the flashlight he used for the street races.

I knew Isaac's older brother too well. I'd made a study of Vic, I knew his tells, I could tell a millisecond before he dropped his arms no matter how he changed it up. That was the jump this race needed if Isaac didn't want to lose money he didn't have.

So, here I was in an attempt to keep my best friend from having that thousand bucks taken straight out of his ass.

I flipped the switch for the trans-brake, stepped on the gas, and listened intently as the engine built RPMs. The little Honda did its best to roar but sounded more like a weed eater with 'roid rage.

Every fiber of my being hyperaware, I watched Vic with a burning intensity that traveled all the way to my white-knuckled grip on the steering wheel.

He always glanced to his left, over his shoulder for headlights in the distance. His way of ensuring the road was clear for the street race he was about to unleash. Though, we were at the track…he'd still do it. Then a step back, raising his arms and jumping into the air simultaneously.

Not yet.

On his fall back down, his upper lip twitched.

I left off the button as soon as his lip wiggled and shot off the line at the exact second he swung his arms downward. Which was a breath before the guy in the tricked-out pickup left and all the head start I needed.

The grating buzz of the engine mutated to a roar—and for four seconds, everything surged by me in a torque powered rush. Nothing else mattered. I wasn't suffocated by the expectations of my family, stifled by the limitations of our small town. No, for those few seconds I existed on a plane apart from who I was.

In this quiet moment, caught between speed and disaster, I lived for the thrill of the race. It was better than sex. Or, better than I imagined sex to be.

I was trembling when I crossed the finish line. I gripped the steering wheel as much to center myself as to hold the car straight.

I didn't need to look over my shoulder to know I'd won, I'd never seen the pickup.

There were no chutes to pull, so I let off the gas and coasted to the very end of the track where there were no lights and Isaac waited in the golf cart.

As soon as the black truck took the turn toward the pits, Isaac hopped off the golf cart and tossed my hoodie into the air in celebration. His elation apparent.

I killed the engine and stopped the small, annoying, yellow car. My chest thick and tight with the full body punch of the high of winning. I'd never done drugs. I doubted any of them could ever compare to what I felt as I killed the engine and climbed from the car, leaving Isaac's helmet and race jacket behind.

"Got him!" I shouted and jumped on Isaac—who caught me in midair with a wiry strength nothing short of impressive.

"Yes! Girl, you are on fire! Treed the shit outta that guy. I saw it from here."

He dropped me to the ground where I retrieved my hoodie and ran my hands through my hair. "Next time, don't write checks your ass can't cash." I scolded him but smiled victoriously.

"You drive like that and I'll write all sorts of checks, Casey!" His eyes were wide and bright even in the darkness.

We did a jumping fist-bump we'd perfected in middle school. I didn't have the heart to rub it in his face that I was the one who saved his ass—again. I wanted my friends to be happy, especially those as important to me as Isaac. But I'd never tell *him* that. Then he might get all sappy and sentimental.

Ain't nobody got time for that. I wanted to *drive*. I was ready to climb back in and do it all over again. Run a hot lap, double or nothing.

Isaac had other ideas. Which included how he got all the adulation and glory. I *should* be used to this part. This wasn't our first hustle.

I told myself I was okay with Isaac getting all the glory, so long as I got to race. In Arkadia, under my dad and brother's watchful gazes this was the closest thing to being a race car driver I could get.

Still, driving the golf cart back while Isaac was the hero in the Honda, slapping high fives and fist bumps…grated.

"Breezy!" he called over the crowd, waving a fan of hundred-dollar bills—half of which were mine. "Let's go celebrate!"

I was down with jettisoning the seed of resentment settling in my gut, but first, to ditch the skinny jeans.

****

The Rooster's gravel parking lot was near to overfilling by the time I wheeled my beat-up old shop truck in beside the building. What better way to celebrate victoriously than rednecks and cigarette smoke.

At least there'd be tequila and dancing.

Isaac rolled his eyes as I hopped out of my truck, wedge heels clattering against the gravel. I'd traded in the no shape men's pants and tank for a teensy-tiny gold fringe dress that left almost all of my incredibly long legs bare.

Thankfully, I'm also small enough in the boob area that going without a bra for the strapless getup wasn't an issue.

I wiggled my hips and sent the sparkling jangly bits shimmering. "You said it was a party."

"I *didn't* plan on defending your honor all night."

I snorted. Through high school and beyond, Isaac and my other surrogate brothers had ruined every opportunity for anything resembling sex in my life. Hell, my sister had ended up *engaged* to one of them. Dating within the circle was the only way I saw working around the proverbial chastity belt my brother Aiden and his bunch had made for me. And that was just too weird.

"Since when did you become chivalrous, Lancelot?"

He took one look around, gestured with his hand across the dirt parking lot that had long since forgotten it was gravel. "Since we're partying in the badlands. If something happens to you here, Vic will tan my ass."

A group of gearheads, the same that had been at Grudge Night, fell in line behind us. A wanna-be outlaw draped his arm around my shoulder and winked at Isaac. His name was Brody, and he smelled like he drowned in Abercrombie to cover up his single guy sleaze. “Ah come on, Isaac. Bree will fit right in with this crowd.”

He did that creepy thing where guys openly ogle you.

I shrugged his arm off and made a face. “If creepy branded a cologne, they’d call it Brody. Don’t you have a dark alley to be in so we could *not* meet?”

Isaac laughed as Brody backed off, scorn twisting his features.

My best friend’s eyes narrowed protectively.

“He’s *your* friend,” I hissed under my breath.

Isaac and I had separated from the rest of the group as we often did. So much alike—the boy version of me in truth. Maybe less of a smartass.

“I don’t have a crew, for real. It’s hard to find people other than you or my brother that actually know what they’re doing. Brody does and if he left, he’d probably take Adam with him. Adam knows his shit too.” Isaac’s voice was pleading. Not that he needed my permission, but it was obvious we both knew I could make his life really hard if I didn’t let Brody’s presence slide.

I cast my eyes to the dark heavens, shaking my arms to rid myself of impending annoyance. A multitude of stars twinkled brightly, a reminder of how far out in the sticks the Rooster Barn was. Each one of those stars was another solar system. Life was much bigger than Arkadia, Texas.

And here I was, at the same shithole bar with the same group of people, doing the same crap we always did. Racing for Isaac, every once in a while, wasn’t enough—I needed more.

"Let's go, Breezy!" Isaac and the others had moved ahead of me now, closer to the entrance.

"She's just worried they ain't gonna let her in, and she got all dressed up for nothing!" Brody snickered, his lips curling up into the shadow of the dark moustache that trailed to his goatee.

Adam, the bigger of the two, a mixed kid with clear green eyes, ribbed him with his elbow.

"If not, I'll bug out with you." Isaac doubled-back. Even he was several months older than me and already twenty-one.

"Nah—usually don't come here with an entourage." I hitched a shoulder, I'd rather them think I was worried about not making it past the doorman than my contemplations of a deeper matter.

Brody snorted. "Yeah, sure, you hang out at the Rooster all the time."

"I told you I could get in, right?" I flipped my hair and stalked by him saucily.

Neither Adam nor Isaac hid their grins.

"Careful now, I'm betting you're overdressed for Bud Light in the parking lot of Daddy's speed shop."

"Just watch." I scanned for my favorite door guy. Dude was large, about Jordan's size, with hammy hands and a booming laugh. I'd once watched him toss Jordan Slater out on his ass as if he'd been the size of a fly.

I caught Kevin's gaze and smiled brightly at Brody when I was waved past the small table where Kevin collected the cover. Beyond, another bouncer let people through the chain across the door. A glance over my shoulder at Isaac proved he wasn't surprised.

"Never had a doubt!" he shouted over the throb of music.

I got to skip the cover charge since Kevin got a discount on parts for his Monte Carlo and free delivery from me—fair exchange in my book.

The plastic, yellow chain didn't move. Long fingers, tinged in the creases with the telltale remnants of grease held it still. My gaze traveled up the length of corded muscle to the tattoos that peeked from beneath a short, white shirtsleeve.

There were moments where you sat back and thought, *Oh fuck*. This was that for me. This doorman wasn't Kevin. Almighty Holder of the Door Chain, spent most of his free time making my life a living hell. If there was any doubt of that, it was swallowed up by the toothy sneer he flashed.

I was dressed like a lady, sort of. And my momma always told me it wasn't ladylike to deck a guy while wearing a dress.

No shit. She really did. Those were her exact words when she pulled me off of a boy who said I was too skinny to be any good on his kickball team. Well, I showed him.

Slow flickers of awareness traveled from my middle, outward. A tightness coiled in my chest. Damn.

My upper lip curled in defense of my physical response to Noah McKay's sexy ass grin. Seriously, he could melt my panties off with a smile like that; before he ripped into me with some sort of scathing remark. Ugh. Why did he have to be so hot?

Chapter Two

I pushed my strappy heels into the concrete, solidifying my foundation and readying for a fight. If Noah denied me entrance, I'd throw a fit, and Kevin damn sure wouldn't get any more deals.

My dad's voice echoed in my head. A stern reminder that Noah worked for the family and should be treated with respect.

Yeah…no.

He raised one perfectly arched eyebrow at Kevin, who nodded his assent across the crowd.

I shivered despite the loathing that tightened my lips when the tall, lanky mechanic leaned close and whispered in my ear. Noah's breath was hot as it blew my hair and cascaded down my neck. "What would big brother say about you hanging out in a place like this?"

With the tip of one finger, I pushed his chin away from me, stopping a millisecond before I traced the paper-thin scar across his lower lip.

Two could play this little game. "I think where I go to shake my ass is going to be of less concern than the fact you let me do it."

I winked, ducked under the chain he raised, and descended into beer-soaked hell. The Rooster Barn claimed to be the loudest honky-tonk in Texas. The loud part was true, the honky-tonk part…not so much.

Gearheads and grease monkeys weren't the

dancing type. So we crowded in the corner, picking up a few more familiar faces. Though, I'd soon consumed enough tequila to forget the names attached to those faces.

I plopped down next to Isaac on a busted old leather couch. He was half wrapped around a pretty girl with an olive complexion and purple tipped dark hair. One of those names I didn't remember. Judging from the row of empty glasses on the table in front of him, I doubted Isaac could either.

"Breezy!" He hooked his free arm around me and the new girl glared daggers. I laughed and undraped his arm from my shoulder.

He glanced at Purple Tips and grinned, his eyes glassy and bloodshot. "See, you can't be my wingman when you're dressed like that, homie."

"Don't be salty." I stood from the couch and downed my shot. "The only place for that is with the tequila. I have no interest in Captain Skinny Jeans. He's all yours."

Bending at the waist, I patted Isaac's cheek before leaving in search of more mind-numbing celebration. I imagined he was neck deep in faux cleavage by the time I threaded through the crowd and onto the dance floor.

I lost myself—almost as much as I had during the race—in the pulsating rhythm on the dance floor. My movements were undulating, gyrating, the sort of thing that forced grown men to shove their paychecks into garter belts.

And you know what? I didn't care. If a stranger slid up behind me and kept pace, we danced. It was nothing short of sex with clothes on, but Isaac was too drunk to bitch at me.

It wasn't every weekend your big sister got married, leaving you the last hatchling still in the nest.

Sure, she'd been living with Jordan for more than a year. But she still had my last name. Raelynn wouldn't be a Casey after this weekend. I was losing my sister all over again, and it hurt. It was a shocking pain, one I wasn't ready for.

All night I'd been doing everything I could to get rid of it.

I'd done the bachelorette party in Galveston Beach last weekend, as a good sister should. We'd hung out on the beach and tonight before the races, we'd done the rehearsal dinner. Through the entire process, I'd smiled and pretended to be happy.

Heaven forbid someone called me selfish or pointed out how many problems I'd already caused. I didn't need to be told how much of a screw-up I was. I knew.

The fact made me sick inside.

I left the dance floor abruptly to find the bar.

Two more shots. Tomorrow would be manis and pedis, hair and makeup, photos and vows. I'd officially lose Raelynn to the big oaf. Jordan Slater would love her forever. Now he'd be her family, not me.

I'd lost my brother, twice. He moved one wife out just to find another one to take her place. I liked Hadley, though. She was a good mom. I might keep her as a sister and get rid of Raelynn if forced to choose. I shouldn't complain. But they were moving on and I was here, just me. It was never my time, nothing was ever about me.

I motioned the bartender for a third shot and

ignored the flirtatious comment from the bald biker guy beside me. Pretty sure at some point it was his grubby hands on my ass on the dance floor.

Eew. No, I did not want to mentally recall that image.

The liquor went down much easier now. Since the crash that took Devin from me—from all of us—everything had been a slow downward spiral of shit I couldn't control. Pretty soon I wouldn't remember how much my life sucked.

Back to the dance floor I went, swaying to the beat of some top forty hip-hop song. I was tall, taller still in these shoes. The tiny gold dress added to the degree of attention my height drew. Pretty soon I wasn't alone.

Not only were my siblings leaving me behind, but both my brother *and* my sister were getting laid. The closest to action like that I'd ever had was the creep I was shaking my ass against. I slapped away the fingers he tried to slip up my skirt.

I shrugged him off with a swing of my long hair, half damp with sweat, and made my way back to the bar. Noah was over with Isaac and the rest of the crew. The two of them had their heads together talking about something important, judging by the animated expression on Isaac's face. Probably telling Noah all about that race he won.

Then McKay turned to me and our gazes caught. Places the dirty dancing hadn't warmed in me heated then.

I turned away and pitched back another shot.

More dancing.

More wandering hands and throbbing bodies from strangers without faces.

Or maybe they had faces and the tequila I drank had faded them away. Whatever. A hard stomp onto the top of their foot usually sent them off in the other direction.

Hot, sweating, and my head swimming, I stumbled from the dance floor to the hallway that led to the women's restroom. I didn't really have to pee, but I needed to catch my breath and find my bearings again. I'd crossed the threshold of self-control that usually got me in trouble.

I mean, yeah, I'd complain that I'd never made it past third base. But in truth, I hadn't found anyone I wanted to take me home yet. Well, there were a few seconds when Noah McKay had gone to work for us that I might have contemplated him.

Especially nights like tonight when I couldn't tell one face from another.

Collapsing with my back against the wall, I took my place in line with a sad-looking group of what might pass as ladies. Too much makeup, hairspray, and perfume. They all glared at me, making it no secret that my youth was offensive.

If I'd had the energy, I'd have flicked them off.

There was a sort of buzzing hum of conversation as attention shifted from me to the guy who slipped into the hallway. He was that sort of guy, long-legged and lean, with the T-shirt tight enough you could see the muscle vibrate beneath the material.

He took up a post against the wall across from me. Which did little to put me in the good graces of my companions. Tall Dark and Fuck Me Now stretched one arm across his chest and hooked it on his elbow.

I did my best to ignore Noah McKay. The line

steadily moved forward to make room for two more jealous bitches. All the while he and I stayed locked in the equivalent of a third-grade silent staring contest.

Annoyed, I broke first and fisted a hand on my hip. "What?"

His head tilted to one side and his chin jutted forward, but he didn't answer. I searched his dark blue eyes for any sign of what was going on in his head.

Nothing.

I braced for whatever asshole thing he was going to say to me, for the judgment he was going to pass. When even that didn't happen, I dropped my arm and huffed a sigh filled with resentment. I'd crushed on him when he first went to work for Dad and Aiden. Right up until I figured out that there was something about me that rubbed him the wrong way.

"Ugh." I turned as the bathroom opened for my turn. Noah's wide palm on the door kept it from shutting.

I didn't bother fighting him on it. I wasn't afraid of him. This wasn't my first dressing down by the holier than thou Noah McKay. The prick.

And then he surprised me—he followed me in and locked the door behind him.

Oh boy, too bad this wouldn't end up like my first fantasies of him.

When I turned back, ready for a fight—fight wasn't what I saw in his eyes. My body responded, almost like it had a mind of its own. Gooseflesh despite the heat, my nipples hardened, and my stomach tightened. *Damn.*

Then whatever it was I saw vanished, replaced with a cruel twist of his lips.

“What do you think you’re doing, Breanna?”

“Having a great night out. Or I was until you locked me in the bathroom.”

He pinched the bridge of his nose as if I were giving him a headache. “In less than two hours you’ve had at least four guys all over you. Your friends are flat wasted, and I’m pretty sure you’ve drunk your weight in Jose.”

I hitched myself up onto the small sink, my knees practically brushing his middle as he wedged himself between me and the lone stall door. Above us the fluorescent light flickered behind its dirty, beige cover.

“Which is it that you object to the most, McKay? My drunken debauchery or my whorish ways?”

The dark blue of his eyes got lost behind thick lashes when they narrowed. “Currently? Your tone.”

I gripped the edge of the sink for balance and leaned close to him, rubbed my cheek against his, much as he’d done on my way in. The stubble there tickled my skin in a way that added a huskiness to my tone when I whispered, “Fuck you, Noah McKay. Remind me of why I’m supposed to give a shit what you think?”

There were a great many ways he could react. One of these days I’d push him to a point that he’d snap on me. Why he gave two shits was lost on me.

I wasn’t remotely prepared when his hands clutched my knees, their calloused strength sending coiling heat up my body, straight to all the places I’ve never known existed, and drying my mouth.

His eyes were filled with heavy-lidded arousal when I leaned back and caught his gaze. My heart hammered wildly in my chest, drowning out the irritated pounding on the bathroom door.

Was it the liquor that forced the gentle moan from me when he slid between my legs and grasped my thighs?

Probably not. He hesitated with his rock-hard chest against mine, his breath fanning across my face. I could say no, stop him.

I didn't want to. Our faces were so close, I could practically taste his lips on mine.

With the practiced ease of a predator sinking his teeth into his prey, he caught my mouth with his and kissed me sober.

Urgent, strong fingers dug into my skin as he raked his hands up my legs to my thighs, then higher. The dress inched up past my hips until he took a hard grip on my thighs.

I'd never been fully aroused in my life, not until that moment. *More. More. More.* Desperately I wanted more.

Noah's kiss was shocking, heating me and leaving me covered in chills all at the same time. His tongue took possession, claimed me, and left me practically begging for things I didn't comprehend. I'd seen Noah McKay a thousand times, fantasized about him in a thousand ways, and never once had I imagined he would kiss like this.

"That shut you up," he whispered huskily against my throat, his lips trailing down my neck to my breasts. I wanted that hot, sweet mouth there, and other places too.

This was a first for me. Desire. Potent, strong, and invigorating. I could escape all the things in my life that weren't going my way. For the first time, I wanted a guy bad enough to lose my virginity.

Doing just that was suddenly *very* important.

"Noah," I gasped and for the first time touched him. I pushed his shirt up and allowed myself to stroke the soft skin that stretched across corded muscle. *Holy shit.*

Moisture pooled in my mouth and other places as I sought out his lips again. This time I kissed him, *hard.* We were both gasping when the banging on the door reached its crescendo.

Noah caught my gaze and with one look shattered whatever goodwill I'd had until that moment. My pride bruised but didn't break at the regret that flashed in his eyes.

"I'm sorry, Breanna." He pushed away from the counter and me. "I shouldn't have done that."

Chapter Three

Silence was deafening when you're swimming in your own disillusion. I sat on that cold, time-stained sink for what seemed like eternity after the door shut behind Noah. It took that long for my body to stop trembling and my head to stop spinning.

I blamed the flush on my chest and the bad taste in my mouth on being well on my way to drunk. A guy couldn't make me feel like this, no way. Especially not Noah McKay's punk ass.

He walked away from me.

Anger, the one emotion I was *always* prepared for flared to life white hot. The tears that burned at the back of my eyes weren't sad. Ashamed, betrayed even, but I was pissed. The dilapidated counter groaned as I squeezed it.

He kissed me stupid, turned me inside out, then just walked away. The look in his eyes spoke volumes. He hadn't *wanted* to kiss me.

And yet? He'd responded to me, hell he'd let off that trans-brake and sent us careening down the track. How could he have *not* wanted it?

I wouldn't call myself a genius or anything, but I wasn't stupid. Confusion was new for me, and I didn't like it at all. If I ever got my fingers around his neck, I would throttle him. That he was an employee be damned.

No longer shaking, I hopped from the counter and prayed my knees were steady. They held, barely. Long enough for me to jerk open the door and flick off the bitch with the teased hair that tried for a snarky remark.

I wasn't in the mood.

Isaac was still on the beat-up couch, mostly passed out in Purple Tips' lap.

"You good?" I lifted my leg and toed him in the stomach with my sandal.

Fighting to control my temper, I ignored the stink eye his *date* was giving me. "Yo, Morales, you good?"

His eyes fluttered open and his lips slowly spread into the drunken impression of a grin. "Yeah, Breezy, I'm solid."

It was past time to go, and we always left together. That was the plan. Plus, I wasn't leaving him here like this. I picked up his arm and dropped it limply on his side. "More like a limp noodle."

"He ain't limp, bitch." Purple Tips stroked his face, and his smile grew even goofier.

Good Lord, he was a moron when he was drunk.

"Suck it, Elvira Fake Tits." I snapped and jerked Isaac up by his shirtfront.

"Whoa!" He was laughing as he fell against me.

The chick's face twisted in outrage. I gave her my mom's thousand-yard stare, and she backed right down. I'd have flicked her off, too, but was too busy steadying a swaying Isaac.

"We're leaving," I told him with a grunt as I hefted one arm over my shoulder.

"My tab—"

I reached into his pocket, pulled out a wad of cash, and tossed two bills on the rickety table. The rest I fisted as we started an inebriated impression of a two-step toward the exit.

This was all I needed, a drunk best friend when I needed him to be coherent. Not necessarily to defend my honor, but to at least listen as I unloaded about the bathroom make-out session.

We made it through the door and to the parking lot before Brody chased after us. Followed by Adam and a few of those fuzzy faces I couldn't remember.

"Isaac, bro, where you going? The party's just getting started!" Brody's voice echoed off the cars in the parking lot.

Isaac's abrupt stop nearly toppled us both from the sidewalk. I kept us from eating gravel—but only barely.

"Yo, Brody!" Isaac threw a hand up in the air in a wobbly salute.

"No, we're leaving." I tugged him back forward to the cars. Usually, he listened to me. That he wasn't was the most aggravating fact. If not for the jumbled-up emotions Noah left me with, I would probably be shouting at Isaac by now.

"You don't want to go, do ya, bro?" Brody lunged forward but didn't reach for Isaac.

Instead, he caught me by my elbow. He didn't know me well but released his grip when the blatant indignation must have shown on my face.

I was good and ready for a fight. As Brody's hand fell away, Breanna Casey roared to life.

"You know what, Isaac. Stay your drunk ass with this chump." I reached into his pocket again and came up with his keys. "But, I'm keeping these and the money."

Which, I figured, was the only real reason all these

people were flocking to Isaac tonight, anyway. Had he not been shit faced he'd have seen it too.

"Chump?" Brody snorted, his face mocking.

"Yeah. A chump. A wasted white boy with no cash, no car, and no girl. You're a pretender. Ain't shit, won't never be shit."

He moved as if he'd step to me—then thought better of it. Apparently remembering who'd come after him if he did. Jordan Slater, Aiden Casey, and Vic Morales were their own brand of badass.

"Whatever, man."

"If you about it, Brody, be about it."

Isaac was oblivious, fumbling for a cigarette. I sighed. It wasn't worth it. Fisting Isaac's keys and cash, I gave Brody my own one-fingered salute.

On a sharp pivot, I went the other direction.

"See you at the wedding!" Isaac's wobbly shout chased me.

Another thing I didn't want to think about. No more sister. No race car. Making deliveries for my dad. Stuck in this stupid shit town.

How dare Noah make out with me, make me feel things, and then just walk away. The ass. He probably did it on purpose to make me look stupid.

Well, I wasn't. I wouldn't be falling for that one again. Fool me once and all that.

The early morning darkness left the air with a chill that cooled my skin, early spring making itself known. I was halfway to my truck—away from the lights and crowd at the door—when Mr. Grabby Hands from the dance floor showed up.

"Where you off to, sugar?" he crooned.

I winced. Not attractive. I wasn't anyone's sugar. I

absently patted my hip for a pocket full of peppermints that was nonexistent in the tiny dress.

Shit.

Inside he'd given the impression of a dude in his early thirties with a semi-appealing face. Now, with the alcohol fog lifted, he was a skeevy looking guy in his forties who'd spent at least a nickel in prison.

He grabbed me by the waist, and I did the only thing a girl like me could do—I punched him right in the nose. "Get lost, pervert."

Shaking my now throbbing free hand I continued on my way, satisfied that I finally expelled some of the anger that ebbed inside me.

His two buddies stepped in front of me. "Come on now, honey. You don't move like that and not want to party. Not when you got that kind of cash on you."

Double shit.

I had most of Isaac's winnings in my hand, in the middle of the parking lot of the Rooster. I knew better than to do something like that. Noah and his kiss had me all screwed up.

"You can't be serious." I laughed; I couldn't help it. Until this moment I'd figured idiots like this only lived in after-school specials and fathers' nightmares. Especially in Arkadia, where my brothers' reputations kept me in a protective wrapping.

One of them backed me into the guy with the swelling nose. "Oh, I'm gonna make you like this, bitch."

For the first time that night, hell maybe in my entire life, real fear sliced through me like a blade. It cut right into the core of me, turning everything cold and my hands clammy. The third guy, standing off to the side, steadily eyed the roll of bills I'd taken from Isaac.

"Bitch I may be, but my nuts are bigger than yours." I stabbed my spiked heel into his foot as hard as I could. When he stumbled back and wrapped his arms around my middle I lashed out with my feet, keeping the money I'd raced for tucked close to my body.

Dude smelled worse up close. His deodorant desperately needed reapplication. I swallowed down bile as I fought against his hold. Behind me, he stumbled but held fast like a wall. My heart pounded in my throat.

I kicked and screamed, more angry than scared now—the upside to adrenaline. I nailed at least one of his buddies in the eye with my heel.

"Let her go, mother fucker," came a menacing rumble from behind me. My savior jerked the guy around by the neck and threw him to the ground as if he'd weighed nothing.

I stumbled, the money and Isaac's keys hitting the gravel. I followed, landing hard on my knees and crawling after it. Snatching it from the ground before the one guy who'd been watching it could grab it.

We were garnering the attention of the people gathered at the door, blocking the cavalry's exit. The shouts from Kevin and the other bouncers had risen above the din.

Noah McKay was wiry, almost twenty years younger, but no less intimidating. There were three of them and one of him. But as I scrambled to my feet behind him, his feet wide set and his arms loose and ready at his sides—I liked his odds.

He landed a gut punch to the third goon before

slamming his knee into the guy's face and sending him to the ground too. I'd seen my brother fight and Jordan. Hell, all of them. But none of them moved like Noah.

Each motion effortless and clean, no energy wasted. If anyone watching had ever wondered how he'd ended up a doorman at a place like this—they didn't now.

This was one of the single most sexy things I'd ever seen. Not a damn one of them landed a punch. Granted, they were drunk, and he wasn't. It was like watching a choreographed stunt sequence.

I remembered being told he was in the Marines before coming to Arkadia. The way he fought now was a violent reminder.

Dude who'd gone for the money pulled out a gun and fired once in the air. The sound of the shot from the black handgun reverberated off the side of the building and broke through the night.

My chest seized tight as he aimed it right at me.

"I ain't playing this shit. The money, now, bitch."

Chapter Four

I froze with shock. This wasn't sexy or funny anymore. Reality went off like a bomb, slapped me in the face, and left me reeling. Eight hundred bucks wasn't worth dying over, not in the grand scheme of things.

But I was stupid enough to cling to it like a lifeline. I'd won this money—half of it. Fair and square.

"The money, hand it over." Goon with a gun reached for the roll of cash with his free hand.

Clutching it tightly, I took a step back, opening a space between the two of us that hadn't been there before. The *hell* if I'd just hand over my money, fear or no fear. This was a nice chunk to put away to get out of this town, to *be* somebody. Money I raced for.

The silver barrel of the gun glinted against steel painted black. Panic swallowed up my smart-ass retort. At any moment a ball of hot, lethal metal would come flying out of that dark hole and end me.

I blinked once and opened my eyes. The back of Noah's head filled my field of vision. He'd slid in the space between the gun and I and walked forward, shouting words I couldn't hear over the resounding throb of blood in my ears.

For the first few steps, the guy's jowls vibrated with shock. Noah took another step until the barrel pressed against his forehead.

I gulped down tequila laced bile.

"You're not going to shoot anybody. Not her, not me. You shoot me, fine, I'll be dead and you'll be in prison." His words were coated with quiet menace. "You know what I hate? Pussies who pull guns with no intention of squeezing the trigger."

The other two—the would be rapists—scrambled away from the scene, abandoning their friend to this crazy guy who wasn't the least bit intimidated by the weapon. I didn't though. I stayed stark still, watching it unfold like a bad dream. If Noah died that would suck on an epic level, one I couldn't comprehend.

Losing someone was always horrible. Even if you only liked him at the damnedest times. Like now. Emotion clutched my heart and propelled me after the two men.

Apparently tired of the bullshit, Noah moved with a speed I hadn't imagined possible. With a quick, twist of the guy's wrist, he had the gun. With an ease borne of practice the chamber emptied with a pop and the magazine tumbled to the hard-packed rocky ground.

The other guy, outrage pulling his features tight and reddening his cheeks, lunged. Noah cracked the butt of the weapon across the dude's face hard enough to send him sprawling on top of the discarded rounds, unconscious.

Nostrils flaring, white knuckling the gun, Noah rounded on me. Damn, the violent edge flickering in his eyes was sexier than anything I'd ever seen. I stopped breathing.

"I'm taking her home," he shouted at Kevin.

The doorman made a rather impressed face and nodded before disappearing around the corner of the building.

When the fingers of Noah's free hand encircled my wrist, the electric shock jerked my breath out in an audible whoosh. I stumbled along after him, mentally cursing the strappy sandals.

At my truck, he spoke to me for the first time. The adrenaline rolling off him was so potent I could almost touch it. His chest rose and fell heavily with each breath and his blue eyes were wild, dangerous. "Keys, Breanna."

Pulling free from his grasp, I moved to the fender with awkward jerky motions and spoke dumbly. "I didn't have pockets. So—" I reached into the front wheel well and dug out my key.

He took it and opened the door, gesturing me inside. I took one long, assessing look at him. The tension loosened from his shoulders, his nostrils had stopped flaring, and the violence in his eyes dimmed somewhat.

A good distance away, my attackers were being hefted up and collected by Rooster security.

The gripping aftereffects of the moment still clung to me. I swallowed once and said quietly, "I can't go home right now."

He bit his bottom lip and held my gaze until I fidgeted with the money and keys I still held. "Fine. Get in."

I did, stopping long enough to pull my skirt down as far as possible for modesty's sake.

Noah sighed. "I've already seen it, Breanna. Move over."

I cracked my window, letting in the cool breeze. But, that did little to soothe the stifling, thick air that weighed down on me. It was weird riding shotgun in my own truck, weirder still, with Noah McKay driving it.

The echo of my fist against the dashboard broke through the sound of my truck's engine picking up speed on the highway. The glove box popped open with a click. It was filled with empty candy wrappers, old delivery orders, and random bits of paper. I slid the wad of money to the side of it and tossed in Isaac's keys.

Noah's face was illuminated by the strobing orange light from the passing utility poles, allowing me to catch the sidelong annoyed expression he gave when he saw the trash.

My anxiety peaked at that moment. My hands shook as I dug through the mess searching furiously for a piece of candy, a prepackaged cookie, hell a piece of gum would work. Anything sugar laden to appease the gripping mortification seeping in.

I didn't care what he thought of the mess in my glove box. This was spring in Texas, what did he expect to find—gloves? No, everything hit me in that moment. The kiss, Isaac's bizarre drunken betrayal, the gun, and my sister getting married in right around twelve hours.

Like a fiend my face heated, my breath hitched, and beads of sweat formed between my shoulder blades.

Noah's foot lifted from the accelerator and the engine throttled down. "Bre—"

"Oh, thank God!" My fingers wrapped around the small yellow box of lemon drops pushed to the back of the compartment and long since forgotten. Tonight, they were my saving grace.

I ripped the box open like a madwoman and

plopped two in my mouth. I didn't even flinch at the sour first few seconds, instead bit them both in half and let the sweet lemony goodness melt on my tongue. With my eyes closed I spent several long seconds steadying my breath and allowing the candy to soothe me. When I looked, Noah shot me a glance from the driver's seat as he headed down the highway.

"What?" I sat back in the seat and plucked another piece into my mouth. "Something wrong?"

He snorted. "Are you okay?"

"Oh yeah. I mean no, but I will be. I don't think I'm going to freak out or throw up." At least, not as long as he didn't look at me like I was insane.

I was attacked in a parking lot, someone pointed a gun at my face. It would take more than lemon drops to make that go away. But they helped.

"Candy?" And there it was.

"Don't knock it until you try it. Beats smoking." I gestured with my chin at the pack of cigarettes beside his thigh.

"You smoke?"

"Eh, smoked. Tasted like shit. I thought I was being cool."

His face softened, but he shook his head like he didn't believe me.

"Plus, Devin gave me shit about it before he died. After…I just, stopped. Maybe he was right."

Noah stuck out his hand. "Gimme."

I shook out two into his palm, and he dropped them between his lips. I made the mistake of watching him toss the candy around in his mouth and had to turn away.

Aside from the insanity of the fight, there had been

something else. I'd always known Noah had an edge to him, but this was sharper and more violent. Sexier, somehow. Was it wrong of me to find it hot that a guy stepped in front of a gun for me? Probably. Was I going to let that bother me? Not likely.

The rest of it? Yeah, I was still pissed. Which unsurprisingly was difficult. He had saved my life and oddly turned me on while doing it. "For the love of all things holy." I groaned and let my head rap against the back glass.

Adrenaline, anger, whatever it had been that left me momentarily sober slowly sank away. The passing headlights of traffic warbled in my vision and my stomach rolled.

It was becoming quickly apparent that I wasn't as okay as I thought I was. He could have died. I could have died. But no—Noah could have died and it would have been my fault.

Never in my life had my emotions been more mixed up.

"Hey, pull over in the school parking lot." I sat up and kicked off my heels. I needed to be as far away from this version of myself as possible.

Chapter Five

Noah swung my truck into the empty lot of the elementary school. As if reading my mind, he pulled into a dark parking space.

"Hop out, I've got to get to my clothes."

He obliged as I did the same on the passenger side. I flipped the seat forward and began digging around for the cloth backpack that held my cutoffs and T-shirt.

"You're changing now?" He lit a cigarette and watched me stoically, like he didn't just lay an epic beat down on three guys.

The way I felt, what I needed to do, wasn't any of his business—of anyone's business. Usually, I made it a point *not* to lie. But there were parts of myself that were for me only. Especially with him. I wasn't giving him any more ammunition to fire at me.

"If my brother or Jordan sees me dressed like this—they'll throw a fit. I'm not taking any chances."

Nothing. No response, not a word. It was like being interrogated by my high school principal…if Mr. Harrison was hot, had kissed me stupid, and defended more than my honor. Okay—it was nothing like that. But still, I was antsy under his scrutiny and clutched my change of clothes like a battle shield to protect myself.

My insecurities, the pain he'd caused me—still not fully eclipsed by what he'd done for me—was too fresh and too raw. Frankly, a guy had never done that to me before. None of it.

"I don't get it"—I waved the small swatch of denim at him over the bed of the truck—"what's with the silent treatment?"

He leaned against the rear fender and gazed across the open expanse of the back. It was dark, but a passing car lit his face just enough for me to make out something I hadn't expected. His jaw was tight, his eyes dilated, and for a moment I thought I saw him tremble.

I glanced away quickly. "You okay?" I tugged the jeans up my hips.

"Yup."

I wasn't buying it. No matter how much we pretended and lied. Neither of us was okay.

"Close your eyes."

Not only did he oblige, but he spun to face the opposite direction. I didn't bother with a bra, just shed the dress and jerked a T-shirt over my head.

Dressed more like myself and thus standing on firmer ground, I tossed my stuff behind the seat and pushed it back. "All right, I'm decent."

Never would I have thought being naked in front of Noah, even with his back turned, would leave me so vulnerable. A compounding of the entire night and too many shots of tequila, piled on. I had at least battled back the nausea by the time I climbed into the passenger seat.

"So, what's the plan?" My voice was much calmer than I felt.

"I'm taking you home." There was a loud metallic thud as he shut his door and put the truck in gear, his profile rigid.

Panic squeezed my throat so tight I croaked, "Y…yo…you can't do that."

He stopped shy of pulling out of the parking lot. "Why the hell not?"

"Because—" Why? I should go home. Raelynn was home, she was getting married in the morning. "—I was drunk at a club I shouldn't have been at, got attacked, *and* a gun pulled on me. Think I wanna listen to how irresponsible I am? How shitty and selfish it is of me to choose the night before my sister's wedding to cause all this drama? No thank you. You can take me back and I'll drop you off at your car. I'm good to drive."

He snorted. "Okay, sure." The sarcasm dripped from both words.

"Then take me to Isaac's house, I'll have him take me to get my truck tomorrow." It wouldn't be the first time I crashed in Isaac's room and forced him to the couch.

"Considering the condition he was in and how his friends treated you, *not* gonna happen." He shook his head like he was speaking to an idiot. "I'm taking you home."

I bristled. "No, you're not."

"*Yes*, I am."

Slowly I pivoted in my seat. "No, you aren't."

I snatched my phone from the dash and jumped out before he could leave. The asphalt was surprisingly cool on my feet as I crossed the empty parking lot and made a beeline straight for the swings on the playground.

Behind me, he cussed. The slam of the driver's door echoed against the school building. I shivered at the lonely, painful sound.

"Get in the fucking truck, Breanna."

"Last time I checked, you weren't the boss of me, *Noah*," I shot over my shoulder. No way in hell he was going to tell me what to do and treat me like a child. Not after he'd treated me like a cheap whore.

The swing creaked and the chains rattled as I turned and plopped onto the seat. Noah had crossed the distance between us, his nostrils flaring with the anger I was accustomed to from him.

"This is ridiculous."

"Hey, I didn't ask you to commandeer my truck and become keeper of all things Breanna. You did that all on your own, pal."

He grabbed both chains and hauled them upward, so that my feet dangled off the ground. The grand display of testicular fortitude did little to dissuade my stubborn nature.

"I grew up with Jordan Slater's huge self, Noah. You don't intimidate me." Obstinate as I was, the lying to him was getting easier.

He did though. I'd watched the crazy jerk walk right into the barrel of a gun and never flinch. Who does that? Plus, I'd had those hands on me. The things they could do, paired with what he could do? Oh yeah, I was shaking in my proverbial boots. Damn him.

Eye to eye, he studied me and his lip curled. "You're saying I should have left you in the parking lot with those thugs? Turned my back and let you get robbed or worse?"

"I had it under control." More lies. Acid lurched in my gut and moisture stung against my eyes. He was right, though. He'd saved me, I hated him for it, and I didn't understand why.

I jutted my chin out in defiance.

"Are you fucking serious right now?" He dropped the swing. The sudden fall took my stomach, and the jerking stop plunged it right back into my middle.

I nearly puked. If I spent any more time around Noah, I was going to need some serious antacid or something.

I laughed, because I couldn't think of anything else to do. "I have to admit, your hero shit was sort of hot." Except, dodge, and evade, turn the argument in a different direction.

That should set him off.

He pressed the heels of his hands to his temples and his eyes widened. "That was *hot*? Have you lost your goddamn mind, Breanna?" He tossed his hands in the air. "Nothing about what happened was hot. Putting someone in a position where they have to hurt someone else or damn near get shot, is *not* hot."

He spun and kicked a rock, it clamored against a piece of chain-link fence. When he spoke to me that way, as if I were stupid and childish, I wanted to throttle him.

He was right. I knew that and I was hiding behind my lies. But he didn't have to be so cruel. I didn't put him in that position. *Shit happens*.

"Yeah, you know all about putting people in positions, don't you?" I wrapped my fingers around the chains to keep from trembling and squeezed my eyes shut. "Get bent, Noah."

The entire night flew by, like someone pressed the fast-forward button on my memories. The race, the dancing, the way he'd kissed the devil out of me, the attack, Noah's reaction.

The night air was sweet when I inhaled a steadying breath. He always did this to me, turned me upside down. Until those few, foolishly provocative moments in the bathroom, I hadn't realized why. How could it be possible that the only guy in my life to really affect me, had to be Noah McKay? I'd only *thought* I had a crush on Devin. It was nothing compared to this.

Memories of Devin flooded in, drowning out everything else the way they often did. The way his entire face lit up when he smiled. The sweet way he'd hug me and tell me about his day and ask about mine. How he was a friend to me, always. I was never just the dumb baby sister.

What would he think of Noah?

Defeated with my current lot in life, I leaned my head against the cool metal links. I couldn't go home, not like this.

"I'm sorry." I had nothing else to say. There was something about Noah tonight, that kept me from pushing when I usually would have. I was tired of lying, tired of it all.

He laughed without humor. "You think it's that easy? This is so much bigger than something you can just apologize for. Breanna, you can't go around half-dressed throwing yourself on any guy within a twenty-foot radius because you think you've got it handled or because watching someone get the shit kicked out of them is attractive."

"I don't do that." I bristled and stood from the swing. I was tall enough that standing in bare feet put me on more even footing with Noah, who was easily six feet tall.

"Don't you?" In an instant, he was so close I could smell him. His chest brushed against mine, which drew my nipples to full attention and left my mouth dry as a Texas river bed.

Dizzy and drunk, caught between Noah and the swing, I faltered. "N…no…"

He traced my bottom lip with his thumb, and it took every ounce of willpower I had not to suck the digit into my mouth. How could someone I despised so much, fill me with such want. I shuddered and shifted my weight to my heels, searching for solid ground.

"Then what do you call what happened at the club?"

The spell he'd cast on me shattered, shards of desire cast away in tiny molten pieces, replaced now by white-hot fury. "Oh hell no. *You* followed *me* into that bathroom, without an invitation. You're the one who kissed me, put your hands all over me, then stormed off without a word."

With a loud smack, I pushed against his chest. Obviously ill-prepared for the force of my shove, Noah staggered back. Room to breathe in, I stepped around him and headed for the truck. "Fuck off, McKay. I'm going home."

"I've got your keys, Breanna." There was the condescension, the attitude that I was too stupid to live.

I laughed. "I'm a Casey, you asshat. I don't need keys." When I was a kid, my dad ran repos part-time. I learned early how to hotwire older model vehicles. My old Ford was easy to pop out the ignition. I had a screwdriver in the glove box for such an occurrence.

The driver's side door was barely open before Noah caged me with his arms and shut it with a loud crack. I was trapped between the cold steel of the truck and the warm iron of his body. My pulse raced and my mouth went dry again. I wasn't the least bit afraid. No, fear was not the emotion that hovered at the core of me.

"How do you do this to me, Breanna? One second I want to strangle you, the next I want to kiss you. And the moment I see another man's hands on you I want to kill him. You think that was all about you out there? No, the moment that bastard touched you I had to fuck him up.

"You make me lose control."

Chapter Six

The symphony of his breathing and the occasional passing of a car on the highway taunted me. His lips so close he might kiss me again. Only this time, I couldn't blame my desire for that on alcohol. I'd found sober in the parking lot of the Rooster and been running on fumes ever since.

I avoided his gaze as long as I could, focusing instead on that scar on his plump bottom lip. The need to trace it with my tongue was so strong my stomach coiled tightly. Brave enough to peek, I was caught in something that took me on the wildest ride of my life. Infinite possibilities were reflected back at me. Not that happily ever after stuff, but the sort of things that people did in the dark…with their clothes off.

I swallowed hard. His earlier rejection all but forgotten.

Then, his eyes softened and everything about him changed. The sudden shift sent me reeling. The sex stuff I could handle, even with my limited experience. But this?

My entire life I always relied on myself, despite any outward appearances. The only person who knew who I really was or the thoughts that tumbled around incessantly in my brain was me.

Devin had come close once but even then he'd only seen Raelynn. Never me.

Backlit by the moon, the keen intelligence in his dark blue eyes missed nothing. There was little doubt he saw right through me and read between all the lines tattooed on my soul. To keep from staggering, I slowly pivoted to face him. I couldn't stop myself, no matter how dangerous I knew letting him kiss me again would be.

The only real crush I'd ever had was Devin and he'd loved my sister. Never once had he looked at me the way Noah was, no one had.

"I can't go home." I pleaded with a whisper and my anger dissipated.

"Why?" His arms fell away and he took the same position he had in the hallway, his left arm stretched across his chest and hooked to his right elbow with that arm hanging loose.

Tears stung the back of my eyes, I blinked them away furiously. There were so many reasons I couldn't go home. How did I choose just one?

"I just can't, okay? You can take me to Isaac and Vic's, I'll be fine there. Okay? Vic won't be wasted, and he's not going to let Brody and his crew hang around. He's as much a big brother to me as Aiden."

Noah inspected me, searching with his gaze to the hidden parts of me. Fear gripped my belly and squeezed.

"You could go home with me."

My heart raced, took a flying leap, and settled somewhere in the middle of my throat. Every fiber of my being was shouting for me to say yes. Even after the way he'd walked out on me at the club.

This was what I'd wanted all along, someone that made me tingle in all the right places, someone I could chase the rush with.

"Why would I do that?"

He smiled in the sort of way that drove women—including me—wild. "Because we both know I wasn't the only one who wanted that kiss."

He wanted it. I opened my mouth, shut it again. Stalling was unlike me. If I thought something, I said it. Why had I paused now? I wasn't about to let my physical reaction to Noah stop me from being myself.

"Then why'd you leave me like you did?"

He tilted his head but said nothing.

I raced for the rush in the same way a junkie goes for a score. The gas pedal was my drug. That I couldn't do it as often as I wanted drove me insane. Tonight was just a taste, a brush of flavor on my tongue to tease me. Sometimes I had to find something different to chase, to keep the resentment at bay.

When Noah touched me, the visceral reaction was so similar it was terrifying. I'd heard the expression *sparks fly* but never experienced it before now. Maybe if I went thrill seeking with Noah, I'd wipe the smug look off his face.

I studied him. His face was angular and perfect, his mouth so tense the scar that stretched across the length of his bottom lip was pulled white.

He was baiting me. My gaze narrowed and I had to fight to keep my upper lip from curling in a snarl.

"You want me to say yes, so you have proof that I throw myself at guys, so you can win that argument?" I trembled, though this time not from barely contained arousal.

He balked but not before I caught a flash of surprise on his face.

"Fine, take me home. Whatever. Just so long as I don't have to deal with you anymore tonight."

"Breanna!"

He reached for me, but I dodged him.

I stalked around the truck and jerked open the passenger door with more effort than necessary. My nostrils flared as I stared straight ahead, refusing to so much as acknowledge his existence when he climbed in.

I could say some pretty awful shit when I was mad, especially if you hurt me. I weighed my options and nothing I had to say to Noah right then was worth my dad firing me over.

"I wasn't baiting you." His voice was soft, like silk, as it slid across the truck and straight into my senses.

My lips twisted. Even his voice was sexy.

I snorted. "Yeah, sure. And if I'd agreed to go home with you, then what?"

He covered his eyes with his right hand, then rubbed it down his face. I'd been around him long enough, annoyed him enough to be well acquainted with the action. "You're like this itch I can't scratch. Half the time I want to throttle you, the other half…I want to kiss you until you can't come up with a smart-ass retort."

Well then.

This was going nowhere or somewhere too fast. I wasn't sure which and in situations like this, I generally ended up doing something stupid. I'd been trying really hard not to keep up that tradition.

"Wow, I found a way to shut her up."

I cut a glance across the dark cab. "I *will* hit you."

A self-satisfied smirk could speak volumes and did little to dull my desire to smack it right off his face. By the time he pulled into my driveway, I was about ready to explode with arousal laced annoyance. Damn it if that smug smile wasn't sexy.

"I'll come get my truck from you tomorrow, text me the address." He had my phone number. Hell, I probably still had his smart-ass text messages to prove it.

I hopped out of the truck and slammed the door but not before he called out the passenger window. "Breanna, you're gorgeous. The guys at a place like the Rooster don't stand a chance. You line them up and they'll get knocked down. Eventually someone's going to get hurt. I really don't want it to be you."

"Why do you care about what happens to me?" Noah just said I was gorgeous, no one outside of my family had ever said something like that to me.

"Beats the hell out of me, half the time I'd like to bend you over my knee myself." He grinned and something sexy flashed in his eyes.

Whoa. The threat was twisted, the danger just enough that my pulse raced and my cheeks burned. Images of Noah doing just that left me feeling all sorts of things that weren't any bit of good.

I didn't run inside to the safety of home, but I walked swiftly to the porch. Noah turned everything upside down and I couldn't right it again.

There was no point sneaking into the house, not when the light in Raelynn's old room was on. Superstition and tradition dictated she spend one last night at home in her old room.

Tomorrow she'd be married, no longer a Casey.

Her new last name, however, would be just as synonymous as ours was in the street racing scene. The merging of two Arkadia dynasties.

The strange tug of fear in my stomach, the one that whispered I was losing my sister, urged me to turn back and stop Noah from backing out of my driveway. I was strong enough not to do that, but I did glance over my shoulder as he took off, and watched the taillights fade away with a tinge of regret.

I could have gone home with Noah and for a little while, forget all the things that were moving on without me. But doing so would change a big part of who I was. I couldn't do that until it was on my own terms.

My virginity was an important thing to me. I found a sense of power in it, knowing that I had something most guys would always want. Sure, one day I wanted to find a guy who made me feel all tingly and warm. One who made me feel things no one else had.

Noah did all of that. He also pissed me off, drove me crazy, and more often than not, hurt my feelings. He put me at a disadvantage no one else ever had.

I was *not* going to tell him that, I'd never give him the satisfaction. I was an emotional mess, the scariness of the scene in the parking lot and the man himself began to settle in. Noah wasn't the only one who lost control.

With my fingers on the knob, I braced myself to deal with Raelynn. She would probably be a bundle of pre-wedding nerves and expect me to deal with those. Considering how frayed mine were, I wasn't so sure I'd be any help.

If I took a deep breath my body would shake with the remnants of what had happened. Worse, once I went to bed I'd probably have nightmares about the gun pressed to his forehead or the girl equivalent of a wet dream. At least I could quasi-look forward to the latter.

What I didn't look forward to was the beautiful, yet frazzled mess of my big sister standing in the hallway when I walked in. Her eyes were accusatory and annoyed. Uh oh. She'd probably heard about what happened.

On a deep breath I stepped fully into the house, prepared for a sort of sibling battle. "Where were you?" My sister's voice held a note of relief that stopped me from snapping out in annoyance as I brushed by her.

I hesitated in my bedroom doorway, before turning to the bathroom instead. I smelled of cigarettes and bad intentions. "Out with Isaac and the guys." It wasn't completely a lie. Maybe she didn't know after all. Raelynn would be losing her shit if she'd heard about the gun.

"He won some big money at Grudge Night." I deflected as best I could.

Usually lying about the racing, the winning, didn't grate on my nerves so badly. But as I glanced at my sister, all worried and glowing the night before her wedding…it did.

Everyone could be happy and excited for Raelynn and Jordan, ecstatic for Aiden and Hadley, and here I was with jack shit. Because the things I did well and made me happy, nobody wanted me to do. It was too dangerous; I wasn't experienced enough. "Breanna, why don't you find a girl hobby? Maybe dance like Raelynn."

Nope, sorry Mom and Dad I don't want to do those things. I just wanted to go fast, for someone to look at me and think I was doing something right when I did.

"You don't look like you had much fun." Raelynn gave me a supporting smile and leaned in the bathroom doorway as I started the shower.

My lip curled. "It could have been better." Minus a few instances. I'd had fun behind the wheel of Isaac's ricer *and* making out with Noah. It was the rest of the night that had exhausted me.

Little lines formed between her eyebrows, her otherwise pretty face marred for a moment. She fidgeted but said nothing, only gazed at me without seeing me, as I got undressed. You could almost hear the cogs in her brain turning. Something bothered my sister; it was written in the lines on her forehead and the rigidness of her body.

She'd tell me whatever it was, when she was ready to do so. No point in standing around waiting. So, I climbed into the shower.

"You disappeared during my rehearsal dinner, the only one I'm ever going to have. That was *important* to me, Bree."

I battled back the guilt and bit my lip to keep from saying that me leaving wasn't strange, but her being upset was. Arguing with her would wake my parents and draw attention to the fact that I'd stayed out all night before Raelynn's wedding. Not the brightest idea.

Since our huge fight before Devin died last year, I put forth an actual effort to not verbally throttle my sister anytime she got all high and mighty with me.

"Everything was over, Rae. We'd rehearsed, we'd eaten, people gave stupid mushy toasts while Jordan mooned over you like the big dolt he is. What more do you want from me?" The scalding water cascaded down my back. I hadn't shut the door, she'd have just opened it and come in anyway.

"You know, this weekend isn't about you."

"A fact made perfectly obvious every spare second of every single day the past few weeks. I'm hot, tired, and smell like cigarette smoke. I want a shower where I don't have to be accosted by you, Bridezilla."

Her silhouette dropped the lip on the toilet and sat down.

I worked shampoo through my long tresses. "Jesus, Rae, can't I shower in peace?"

"This is going to be a shotgun wedding."

Chapter Seven

Sudsy foam went flying everywhere as I jerked the curtain back enough to stick my head out. "What are you talking about?"

My breath caught and my head swam. Of course I knew what shotgun wedding meant. I just hadn't expected to hear the phrase coming from my sister's mouth a few short hours before the dawn of her big day.

"I'm pregnant, Bree."

"Fuck." Not trusting my facial expressions, I slid under the stream of water, let the curtain fall in place, and rinsed my hair slowly.

At the pajama bachelorette party at Hadley's, Raelynn had stamped out the topic of wine under the guise of Cara being so young. I'd thought that was stupid, it wasn't like Cara would have to sneak around to find liquor if she wanted to.

It all made sense now.

My sister wasn't just getting married, she was going to have a baby. This was *big*.

"Have you told Jordan?"

"Nope. Just you. I assumed, because I'm late." She stood from the toilet and paced the small bathroom. "I wasn't sure until a few hours ago. I got sick after the rehearsal dinner, have been getting sick for a few weeks. So, I took a test."

She sounded so small, so unlike Raelynn, that it

broke me. This should be a happy event.

"He's going to flip out." He'd be a good father. Hell, he was awesome with Aiden's kids.

Her voice quavered. "That's what I'm scared of."

I squirted a healthy dose of shower gel into the purple loofah and lathered it up. "Nah. I meant he'll be ecstatic."

"And I'll be hormonal and fat for the next nine months."

That was a long time. I'd have to skip town or something, I couldn't handle Mom doting and panicking over a pregnant Raelynn. Not to mention hormones. Rae lived beside us, I worked with her every day, I couldn't deal. "I'm outta here until you squeeze out that crotch fruit."

She choked and sputtered a cough. "Crotch fruit?"

"Yup. You heard me. No way I'm sticking around with you all emotional and pregnant. I'm pooling my resources and getting a ticket to anywhere but here."

When she laughed, I couldn't help but smile. I was only half serious and my comments served their purpose as she wasn't all shaky sounding.

The leaving part wasn't a half bad idea if I was honest with myself. Not only was I losing my sister, now she was a mom too and here I was…stuck.

Both my siblings were parents now, and I'd never even practiced making babies. I covered myself in berry scented body wash and held my tongue. I couldn't tell her about what happened tonight, not now. Every time I thought I could confide in Raelynn, something always came up.

"I love you, Breanna." Her words came as if she could sense the sudden emptiness in my heart.

"Love you, too."

"Will you stay with me until I fall asleep?"

I rinsed the suds from my body and clean now, shut off the water. "Yeah, if you'll hand me a towel."

This was my last night with Raelynn, my sister. After this she would be Jordan's wife Raelynn, no longer a Casey, and now proliferous procreator of crotch fruit. The already short list of things we had in common was now *exponentially* shorter.

Not long after I'd brushed the tangles from my hair and donned pajamas, I curled up beside Raelynn in my bed. My room had the blackout curtains that would offer us a few hours of rest.

"Are you bringing a date?" she asked softly as if she feared sleeping as much as all the changes that lay ahead of us.

"Isaac was supposed to come with me."

"He's not?"

I snorted. "If he manages to wake up in time, he's going to have one hell of a hangover."

"One of *those* nights, huh?"

"Definitely." I grumbled on a sigh, punched my pillow, and settled into the bed.

She laughed, one of the more comforting sounds in my life. There'd been times when I hadn't heard it much. I was glad now was not one of those moments. Yes it was all about her, but if I stopped thinking of myself for two seconds…she deserved to be happy.

"Bring someone else."

What sort of wedding date would Noah be? Would he wear a suit, maybe a tie? The idea of him in a tie made me smile in the dark. "Cara and Vic are already in the wedding, Rae."

"No, I meant a *real* date."

I pulled the comforter up to my chin and shrugged. "Vic is a real date. He's cute, he qualifies."

"Would you sleep with him?" Her tone was sassy, much more like Raelynn than she had been while I was showering.

I made a face in the semi-darkness before shaking my head. Vic was a good looking guy, a ladies' man. However, not for this lady. "That's like me asking you if *you'd* bang Vic."

"Well, what about Isaac? Would you sleep with him?"

I laughed outright. "Yeah…no. Not in this lifetime."

"Matt Foster?"

"Came close, but no." I rolled to face her. "What is this, twenty questions about who I'd have sex with?"

"Well, you're super-hot with no boyfriend."

I flopped back on the bed. "I haven't found anyone that revs my engine." Mostly, anyway.

"Did Matt Foster?"

I snorted a laugh. "Hell no. I could have, but he was too much of a pushover. I need someone…stronger?"

"Devin?"

My stomach pulled tight. Sure, I'd cared a lot for Devin McAllister. He'd taught me how to street race, listened to my hopes and dreams. I'd thought the world of him and probably would have slept with him, had he not always been in love with my sister.

He was gone now, though, so any answer I might have given was pointless.

"Raelynn," I said tightly, fighting against the

emotion in my voice. "Let's not go there."

She stayed quiet for a few seconds. "Noah's pretty strong."

"Hell no! No, fucking way, that asshole…" The vehement disagreement came far too quickly. Because well, several hours ago I'd have done a whole lot with Noah McKay.

Raelynn laughed. "Thou doth protest too much."

I grunted, but it was the only response I could come up with in that moment.

My sister had this way of sitting quietly and not saying a word until I exploded with all the words I shouldn't say to begin with. The bedroom grew so quiet I could hear the second hand tick away on the wall.

I sighed. At least I knew for a fact she hadn't yet heard about what happened last night. "He's hot, but he's seriously an asshole. If I could have sex with him and never have to talk to him that'd be great."

"Breanna!" She scoffed but laughed brightly.

"And on that note, I'm going to sleep."

Where hopefully I didn't dream about Noah McKay.

****

I hadn't dreamed at all. But standing there in a knee-length purple dress with lace trim and cowboy boots; I was encased in a nightmare.

"Wait, what?"

Hadley handed me the bouquet highlighted with sprigs of lavender. "Yup, it was you all along. We figured you'd freak, so we just pretended it was me."

"I…cannot…be…maid…of…honor." Horror at the very thought settled on me like a cloak of daggers. This was a girl thing. Something more suited for the romantic-minded Hadley, not me.

"Too late." Cara—my supposed friend—giggled with bubbling delight.

I glared at her. "Shut up. You're only here because Jordan has more friends than Raelynn does."

My sister made a strangled noise that I assumed was directed at me.

"True." Cara's eyes sparkled as she blew a strawberry blond curl from her face. "But, I can think of worse things to do tonight."

"You are not a place filler." Raelynn struggled with the white silk stocking she tugged up her thigh. Thankfully, she wasn't green in the gills yet, no baby bump either. "Cara is family. Has been since the day she helped me win five hundred bucks."

"When did that happen?" I scowled. Cara was my friend, not hers.

"See, it's not always about you, Breanna." Cara stuck her tongue out at me before kneeling to help Raelynn with the girly things she was wearing under the mountain of white satin and beadwork.

"Says the bridesmaid who wasn't just told she had to make a speech in front of everyone about a wedding she thinks is silly since you two are already living together and—"

Rae shot me an icy blue glare that stopped me cold. No dimple winking smile from that Casey. *Your secret is safe with me, damn.*

"Breanna Diane!" My mother snapped. "This is your sister's special day and you will not be disrespectful."

The estrogen stuffed room grew smaller, more suffocating. Mom was right. I went to the bride, stood behind her and caught her gaze in the mirror. “Sorry, Rae, I’m just freaking out.”

“You’re telling me.” She snorted.

“My eye is twitching.” I pressed the tips of two fingers to the nervous, jumping eyelid. A cool, long-stemmed glass found its way into my free hand.

“Oh, Hadley, you’re a goddess.” The cool liquid bubbled down my throat. I finished the champagne in several quick swallows.

“That’s what I keep telling you.” The cute blonde—my soon to be sister-in-law—flounced past as I stepped out of my mom’s way.

She finished tying the back of Raelynn’s gown, with strong but trembling fingers. I’d focused so much on myself the past few days, I hadn’t thought of Mom—proud, scared, sad, and happy all rolled into one.

Or at least that’s how I felt.

Raelynn did a sweeping turn with the four of us crowding around her.

“Whoa.” I’ve heard brides glow, that pregnant women glow, but the incandescent shimmer that radiated from my big sister was mesmerizing. “Raelynn, you’re beautiful. Like a princess.”

I set the empty glass on a table to keep from dropping it. *Radiant.*

Blue eyes caught my gaze and held, turning a little glassy. “I need you to do this for me, Bree.”

“Yeah, yeah. I’ll do it.” I gave her a chaste hug, so as not to mess up the dress and hair. Then promptly downed the glass Hadley handed Raelynn. I winked at my sister as I placed hers beside mine.

We were all baptized in the First Baptist Church of

Arkadia. Outside was the prettiest gazebo I'd ever strung thousands of tiny white roses on. My sister would get married there before heading out to Cara's place for a giant party.

Mom and Raelynn kept calling it a reception…but it was more champagne and cake—that's a party. Where, as maid of honor, I now had to make a speech.

I pulled an emergency peppermint from the inadequate cleavage left by the getup I wore. Even the spicy-sweetness didn't calm me.

"We switched, so remember you go down the aisle right before Rae," Hadley whispered as we lined up inside the foyer. People were already being seated, Aiden walked Mom to the front row.

"It's not rocket science, Hadley. I walk out before Raelynn and Dad. Got it. At least I don't have to chase after Luke." Switching with Hadley meant that she would walk the aisle behind her son.

To me, that's exactly what my brother's children were. Hadley's children. She was a definite upgrade from their birth mother.

As Hadley and Cara readied my nephew, I turned back to my sister. Raelynn was always gorgeous, but today she took my breath away. The full satin skirt with a beaded corset top made the most beautiful dress.

"Oh! Hadley, we almost forgot."

The perky blonde spun around as I snatched a tiny key chain from its perch inside my bouquet.

"Forgot what?" Raelynn's perfect bridal makeup job twisted in panic.

"These." Hadley pulled off her necklace, a perfect teardrop necklace. "Something old and borrowed, it was my grandmother's."

Cara knelt and slid a pretty pink garter up the bride's leg. "Something new—I picked it out." She beamed.

I clutched a blue, piston-shaped key chain. When Rae saw it in my hand, her eyes welled again. The emotion that passed between us was strong enough that both Hadley and Cara stared, confused.

Sheepishly, I shrugged. "When I got my license, I snatched this off Devin's keys. It's been on my key ring ever since."

I tucked it in her bouquet and whispered in her ear. "He'd be here, standing there with Jordan and the guys."

There was a soft whoosh—something between a sigh and a gasp—from Raelynn. Her bright blue eyes shone with unshed tears and emotion I didn't want to process. Not now, maybe not ever.

"Thank you, Breanna." She kissed my cheek, a tear brushing against my temple.

I straightened. "Something blue."

Then the organ started and someone shoved little Luke out the door, Hadley slipping out in step behind him.

"Showtime!" Dad came in, looking dapper in his dark suit and tie. My heart swelled a little. I couldn't think of a time he'd ever been so dressed up.

The slide click of the photographer snapping away drowned out the music while I straightened Rae's veil one last time.

Then it was my turn.

"Here goes nothing. Our last moment as the Casey sisters."

"No." Dad pulled both of us to him. "You'll always

be my girls."

I kissed his cheek and hers, then headed down the red-carpeted aisle hiding the massive lump in my throat behind a megawatt smile.

Chapter Eight

All eyes were on me. With each step upon the red carpet toward the gazebo outside the church, my skin nearly crawled right off my body. Oh, I liked attention and all. But, not for just walking down an aisle in a dress. I wasn't earning this; I was a purple spectacle in cowboy boots.

Noah was there. His presence, like warm honey, poured all over me, slowing me down. I hitched my breath, gripped the lavender bouquet tighter, and trudged on. I didn't search the crowd for him for fear I'd trip and get caught in the gooey awareness.

My gaze was trained forward toward the decorated wooden structure where Jordan and the rest of the wedding party waited. He, my brother, Vic, and Isaac looked like something out of a romance novel in their suits and purple vests.

Our gearheads cleaned up nice.

I made it to the gazebo without tripping and falling on my face. When I turned, the music changed. The familiar classical notes floated across the air, carrying the scent of fragrant blossoms as well as heralding the vision in white at the other end of the carpet.

My sister was beautiful as she walked down the aisle, clinging to my father's arm for support. I didn't cry, but emotion clogged my throat when Dad placed her hand in Jordan's.

Patience was not my virtue by any stretch. As soon as I'd handed Raelynn the ring, my gaze swept the crowd. I found Noah almost instantly as if a tractor beam had pulled me right to him.

No suit, but he'd managed black dress pants and a gray shirt with a button loose at the collar. I ripped my gaze away before I drooled on myself. This wasn't the time to envision popping each of the other buttons off.

Get it together, Breanna.

By the time Jordan choked out his I do and the first tear trickled down my sister's cheek, the fake smile I'd plastered on my face had grown real and I wasn't thinking about Noah McKay.

They were going to make wonderful partners. Before they'd given in to each other, something had been missing from each of them. Apart, they were in pieces and together they were whole. I loved them both.

Arm in arm with my brother, I followed the newlyweds past the guests and back into the church. I scanned the crowd one last time over my shoulder and immediately sought out Noah standing off to the side.

All eyes were on the departing bridal party. Though, Noah's were trained right on me.

Damn.

****

My unusual silence came at behest of nerves that gripped my throat tight. Wait staff in black jackets served fancy food I barely touched. I'm sure it was delicious, but what I wouldn't give for a tootsie pop instead, maybe a candy cane. Anything, sweet. Hell at this point I'd even go for chocolate—not my usual style.

My parents had paid for the wedding, but Jordan

had gone all out for the reception. A giant tent had been raised on the Schaver farm. I could throw rocks at the strip of concrete we usually raced on. This should feel like home, not an alien planet with Vic Morales in a tux.

Fitting, though, that Jordan Slater's wedding reception was so close to the finish line where we raced. Full circle, I supposed.

On the other side of the groom, Aiden's arm hung around Hadley's shoulders. His blue eyes twinkled, and a dopey smile curled his lips. Love, made my brother look like a completely different person. Bright, happier, more alive.

I swallowed down the reflux that burned the back of my throat. This was all too much. I was going to suffocate or vomit. I couldn't handle all the—whatever it was hanging in the air. Everyone was all dopey eyed and happy.

"You know, Breezy, when you make those faces I wonder what's going on in there." Vic tapped a finger to my temple.

Very few people got away with calling me Breezy. Vic was one of them. I stabbed a carrot with my fork and made a very dramatic face. "I was thinking, how disgustingly happy in love my brother looks and my sister too, I hope it's not contagious."

Vic laughed outright and cut into his steak. "Love looks good on all of them. Maybe you *should* try it."

I cut my gaze to keep from rolling my eyes. "You first, *hombre*."

Teeth flashed against mocha colored skin and his dark eyes glinted with a charm that could easily move mountains. Add in the slicked-back dark hair and half the women in the room were staring at him already. At least he wasn't all goofy and lovey-dovey.

With his steak knife, Vic gestured the length of himself. "All of this ain't meant to be tied down to one woman, Breezy."

I snorted, loud enough to earn a hard glare from my mother who sat several yards away at the family table.

Side eye from my mom was a regular occurrence.

"Were there two last weekend?" I cocked my head sideways. I'd bunked at Isaac's instead of going home, where tiny tots were running rampant for the weekend.

His grin lit up the entire table. Yup, Vic had no problem with the ladies. "Maybe."

"You're gonna hafta tell me all about that one, someday." It was lost on me how any woman would want to share. I wasn't made like that.

Not that I'd ever want to be in Vic's bed. I loved the guy, sure he was hot, but he wasn't *like* my brother…he *was* my brother.

He winked. "Breezy, if I told you the half of it, your brother would kill me."

This time I didn't hide the emphatic roll of my eyes.

Hadley caught my attention and gestured at her champagne glass.

"Damn," I muttered under my breath.

"What?" Vic looked around, as if I'd just heralded impending doom.

"Maid of Honor speech." I stopped short of banging my head on the table. I grabbed his champagne, downed the entire glass, set it back down and reached for mine. The bubbly liquid fizzled its way down my throat and started to bind itself into something resembling courage.

"Whoa." He covered my hand with his own and squeezed. "Slow down."

He knew me well enough, I didn't have to tell him how scared I was in that moment. Speaking in front of everyone wasn't a problem. Saying the right thing on Raelynn's special day was. Giving voice to emotions and thoughts I spent most of my time ignoring was almost painful.

"Say what's in your heart. She's the only sister you have, you love her, tell her so. That's all you have to do."

He made it sound so simple.

"Here goes nothing," I whispered and stood, shimmying my dress back in place. I tapped my silver fork gently against the rim of the now empty glass. The loud tinkly clang rang out beneath the large tent.

All eyes on me again, I fought not to shift my weight around. Beneath the table, Vic squeezed my calf. This wasn't about all the people here, what they thought of me—of us. I was standing there in a dress, my trembling fingers wrapped around a champagne flute, for my sister.

I dropped the fork. "Oops, shit." There was a surprised hush that followed my blurted expletive. How were any of them really shocked?

Vic caught the utensil as it bounced off the table and headed toward the floor. With a wobbly smile of thanks I shifted my attention to my sister, not the crowd of wedding guests.

She was radiant. Her tanned skin shimmering almost gold and the pale blue of her eyes so bright and happy it almost hurt me to look at her. Her hair was swept up from her pretty face and the veil was long gone. Jordan sat at her side, one large arm wrapped across her bare shoulders.

Both watched me expectantly.

“Apparently, I’m supposed to give a speech and I am woefully unprepared.”

“Not surprising!” a familiar voice heckled.

I jerked my chin to the offender. “Yeah well, you can suck it, Isaac Morales.”

“Breanna Diane!” Mom chirped before my dad could stop her.

Jordan’s shoulders shook a bit as he chuckled, and Raelynn wore a bemused expression.

I took a deep breath. “So, today I lost my sister.” I hurried on before my mom could bust out the middle name again. “I’d say I gained a brother, but the truth is Jordan has always been family. Nothing changing much there. I figured I’d get up here and just manage to piss someone off or say the wrong thing, because I *am* losing my sister. Then I realized, when I saw her slip her hand into Jordan’s, I wasn’t losing anything at all.”

I swallowed, trying to wet my throat that had grown hoarse. “My life is the same right now as it was yesterday, as it will be tomorrow. It’s Raelynn’s life that’s changing. She’s a wife now and one day will be a mother.

“Today is the beginning of a new journey and one that is all hers. I know beyond any doubt that she’ll be amazing in all things. So, while I’m losing the sister I knew—I’m gaining a smart, amazing woman that is going to carve a path in this world I can only hope to follow.”

When she reached for me, I took her hand and

squeezed. Like Vic said, this was all about my sister. "Raelynn, my entire life I've been a poor imitation of you." When she balked, I squeezed the fingers I held and Jordan kissed her hair. "Everything good I am, I learned from you. Thank you, for loving me even when I didn't deserve it and for showing me what being good and kind really means. I hope that every day of the rest of your life is as happy as this one. You deserve no less. I love you."

Then I cut my gaze to Jordan, whose eyes looked a little watery.

I swallowed back my emotion and gave him a stern look. "Be good to her, Slater. Always. Or I'll shove that shiny Malibu right up your big ass."

There was laughter and applause, but I didn't hear any of it. My sister stood fast and grabbed me tight. Neither of us caring about the frilly dresses that were crushed between us.

Her words were the only sound that reached my ears. "Thank you, Breanna. I love you so much. You'll never lose me."

"I know." Much as Jordan had, I kissed my much shorter sister's hair and took my seat, as our brother stood.

Aiden's hair was pulled back from his face, he'd shaved, and looked more than dapper in his tuxedo. Beside him Hadley beamed.

"Baby sister is hard to follow." The crowd laughed, and he smiled, charm oozing from his dimple down to his toes. "Jordan, since the first day I met you I knew you were on the same level I was. I watched, like everyone else, as you tiptoed around Raelynn for years. I couldn't be prouder to have you, officially, as my brother. You're one of the best men, this best man has ever met. Best of luck, Raelynn will no doubt keep you on your toes."

Aiden grinned wildly. "And I'm never going to get used to you kissing my sister."

Hard to follow my ass.

Chapter Nine

The bride and groom danced first, to some mushy song that almost made my eye twitch. As they spun around on the dance floor, Jordan cried. Slow gentle tears tracked down his cheeks. I wasn't such a hardass that I didn't warm as I watched them. His face twisted in amazement. It would be easy to think he was suddenly overcome with emotion that my sister had married him.

Nope. Ten-to-one odds she'd told him about the crotch fruit.

My stomach did an unfamiliar happy tumble and my heart grew light. So, I shoved another forkful of cake in my mouth and thanked God I was alone at the table—no witnesses to my internal bout of sappiness.

"Aren't you just full of surprises?" Noah McKay took a seat beside me at the round table near the dance floor.

I grunted and made a face. *Had he read my damn mind?*

The mouthful of cake was the only reason my lips stayed together. The charcoal shirt and dress slacks did something to him, changed him. No, the rough edges were still there—but smoother now. He'd slicked back the top layer of his hair, drawing attention to canny blue eyes and a snarky smile.

He took a long pull from a beer. I may have spent

too much time caught up in the way his lips wrapped around the bottle. I swallowed the cake without choking—a wedding miracle.

He swallowed with a hiss and grinned. "That's more like it. Your speech was far more eloquent than I'd expected from you. Well done."

My upper lip curled like I'd smelled something bad. "Wow, look at you, using big words. I appreciate the backhanded compliment." Each time I started to think he was hot, he somehow managed to remind me he was a jerk.

"I wasn't trying to start shit. You do that to me and I don't know why…" He trailed off then laughed and took another swig. "I just wanted to say, you did well. I was impressed."

He sighed and rubbed a long-fingered hand across his face. He'd shaved, his perpetual five o'clock shadow was missing. The lack of stubble left him looking younger, sexier. Would his lips feel different, softer?

"Thanks." I bit off the word and cut off further response with another forkful of expensive wedding cake. This was my second piece, I'd cut it myself so it was more butter-cream icing than anything else. Pure sugar and butter, my two favorite food groups.

I focused on the cake and ignored Noah.

"I'm sorry," he said so softly I almost missed it.

Taken aback, I sat up straight and widened my eyes. "Whoa. Did that hurt?"

He laughed and took another drink but didn't have a chance to say anything else as Isaac did a dance around the table and handed me another glass of chilled champagne.

I'd lost count of how many I'd drunk, until my twenty-first birthday I had to make do with pilfering wedding alcohol. At this point, I'd drunk enough to get all sappy about Jordan being a father.

I swallowed half the glass in one sip and beamed at Isaac. "You bring me drinks"—I gestured at Noah with my glass—"and that one is apologizing. I feel special."

"Short bus special, probably." Isaac spun a chair around and straddled it, drinking the same bottled beer as Noah.

"He gets away with giving you a hard time?" Noah raised a brow.

"Yup, he's my best friend."

Isaac and I clinked our drinks together.

"Enough of a best friend to be concerned that the two of you were in a pretty gnarly situation last night." There was a thin layer of attitude coating each of Isaac's words.

I snorted, Noah shrugged, and Isaac's gaze stayed glued to my parking lot hero. "What's this I hear about a fight and a gun?"

Moving slowly, as if he had all the time in the world, Noah set his empty bottle on the table and leaned back in his chair, hands in pockets—not the least bit intimidated by Isaac. "There was a situation and it was handled."

"I heard you got ballsy, McKay, and damn near got my best friend shot." Isaac's cheeks were twitching with a barely contained rage I'd missed earlier. It hadn't been attitude, but anger.

Alarm bells sounded in my head. This was Raelynn's wedding, I couldn't let this turn into a brawl.

"Guys—"

Noah cut me off. "Actually, I stepped in right before she got mugged and gang-raped while her best friend was too drunk to know his ass from a hole in the ground. You were the one that left her alone in the parking lot, bud, not me."

Something shifted. Every word Noah had said was true. Isaac had been drunk, he did leave me out there alone. And the realization settled over Isaac. His eyes widened and his face tightened angrily. Pure, unadulterated hate seemed to ebb off him in waves.

All of this directed right at Noah.

I caught Vic's gaze from across the tent. Apparently, my expression spoke volumes, as he headed straight for our table.

"Isaac." I laid a hand on his arm and spoke softly in hopes of diffusing the situation. "Shit happened, it was handled, and I'm fine."

Silently, I shot daggers at Noah whose lips were slightly upturned in cocky challenge.

Isaac pushed back from the table and stormed off, slamming into Vic's shoulder on his way but never stopping.

"Damn, Breezy, what'd you do this time?" Vic took a seat in the chair his brother had vacated.

I finished my champagne. "Nothing. He's just like a prairie dog. Cute but not so cuddly."

"Ha! She proved the only person he has to be mad at, is himself." Cara plopped down in the seat on Noah's other side. Her shimmering purple dress a reminder that we were still dressed like My Little Pony rejects. "Did some asshole really pull a gun on y'all?"

I'd been laser-focused on Isaac and Noah, I hadn't seen her approach. My eye was twitching. I pressed two fingertips to the jumping eyelid. If Vic knew about what happened at the Rooster, Aiden would soon.

"He already knows." She read my expression expertly and waved at Vic with a perfectly manicured hand. "Everybody does, except maybe the bride and groom. You're front page Arkadia news today, you and Superman here."

Noah was like a stone. No grin now, just quiet contemplation.

"Shit." I slumped into the chair.

"Yeah, *cariño*, I'm betting Aiden's already heard about it."

Cara was the closest female friend I had in the world. She proved it, by reveling in my misery with a wide, bright smile. Her nose was turned up at the end and flecked with a dusting of freckles that grew more faint every year. Golden strawberry curls spiraled in tendrils where her hair had fallen from the fancy up-do we all sported.

She was always cute, tonight she was more than that. Pretty. Or maybe I was just drunk. I should be mad at her for enjoying herself, but I couldn't find the energy. I was officially giving up on life. Even sugar wouldn't fix this.

My fork clattered to the plate with a clang.

My brother would have something to say about this. My only saving grace was that my sister would be off on her honeymoon soon. She'd just make a big deal out of everything, and I'd *never* hear the end of it.

The music was suddenly too loud, the tent in the middle of nowhere too confining. I itched to change and literally let my hair down. When I glanced at Noah, I was caught in the molten steel of his blue gaze. He didn't blink, nor look away.

At the table, Vic and Cara chatted away about the incident at the Rooster. I wasn't really hearing them. Memories of last night flooded back. When my tongue snaked out to wet my lips, Noah smirked and my nipples hardened to attention.

Well, that was new. For the first time in my life, I broke first and tore my eyes away from Noah and the sensual battle of wills.

Holy cheese on a cracker, I was nearly twenty-one years old and never met a guy that made me all girly acting. Now I had, and he drove me insane.

"I can't believe you're here," Cara marveled when Hunter East approached, decked out in a black suit and a bright blue shirt.

If he hadn't already made it to second base with my sister—before Jordan pulled his head out of his ass—Hunter might have made me feel all tingly. Maybe. If I was into the American Pie thing.

He sat down across from me, caught my gaze, and shrugged. "I was invited, why wouldn't I show. Raelynn is a friend."

"And Slater?" Cara snorted and fidgeted in her seat when he turned his attention to her.

Vic laughed.

I rolled my eyes. "Jesus y'all, that was years ago. Pretty sure there's a line of pit-bunnies standing between Hunter and the last time he hooked up with Raelynn. It's fake news."

I hadn't been allowed to stay that night when Rae's ex had shown up in Arkadia. My brother had sent me home. But that guy had hurt my sister, and Hunter stayed behind, with Vic and Aiden, to make sure the psycho never hurt anyone else.

When I was feeling particularly vile about the pretty douche who raped my sister, I imagined they killed him and hid the body where no one would ever find it.

I heard, however, he was dumped off at a hospital with injuries similar to being hit by a semi-truck. To calm myself, I focused on the pretty bouquet of flowers my sister had carried and my soon to be sister-in-law had caught.

Hunter grinned his approval at my support and I smiled. None of this seemed lost on Noah to my right. His gaze fixed on Hunter for a long moment. I held my breath. *Why do I care if he thinks I'm flirting with Hunter?*

"Dance with me, Breanna." As if sensing a disturbance in the force, Vic stood and extended his hand. I'd managed to avoid dancing whenever possible at the wedding. Let's face it, I was really here for the champagne and cake.

The eldest Morales wasn't taking no for an answer. I'd been caught in that hawkeyed stare enough times to know there was no getting out of it.

Hunter gave a couple of two-fingered whistles when Vic led me out on the floor. Not Noah, though, he watched intently. My brother and Hadley, and several other couples turned round and round to a slow song on the dance floor.

No sooner had Vic's hands settled on my hips than Hunter had coaxed Cara from the table and was tucking her against him. Her cheeks were so red, I thought she might pass out.

Vic watched them too, with a sly grin on his face.

"She might start drooling." I chuckled.

"Nah." Vic settled into the rhythm, dancing so naturally he made my gawky self look good. "Give her more credit, she's been a pro—been mooning over that guy for years and hiding it well."

I snorted. It didn't look to me like my wide-eyed friend was hiding much of anything. Especially not her adoration for Hunter East. "Sure."

Maybe it was the champagne, maybe the mood of the evening, but I gave an uncharacteristic wistful sigh. "Why couldn't one of you guys look at me like she looks at him? That would make life so easy."

Vic's sharp eyes widened, like I'd grown fangs and six heads. "That's just weird. One married couple within the crowd is enough for me."

We spun around the dance floor, his hand warm on my hip. The cowboy boots put me at eye level with Vic, but dancing with him wasn't uncomfortable. Noah was tall though, enough I could probably wear heels and still not be taller.

I searched him out then and our gazes caught.

"And *that's* why I asked you to dance. Since we're on the topic of you, mama, and guys who look at you."

I whipped my head around and blinked furiously. "Huh?" I stumbled, but Vic righted me, never missing a step.

His easy laugh rang out and drew the attention of my brother and several others. He winked at Aiden. "Your sister thinks I can't see right through her."

Aiden snorted and shook his head. "Most transparent girl ever, everything shows on her face or tumbles from her mouth."

"Bite me, Aiden." But I only half meant it. He *was*

right.

Vic spun us away from my brother and his fiancée. "So, what's up with McKay?"

My mouth went dry and my heart started racing. To buy some time, I fingered the garter Vic had slid up his bicep after catching Jordan's toss. How was I going to answer *that* question?

Chapter Ten

Vic Morales, race-master extraordinaire could be called a great many things. Stupid, was not one of them. I was forced to think on my feet, while I tried desperately not to step all over his.

"Nothing, really."

He wasn't buying it. His dark gaze narrowed and his lip curled, but he didn't straight up call me out on the lie. "And the incident outside the Rooster last night, he just happened to be there? Or is it just a normal occurrence for you to need rescuing and you neglected to tell me?"

With a shaky step that nearly took out his toes, I stiffened, then was caught in Noah's gaze over Vic's shoulder. Between Noah watching me—apparent jealousy stiffening his body—and Vic's interrogation I was about to lose my mind.

I glanced up at the top of the white tent and tried not to massage the impending twitch. "I've got my dad, Aiden, Jordan, Isaac, and now Noah. I do *not* need another man to preach at me about the hazards and dangers of my life."

"I wasn't going to preach." He twirled me in his arms, which left me dizzy, and softened his tone. "I know better than that, you're going to do whatever the hell you want to do. You can call me you know, especially if my brother's drunk and stupid and not watching your back."

I leaned in, rested my head on Vic's shoulder, and let the stress flow out from my body. Unlike the rest of them, Vic didn't judge. Not even after I'd fought with Raelynn and took Devin's side in the whole debacle. Vic would always have my back.

"I know, I'm sorry. I was drunk too—wasn't thinking."

"I know, mama." He nuzzled his cheek against my hair. "You worry me, you know."

What did I say to that? Sure, my behavior was questionable at times. But my defiance was born from the proverbial chafing at the bit I did daily. This town was too small for me. I needed something…more. Vic liked being the big fish in a little pond with a steady stream of pit bunnies eating up every word he said.

That wasn't me.

"I wanted to talk to you about Noah, anyway."

I jerked back, like he smelled of dirty socks and mealworms. "Huh?" I recognized the tone very well. Vic wasn't often serious, but when he was it would serve everyone well to listen to him. "I thought you two were friends?"

Another spin, this one with a little hip wiggling, Latin flourish. "Oh yeah, I like the kid. I just need to ask you a favor."

My head topsy-turvy, I righted myself quick in his arms. Vic held fast and never missed a step, even as the music changed and the tempo quickened.

When I scrunched my nose and made an impatient gesture, he chuckled. "Just remember, Breezy, some men are too proud to beg."

I must have given him quite the look because Vic

laughed again. "If you want him, great, but don't dance around and act like you don't see what's going on. Don't bait him, as your sister would say—don't poke the bear."

I'm not a fan of being confused and I've never considered myself the dumbest person in the room. That I suddenly seemed like I fit both those descriptions was off-putting.

"I appreciate you looking out and all, but I really have no idea what you're talking about. Noah works for my dad and brother—that's it."

"Uh huh." Vic tossed a glance toward Noah. "That's why he's staring me down like a bull ready to charge?"

"Oh, sweet baby Jesus, what?" I stopped dancing completely and whipped my head around, Vic's platonic grip lodged at my waist.

Noah *was* watching us, his blue eyes narrowed to slits and his nostrils flared. I'd seen that wild look on his face before. It should have scared me. Nope. My nipples went hard, my mouth dried, and I clung a little too tightly to Vic's shoulders.

The tent was suddenly far too small and suffocating. Abruptly the song changed again. Silently I thanked the DJ for offering me a reprieve. To keep from smothering in Vic's good intentions, I pulled away and sought refuge with what was left of my cake.

Let's face it, going back to the table was an epic mistake.

With Vic and Cara on the dance floor and Isaac MIA, that left a surly Noah McKay as the only occupant. And I'd walked straight to him, ready for a fight.

"What's your deal?" I shot as I tucked my purple skirt beneath my ass and sat down—hard.

He opened his mouth and his tongue slipped out and across his bottom lip, then he took seduction a step further and pulled the shiny, succulent flesh between his teeth.

"Sweet baby Jesus." I pushed the cake away and let my forehead drop to the table. I couldn't live like this. I was vastly inexperienced in such things—no matter how much swagger I put on.

He laughed. "My deal? I don't know whether to throttle you or kiss you." He stood from the table and left me to my misery. Thankfully.

"Where's tall, dark, and moody heading?" A winded Cara plopped in the chair beside me. Her cheeks were pink from exertion in a way that made me jealous of the almost ivory tint of her complexion. "And what did you do to piss him off this time?"

"Hell if I know, I gave up on figuring that one out a long time ago." I slowly raised my head from the table.

"If you could channel all that aggression into sexual tension, the two of you'd make one hot couple." She popped a wedding mint into her bow-shaped mouth.

"Yeah, about that—" I flinched.

Her lips formed an O of surprise. "You banged Noah?"

I waved that notion off with a flick of my fingers. "No, but close enough."

"When, where? Give me details, woman!" She scrambled off her seat and around the table to the chair Noah had vacated. I'd known her long enough to know that hearing about someone's sexual escapades was almost as good as the real thing for Cara.

Over the past few years she and I had become close. She was quirky and snarky—a combination that spoke to my heart. "At the Rooster Barn last night. In the bathroom. Oh my God, this makes me sound like a dirty whore."

"Not if you didn't have *actual* sex in the bathroom of the biggest dive in Texas. Sort of trashy maybe, but…"

I snorted. "Gee, thanks."

"Anytime. At least he's super hot. It could be worse."

She was right. Noah was attractive, in that brooding bad boy sort of way. I'd never thought I'd be pulled toward a guy like that. The only other crush I'd had was Devin and he was clean cut, almost perfect. Two things Noah was definitely…not.

Isaac reentered through the back of the tent. Maybe it was the nosy little sister in me, but I'd always been pretty good at spotting when something was about to happen. After the way he'd left, I bristled waiting for him to pick a fight.

My apprehension evaporated. There was a tension in his face. I knew him well enough that it didn't scare me, because it was strain born from excitement.

When he beelined right for Vic, who stood on the other side of the dance floor talking to my brother, I stood from the table. Cara followed suit, falling in step beside me as I headed that way.

Hunter met us there. I wasn't the only one who recognized the type of excitement that was all Arkadia, all the time.

Vic's lips had curled in a ready smile and my

brother's eyes were flashing.

"What's up?" Aiden fiddled with the button on his suit jacket, like he was fending off an impending storm of adrenaline.

Words tumbled quickly from Isaac's mouth. "I just got a call, North Side townies brought some local homies from near Houston. They're trying to hustle a bunch of races and money, since Slater's out for the start of the season with this wedding shit."

Of course the hyenas ventured out once the lion left the jungle. They just didn't realize the level of mistake they were making.

Growing up, if I was hurt or scared I went to Jordan to feel safe. He was always the one to defend and protect. But, if I was angry and upset, I went to my brother to seek vengeance against my enemies.

I was a kid, I was dramatic of course. But Aiden had a wild streak that might have knocked a few teeth out a time or two.

The smirk and narrowing of his eyes was terrifying and amazing. He turned right to Hunter. "Well, everybody ain't on a honeymoon. Let's go show these bastards what's up. Make it happen, Vic."

"On it." The race-master angled his head at Isaac and worked at the knot in his tie. "Let's ride, little brother."

"The kids?" I asked my brother, hoping he wouldn't stick them with Cara. She was a hustler, always working, even if it meant missing races to babysit for my brother and Hadley. But tonight would go a lot smoother with Cara at my side.

"With Mom and Dad for the night." Hadley tossed me her keys. She'd driven Raelynn to the wedding earlier. "Don't crash."

"There won't be a dent in your grocery getter." The look she gave me spoke of how little she believed that. It wasn't my fault my lead foot always got me in trouble.

It wasn't a mom van, but a large four-door, four by four, SUV. While I ran out to get it, Cara cut across the field between the tent and her house.

Five minutes later, she was dressed in jeans and a T-shirt and climbing into the passenger seat. "This is great. I snagged champagne *and* there's a race."

I snorted. The champagne buzz I'd had was long gone, no thanks to Noah. Little buzzes of electricity tingled up from my middle at the thought of Noah showing up at the race.

This was getting out of hand.

****

The road was unlit, desolate, and dirty. The grainy, sandy film that covered the surface clung to the bottom of my old, ratty Vans I'd changed into. I couldn't exactly line my brother up in a bridesmaid dress.

"Because *this* isn't sketchy at all." I cut my gaze to Isaac who walked the length of the quarter mile stretch of road beside me.

He made a face of agreement. "This wasn't Vic's first choice, that's for sure."

Aiden was several yards ahead of us, with the drivers from our crews that would race in the next little while.

"They'll have to pop off quick." I scanned the open field until my gaze landed on the newish subdivision less than a mile away. The crowd alone would draw attention, the second the engines fired up we'd barely have time to do burnouts.

Isaac swallowed hard. "Yeah, I don't think they can get off enough burnouts to stick at the line without someone calling the five-oh."

I'd ride back with my brother, to get the car ready. Vic and Isaac would stay when the out of town guys took their turn to walk the street we'd race on. To keep the headcount low, each driver could bring one crew member to discuss road conditions. But at the end of it, if they ran or not was Vic's call.

Vic was there to keep things fair. Oddly, though he was my brother's friend, Vic was about as straight and honest as they came. Nothing he did intentionally gave Aiden or any of our guys an advantage.

"Do we have time to sweep it, at least at the start?" My voice sounded eerie. It was past midnight, but we had time still until late enough to race.

I made my way to about the three-hundred-foot mark and knelt, raking my finger through the fine layer of silt.

"Whatcha think?" Aiden knelt beside me, keen blue eyes missing nothing.

"It's shit."

"Not the first time any of us have raced on a shit road, Bree."

"Nope." I propped my arms on my knees and tilted my head. My brother and I understood each other, always had. When it came to racing, he was the one man in the family that listened to what I had to say. "But, there aren't any bumps, no cracked pavement, no potholes."

I thought about the situation and wished for the first time in a while I hadn't stopped smoking. This wasn't just any racer, but my brother. The same guy that as an awkward teenager had still managed to kiss my scraped elbow and carry me into the house after I wrecked my Huffy. He had three kids, and a fiancée who loved him to the moon and back. I wasn't going to say send it without certainty he could hold it.

There was a giant weight on Aiden's shoulders, almost forcing him to race. With Jordan not there, someone had to hold up the Street King mantle. Even still, he would trust my judgment.

No pressure.

Noah and I had become integral parts of Aiden's crew, probably one of the only times we didn't fight. I almost huffed a sigh when I thought about what Noah would have to say about my conclusion. "You'll have to change the tune. Let me look at your data from the last race. I think if we cool it off enough, you can stay straight and not ditch it."

I nodded to my left, the side of the road lined with trees. "And pray you get lane choice in the coin flip. That left line is suicide if you get sideways."

"We'll head back to the shop, check on everything and get some food, and see what Vic has to say." Effortlessly, he unfolded from the pavement.

"Sounds good." But did it? I was sending my brother down a road that was barely fit to race and wishing desperately I was behind the wheel instead. Not that I thought I was that much better than he was—I knew it.

Chapter Eleven

Since Aiden and Hadley had moved into the old Bennett place in downtown Arkadia, within two blocks of the courthouse—we very well couldn't all congregate on Main Street at one in the morning.

Instead, we filled the parking lot of my parents' shop with tow rigs and spectator vehicles. Hunter and Aiden—bonded by something I'd rather not think about—had both their rigs and crews. I still hadn't moved past Jordan's arch rival being buds with my brother. Their friendship was a reminder of a void that had been left behind by foolish young love and the lengths Arkadia loyalty would go to right a wrong.

I shook off the melancholy and focused my attention on something other than slowly fading memories. I stood in Aiden's enclosed trailer, bent over a laptop, chasing an elusive white rabbit. Aiden had taught me how to tune a race car not long after he'd started track racing.

Tuning the car, making sense of the zig-zag lines and random numbers of data left an empty place in my soul. I should be driving not tuning, yet here I was.

Because I was better at setting cars up for the street than Aiden was. Balancing my options when there was one giant unknown—the racing surface. I'd spent too many late nights watching Jordan, Vic, and Devin do this very thing. And because this was all I could ever do, if I stayed here.

A lump formed in my throat when I thought of how much we'd lost, who we'd lost. The dark car waiting in the trailer with me was a constant tribute to Devin. Even as it was also a painful reminder of a ghost.

"I think…" I cracked my neck and with the loud pop, out went all my nerves. "I've got it."

Aiden glanced over my shoulder and checked the data. Obviously pleased, he gave me a curt nod of approval.

Time to rock and roll.

I shot a quick text to Isaac. Last check, more than an hour ago, he was finishing street cleanup. He responded immediately, as was the way of best friends.

I turned my phone to my brother so he could read the text. His deep voice was scratchy with pre-race nerves as he called out across the parking lot. "They're staging lookouts now. We're going to have to roll off, push the car to the line, and we'll have two quick burnouts."

"Coin flip at the Wash Out before heading to the race spot. Two car or truck loads can follow us out. That's it, everyone else will have to watch from the vacant lots off Morris Chapel," I barked the orders and took the foil wrapped burger from Cara.

I took a bite, chewed, and cut my gaze at her. "Where'd you get this?"

"I had Brody bring them."

I snarled. That guy. I didn't like him. Suddenly, the burger didn't taste so good. I chucked it and hopped out of the trailer.

She must have read my expression. "I had to ride with *somebody*. Vic's keeping the spectators to a minimum."

When I only made a face, she laughed. "Besides, he's cute."

"We're going to have to have a conversation defining cute. Baby pigs are cute. Skunks are cute. I wouldn't want to ride with or be seen riding with either."

Her eyes darkened, like a cloud rolling over her, as if comparing Brody to a baby pig was offensive. "Yeah well, we can't all have Jordan Slater and Hunter East fighting over us like Raelynn."

She spun and stalked off, and I was left to toss my hands up in exasperation.

The neighborhood near where we were racing was still being developed. Recently paved roads extended past the rows of houses to dirt encased empty lots whose only occupants were the occasional dumpster or port-o-john.

From that area, there'd be a good view of the action and leave the race street empty enough to get out fast if we had to. I still wasn't surprised when Cara's lithe form jogged across the vacant lots toward our staging area.

I cast a look at my brother across the narrow breadth of the trailer. His soon to be wife was nestled against his side, her green eyes practically glowing with adoration. Were it anyone else, I might throw up in my mouth a little. Love, like that, just wasn't real to me. Life was too messy.

But Aiden and Hadley got me right in the feels. She'd loved my brother and his kids as if they were hers since day one. Maybe they were. I was spiritual enough to wonder about that one. Especially since

Hadley and Aiden fit together like they were made for each other.

They deserved blissful happiness and if his ex-wife ever showed her face again, I'd rip it right off and punch her square in the throat.

The happiness of my family meant more to me than I'd ever admit out loud.

"Oh! Oh!" Cara's eager yelps as she ran up had me turning on a lazy pivot.

My dry reaction was in direct contrast to her excitement. Not unusual.

"Isaac has Brody and Adam running interference with the cops a few miles away, so we should be good to go." When I opened my mouth to comment on how little I trusted that duo, she shut me up with a lethal gaze. Cara was feisty in a way that none of the other women in my life were. It wouldn't surprise me if she decked me if I took it too far.

Someone dropped the ramp on the back of the trailer, the doors swinging open with a thunderous reverberation of metal. Orange light cast from the street lamp flickered across the glossy hood of the classic black Camaro.

I was suddenly lost in the grip of my memories. Devin had driven this car once. He'd been different from what I knew. More polished, gentler even. I missed him so much. He'd kept my secrets, calmed me when nobody was looking, and saved my ass more than a few times. Together we'd always been just on the outside, looking in on Jordan and the others.

I thought I'd been in love with Devin. Until…Noah McKay kissed me. Then, everything had shifted, skewed. Sure, it was probably all hormones and crazy physical stuff. But, there was something about Noah that tugged at me, made me question all the things I'd thought I'd known.

With each step, I shook off my inner turmoil. By the time I rounded the back of the trailer to help direct Aiden off the ramp, I was mostly back to myself.

I needed to do something, though, moments like that were happening too often. Aiden and Raelynn were adults now, with lives and partners. Things were changing for them and here I was, still the same me.

I needed to get laid or get a *real* wheel job. Either would keep me from feeling so left behind.

Not that I could explain why doing both things suddenly felt so urgent. Maybe because I was twenty now and still hadn't accomplished anything I'd planned to do. Or because I needed to feel like a woman, not a child.

I stepped around the corner and right into a solid wall of warm, testosterone-infused, male. I'm tall, so my face smacked straight into the column of his throat. I inhaled before I could stop myself and was rewarded with the enticing, spicy aroma that was all Noah.

My head tilted slightly and my gaze rose, propelled by an unseen force, to his. My lips brushed against smooth skin that was usually covered with dark stubble. Why did I know that?

My heart hammered a ricocheting bullet through my chest and I licked my lips a breath before he leaned close enough to brush his mouth against mine. My fingers twisted in the cotton of the white T-shirt he wore.

He tasted of something sweet and forbidden. I slid my tongue across his in search of more and he kissed me back. This was no simple thing, this was a reckoning. Desire sizzled and shot straight through me and out of my feet, anchoring me to the street and him.

When he moaned softly and gripped tightly to my hips, I snapped back to reality. Which wasn't a place where I could run around kissing someone as infuriating as Noah McKay.

Unafraid of confrontation, I jerked my lips from his and glared angrily at him. "You can't do that."

He narrowed his eyes, which did little to deter from the appeal of his kiss-swollen lips. "Do what?"

"Just walk up and kiss me like that in front of everyone."

His laugh was almost a roar of indignation. He shook his head. "Breezy, you ran right into me and gave me that *screw me* look. What did you expect me to do?"

"No way." Adamantly I shook my head. "I bumped into you. My bad. I did *not* give you any sort of look."

At least, I wasn't going to admit I had, despite Vic's earlier advice. Because for those few seconds, pressed against his chest, I wanted to do what the look implied. *Damn.*

"Keep telling yourself that. I know better, you kiss me like you mean it." With a bemused grin he slid past me and left me standing there, gawking.

I wasn't sure which was more infuriating, that he said that or that he was right.

****

Thanks to the subdivisions rapidly developing, the street was better lit than most of our race spots. An incandescent glow covered us with a false sense of security. This was the sort of light put up by suburbanites to deter hooligans and vandals. And, well, people like us doing the things we did.

"I ain't got a good feeling about this." Isaac bounced on the balls of his feet, shaking his arms loose at his sides like a prizefighter.

Tall, lanky, and wiry he hadn't filled out enough to hit a professional weight class. But he was scrappy and cagey. Fighting Vic's little brother wasn't a good idea. I knew, because I'd backed him up more than a time to two.

Up until the other night, he'd always had my back. So when he got feelings about things, I didn't brush them off easily. "Yeah, I trust your brother, but this is sketchy as fuck."

"Stay close, if we get popped I don't want to get caught because I was too busy looking for you." He stiffened, like he had something to prove.

I snorted. "I can take care of myself." I didn't poke the bear, though. No use guilting him over things he already felt bad about.

"Yeah, but are you going to explain to Vic how I let you get arrested if shit goes south, after what happened at the Rooster?" he asked as he followed me to Aiden's car hauler.

Bright white light poured from inside, where Noah and my brother were scurrying about on an adrenaline high. We were all starting to feel the tension mount, you could tell by the tightness of Noah's shoulders and the quick, jerky movements Aiden was making.

We had a short amount of time to get a race off. Especially considering the crowd that had gathered across the expanse of smooth dirt that had once been a hay field. "He ready?" I asked Hadley as she jogged out of the trailer, wrapped in one of Aiden's old race jackets. A reminder that she, too, was family.

"Yeah. Mostly."

With a wiggle, I slid half under the back of the car and unhooked the chains. Across the undercarriage, Noah did the same to the front of the car. Despite how much we argued, we'd worked well together since he'd started helping Aiden race.

I slid out, took my place at the bottom of the ramp, and held up my right arm as Noah climbed in the car. Gears clicked and brake lights winked red when he put the car in neutral, then winked off.

"Back—straight out."

Inside the trailer, Aiden and Isaac gave the classic Camaro a shove from the front. I backed up, one large step at a time as Noah steered the car off the ramp. When I made a fist, he stopped and put the car back in gear.

With all of us working like a well-oiled machine—unloading the car took less than thirty seconds.

Aiden was racing against an older, Fox-body Mustang with a turbo so big he couldn't put a hood on it. I'd seen videos of the guy online, but nothing that made me nervous.

I gave my brother a fist bump just before he slid into the car. I'd done the very same thing at least a thousand times before. The lump that formed in my throat each time Aiden strapped into Devin's car was as painful as it was large.

Tears pricked the back of my eyes. I blinked them back, there was no place for that sort of emotion here. Not when I'd have to explain myself, not when I'd look weak, and not when my brother was finally happy.

I'd thought of Devin more tonight than I had in

months. It wasn't just that I missed him, but everything was changing around me. Much as it had when he died. I couldn't fight the feeling that under the surface of my family's happiness something ugly and mean lurked, threatening that sort of upheaval all over again.

"Is the road that bad?" The sister of my heart's big green eyes filled with worry.

"Oh no, it's not that," I assured her, trying to lighten the heavy dread that must have shown on my face. "Aiden can handle the road—I've got a lot on my mind."

The thunderous roar of my brother's turbo charged racing engine shattered the quiet of the night. The consuming cacophony swallowed up whatever Hadley would have said.

Begrudgingly I fell in step behind Noah, leaving Hadley and Isaac to trail along behind us. I got lucky that nobody saw me earlier when I was practically climbing him like a tree and shoving my tongue down his throat.

A stinging warmth spread from my chest to my cheeks. Just thinking about kissing him made me want to do it all over again. I bit down on the inside of my cheek, hard, to give myself something else to focus on.

Through wisps of hair blown in my face as we walked, I caught him watching me intently. Beneath my stomach, parts of me that had never seen the light of day tingled in a way that I bit my cheek harder.

Forcing my gaze on the back of the sleek black race car as it rumbled to the line, I ignored the sexy guy who ambled along beside me.

Again, Noah and I worked together perfectly as we ran my brother through a smoke inducing burnout. The alcohol based race fuel he ran burned at the back of my throat. I wasn't going to complain, I lived for this. The burn was just part of the experience, part of the love I had for racing.

I wished I was the one behind the wheel. Mentally, I went through the process inside the car—at the same time I lined Aiden up at the start.

Slide the car in gear, let off the brake, roll backward. Angle my hand to direct Noah in front of the car, keep Aiden rolling back into the rubber left by the burnout. Check the gears, brake, put car in low, bump in, hold the trans-brake.

With a fist rap on the fender, Noah jogged back to where I stood.

I held my breath as Hadley stuck her fingers in mine and gripped tightly.

The race was won before it began. Not set in his rubber good enough, the Mustang spun at the line and kicked sideways, leaving Vic dashing into the lane my brother's car had already vacated. My tune held, shooting Aiden straight down the orange lit street in a cacophony of screaming engine and tires on concrete.

If he got a little loose at the big end, we couldn't tell, we were too busy running up the street behind him—cheering like we'd won the biggest race of the year.

I stayed behind at the start line when Noah and Hadley took the trailer to the other end of the street to pick up Aiden and the Camaro.

"I live for this." Cara grabbed my arm and tugged on it. "It's even worth the burn from the m-five."

I grinned. That Cara shared my love for street racing was one of the reasons I liked her so much.

Matt Foster winked as he walked Hunter's now sleek, black compact pickup to the line. I'd dated Matt once, a long time ago. Cute enough, but he wasn't my type for real. I'd never gotten that tingly, warm feeling when he'd kissed me.

Just then, Matt looked over at me and grinned as Hunter fired up his engine. He was racing an absurd eighties model Buick. A sleeper, the sort of car that looked anything like a race car but sounded like a scalded dog running hell bent for leather. Not the sort of race you took for granted.

This was going to be good.

The drivers left at the exact same time, blowing past Vic and making quick work of the recently swept road. Second race won. We all waited with bated breath for the call to roll down the line.

"East has it by a car!" Vic shouted and we all cheered.

Hunter was on his return, when the one word I never wanted to hear echoed through the crowd.

"Cops!"

Chapter Twelve

In the distance, sirens wailed, drowned out only by the throb of Hunter's engine. The crowd at the start line dispersed in the chaos of a giant disturbed anthill. I jumped in front of the black race truck as he accelerated and everyone scattered.

Hunter was one of the only drivers whose vehicle was mostly street legal. He could get out of here safely and fast.

When he stopped I grabbed Cara by the hand and dashed around the front bumper. My chest was heaving and my heart pounded. I missed the handle on the door twice before I jerked it open. "Get her the fuck out of here!"

I shoved her through the roll cage and into the space where a passenger seat had once been. Cara wasn't looking at juvie if she got caught, and Rascal would kill me if she ended up in jail.

"Bree, no—" The other thing that made Cara a great friend was her loyalty.

Right now, it was making my eye twitch.

"Just go!" I shouted as I slammed the door.

With a bark of tires, Hunter tore out the other end of the street, blazing past two cops who were closing off the intersection.

"Bree!"

I whipped my head around in the direction of

Isaac's voice. Across the dirty pavement panic stretched his features.

I wouldn't get to him in time.

Aiden's rig was too far away. I had to come up with something and fast.

Isaac caught my gaze and must have recognized the determination there, because he spun and ran toward Vic's car.

Flashing blue and red lights were bearing down on me, clouding my vision until I couldn't even see my brother's taillights in the distance.

There was a stoic, painful feeling that settled in the pit of my stomach. Aiden wasn't coming for me—he couldn't. This was a perfect metaphor for my life. I was being left behind, while everyone else scattered in different directions.

Everyone was running *away* from the rows of identical brick and siding houses, in the direction of their parked cars.

I took off in the opposite direction. I ran across the construction site, dodging the various pieces of construction equipment placed sporadically all over the vacant and just cleared lots. Soft dirt under my boots cushioned the sound of my footfalls. Not that they could be heard over the engines that roared and sirens that blared.

This was pure, unadulterated pandemonium.

In the distance dogs barked and howled in response to the uproar. People walked out onto their porches.

If I was fast enough—which I was with long ass legs and years of running from my brother and his friends—I could make it across the street and between two houses before the cops could get around from the other street.

My current plan was to hang out until someone could come back for me. My brother wouldn't just leave me, would he? So much had changed, I didn't know anymore.

My legs pumped harder as everyone scattered.

I cleared the vacant lots, hopped from the curb, and nearly ran right into the front end of a third-gen Camaro.

The narrow, black fender was one I was all too familiar with.

"Get in!" Noah commanded and slapped the outside of his door.

I didn't wait for him to tell me a second time. Adrenaline screamed through my body, causing me to almost trip as I jumped into his passenger seat.

Noah slammed the car in gear, popped the clutch, and launched like a rocket. He left a trail of screaming rubber and smoke as I fought my trembling fingers to hook up the racing harness that had replaced the seatbelt.

He tore around one corner, passing a squad car as if it stood still—Noah's tachometer still winding ever upward.

The cop spun around as Noah moved through the gears and exited the neighborhood like a targeted missile. I'd never ridden in a car going this fast and not been driving. What had before been a throat tightening urgency turned to something else.

The car roared and my fear mounted. Vic was right, our resident mechanic's car was much more than it seemed. This was a damn race car. One that could hold the high end without blowing the motor.

"They can't chase you if the speeds get too dangerous." I wasn't a great legal mind. But I damn sure didn't want to go to jail tonight.

"Hold on," he spat over the roar of the engine as the blue lights lit up the back glass.

For the first time, I peered at him. His determined expression was a good sign. He wasn't planning on getting caught. I grabbed onto the edges of the racing seat and held on as he tore through another intersection.

By third gear we'd picked up another pursuer.

Noah had been parked on an adjacent street. He would have had a clear shot out of there. He'd doubled back. The depth of that act wasn't lost on me.

"My brother tell you to come get me?" The question slipped out. But in truth, I had to know.

Fourth gear and gaining distance on the cops. I no longer heard the sirens and I could see the highway.

"He didn't have to." He downshifted, braked, and turned the wheel all at the same time. I wasn't going to jail and Noah hadn't left me behind. Maybe he didn't hate me. The fear faded and was replaced by something else.

I clutched the sides of the seat, my stomach tumbled to my feet, and I grinned like a maniac as we took the turn at a dangerous speed.

I lived for this shit.

Third gear again, fourth, and by fifth we were on the highway and the cops were long gone.

"Woo!" I screamed and unbuckled. I stomped my booted feet on the floorboard and shook my hair in the cold wind that blasted through the open windows. "Now *that* is some driving, McKay!"

His lip curled. "That's what you call fun?"

I turned fully toward him in the seat. “Fuck yes. And you do too. Don’t try to pretend you didn’t get off on that shit.”

Amusement shifted on his face and excitement danced in dark blue eyes illuminated by the white dash lights.

I socked his shoulder and laughed. “See, you loved it.”

From the driver’s seat, while he drove entirely too fast down the four lane stretch of black top, he cast a glance at me. It was one of those looks that made me want to cover my private parts. Or maybe strip naked and let him see it all. I bit my lip and did neither, though it wouldn’t take much for him to have me do either.

Everything in my life had changed so much, I was left with this big chunk of myself gone. Things I’d thought should be a certain way weren’t. Life wasn’t as easy as I’d thought it was going to be. And that realization left me unsteady and unsure.

I settled back in the seat and studied Noah. The knowledge of what could happen when I was alone with him hung unspoken between us. The hole inside me began to disappear. I could forget about all the things that weren’t going the way I wanted them to. So long as I was with him.

Kissing Noah had made it easy to forget who I was. There was something in the way he never seemed to give a damn and yet always showed up when I needed him.

If I closed my eyes I could see him with the barrel of the gun pressed against his forehead, daring the redneck to pull the trigger. The reckless insanity of it was one of the sexiest things I'd ever seen. Sharper, roughened edges hadn't attracted me until now. Noah had the sort that cut deep.

He was the escape I craved, no matter how infuriating he was. But what could I do about it?

As the needle on the speedometer crept farther from the one-hundred-mark, I made a decision. The car wasn't the only thing that could move fast.

Noah drove the long way around Arkadia. He finally stopped at a gas station not far from my parents' house. He was taking me home. I wasn't so sure I wanted this night to end just yet.

While he got out to pump, his phone vibrated on the console. I'm not normally nosy, but it was Aiden's number that flashed across the scene.

My brother who hadn't been there to save me like he should have been.

With a sigh, I checked the message.

Is Breanna with you?

I glanced over my shoulder at Noah, lounging on the fender.

I responded back to Aiden.

No.

Served his ass right. Out of all of them, nobody took the chance to come back for me but Noah. Let him think I was missing or whatever. This was my life to live my way. If they all wanted to forget about me, I could accommodate.

Hit me up if you hear from her.

I deleted all three messages and left the phone lying as I'd found it. If I was reading Noah right, it shouldn't be that hard to convince him to take me anywhere but home. There were a million excuses I could make, but none of them were the honest answer.

I'd been drawn to Devin because of how different he was. *His* edges were smoother than what I knew. Not Noah. And he was as far from that as any man I'd ever known.

Tonight, last night, I'd seen something behind the facade he put on for everyone. He wore a mask, like I did. Not that I would tell anyone that. The snark, the sass, was what kept me safe—sane.

Noah was the sort of guy who would meet head on whatever it was churning inside me.

I watched Noah intently as he climbed back in and fired up the Camaro. We were in the clear, he'd saved me again. I should have been annoyed, but I wasn't. Somehow, he had made me want him on a level I'd never experienced before.

I leaned across the console and whispered against his ear. "I can't recall a time I've seen you clean shaven."

I sank my teeth into the soft skin of his ear lobe and soothed the skin with a suckling kiss. The rush that came with the bold action was new and thrilling.

"I don't do it often."

The roughened texture of his voice drove me half mad and bolstered my newfound womanly courage. My fingers danced across his chest, to where his heart hammered beneath my touch.

Behind his ear and lower, I kissed my way to his jaw, and Noah growled. He managed to pull from the station without peeling rubber from the tires.

"Do you understand what you're doing here, Breanna?"

I pulled away enough to study him as he changed

lanes without so much as a flick of his wrist at the wheel.

"You keep that up and I'm not taking you home *or* to your friend's house."

All but crawling onto his lap, I answered him with a scorching kiss. My eyes closed, as the car sped through the night. When I opened them, Noah's had grown heavy with obvious arousal but stayed focused on the road.

He'd yet to even touch me.

Fear was always one of my biggest motivators. If ever I'd been afraid of something, I searched it out and threw myself completely into whatever it was.

Strange that the thing that scared me the most, was the way I felt inside when I slipped my hand in his and settled in my seat.

"I don't want you to take me home."

He didn't. I knew that Noah had a room at the old motel turned studio apartment complex. When we pulled in, the knots in my stomach jerked tight. There was no going back. Gumption was something I had more than enough of.

I didn't hesitate as I climbed from the car and followed him into room one-oh-eight.

The small apartment was neat and clean, the bed made perfectly. Not a dish left out in the kitchenette or a pair of sneakers left lying around.

Everything was perfect, military precise. The one room abode practically reeked of Noah's presence.

I kicked off my boots and left my socks in them, leaving Noah to lock the door behind us while I did a circuit around the apartment. My movements were courage boosting, until I turned and let my eyes roam over him, for the first time, without worrying that I would get caught checking him out.

"What?" He arched an eyebrow.

I shrugged with an impish smile. "You're hot, McKay. Can't I appreciate the goods?"

When he grinned without sarcasm or annoyance, my insides turned to wobbly jelly. He was so much more than that. Perfect in his imperfections. Tall and lean but riddled with wiry muscle. His shoulders were broad, his hips narrow. His perfect lips were marred by a scar. And his blue eyes so dark you could barely see the color.

Especially now, when his entire body was so tense that I was almost afraid to touch him for fear he'd snap.

I stood barefoot on the carpet, waiting. For what, I didn't know. Still he watched me, not saying a word. His only movement was to cross one arm over his body and grip the other elbow. A movement I'd seen him do a hundred times at the shop.

The silence began to echo in my ears.

"This has to be you, Breanna. I don't trust myself, not when I've wanted this so bad for so long."

My heart and my loins battled for dominance within me. He wanted me? That was big news, because he sure as hell didn't act like it.

I closed my eyes and took a deep breath. I'd never done this before. Where was I supposed to start? In the car it had seemed so simple, flirting, touching, but now…

When I opened my eyes, he was leaned against the wall by the door.

With hands that trembled slightly, I unhooked the button of my jeans, slid them down my hips, and stepped out of them. The air around me was cool on my legs but wasn't the cause of the goose bumps across my skin.

There was no going back. I gripped the hem of my shirt.

When he licked his lips, I came undone.

I was a woman who prided myself in my confidence, knew my assets and what worked. But when Noah looked at me like that, I forgot everything.

"Noah," I all but croaked his name.

"For the love of God, don't stop," he whispered.

Suddenly all the blood in my body rushed to my girly bits. No more chills because my skin was super-heated. I tugged the shirt up my middle and off, then let it drop to the floor.

I stood before him in nothing but the matching purple satin I bought to wear beneath the bridesmaid dress.

His eyes were sleepy and hungry at the same time, as his gaze swept over me. He hadn't even touched me and I was almost a puddle on the floor.

I took two steps toward him. The nagging fear in the back of my mind was that he would stop me and laugh, humiliate me.

He didn't. Instead, he closed the distance between us, tugged at the pins that held my hair up, then snatched the band from it. I held on to his hips as he pushed his fingers through my hair.

He kissed me, slowly, exploring my mouth with his tongue and driving me out of my mind. It wasn't fair that one man should taste so good, smell so good, *feel so good.* I urged my body against his, relishing in the cotton of his T-shirt against my bare belly.

When he moaned breathlessly against my lips, I smiled. This was everything I'd imagined and more.

His hands warm and incessant, slipped from my hair to cup my breasts, and stroke across my satin-covered nipples in a way I'd never known would feel so…delicious.

I clung to him as he lifted me and wrapped my legs around his waist.

He ripped his mouth from mine when he stopped at the bed. Our chests heaved, my heart raced. The last thing I'd wanted him to do was to stop.

"Last chance to back out. Once I start, I'm not going to be able to stop touching you." His voice cracked, and he swallowed hard.

I smiled with a laugh. Yeah, this was going to happen. But if he needed confirmation, I could give him that.

"I *want* you, Noah. I *want* this."

Chapter Thirteen

He claimed my mouth, kissing me until I couldn't do anything but tremble like a damsel in distress. His incessant hands slid around to cup my ass. That in and of itself was an assault on my senses I was ill prepared for.

No one had touched me like that before. When he squeezed, I moaned. My desperation for what I knew he could offer me overrode any apprehension I might have had. I needed this, even if it was for just one night.

He carried me to the bed and tumbled with me atop it. I gripped at his shirt, desperate to touch skin. He moved away from me, though, and slipped his fingers beneath my bra. Noah laughed against my lips, before tearing the satin from my skin.

Noah kissed me everywhere, like a man possessed. Each touch, each kiss, was a bolt of lightning shocking straight through my system.

He left me little time to contemplate what would happen next. I was too busy relishing the now.

There were condoms in the drawer by his bed, of course there were. He was Mr. Perfectionist, of course he'd be prepared. He broke away from me long enough to shed his clothes and put one on.

I peeked then, for the first time, let myself look at him. I'd seen guys naked before. I'd chased around Aiden's friends my entire life. That bunch wasn't afraid to streak or skinny dip.

But never had any of them been built like Noah. He was tall and lean. Every inch of him seemed to be chiseled from stone. A set of dog tags hung against a defined chest that ran to a narrow waist. A round, puckered scar on his bottom right abdomen was the only mar to the perfection.

He was beautiful. I itched to touch him, to trace my fingertips across the tattoo that ran down his side. *Semper Fidelis*. When he shifted, I glimpsed the Marine Insignia—globe, eagle, and anchor—took up most of the back of his left shoulder. Only this eagle was angry, its talons sharpened for battle.

I shivered. It was easy to forget he'd had a life before Arkadia.

When he came back to the bed, I reached for him. My fingers were more tentative than I intended, as I sought out which muscles would jump beneath my touch. When I found a sensitive spot, I used my mouth to chase the thin line of dark hair down the bottom of his abdomen.

He stopped me with a groan. "No, Breanna."

The sound of my name like that, whispered with desire and need, was the most intoxicating thing I'd experienced in my life. How could I have more of it? I never wanted that feeling to stop.

Here I wasn't stuck, I wasn't waiting on something in life to happen on me. No one was leaving me behind.

Noah captured my nipple in his mouth as he pushed my panties down my hips. I'd never been truly aroused before. But beneath him I writhed hot, wet, and wanting. My heart pounded, and my breath caught as he parted my legs.

His lips were on mine when he slid inside me. The pain was sharp, but momentary, and quickly washed away into a steady, warm rhythm that kept me on edge waiting for something.

I clutched his shoulders, mumbled his name, and when I reached the point where the world exploded around me—I did so, wrapped around Noah.

Not bad for my first time. All the horror stories from Cara, my sister, and Hadley left me little hope. But Noah was much different. Pretty sure I was glowing, warm and languid as gentle aftershocks rolled over me.

He lay atop me, sweating with his chest heaving, but said nothing. He hadn't even looked at me or touched me.

When he abruptly rolled off me and padded to the bathroom I chalked it up to Noah being his usual surly self. I snatched up my panties and shirt and pulled the shirt over my head, thankful my first time hadn't been as painful as described and that I'd actually enjoyed it.

He stepped from the bathroom naked and as glorious as he had been before. At least until I met his gaze. Anger, barely contained shot straight into my gut and jerked my back straight.

Confused, I shook my head. Had I done something wrong, was it not as good for him? The fickle confidence of the female psyche was something usually lost on me. Until now. Something coiled in my chest and whispered my inadequacies in my ear.

So, I handled my feelings my way. I stalked past him into the bathroom to clean up. I had no idea what had him acting like an ass, but it wasn't my problem.

Apparently Noah, no matter how hot, would

always be a jerk.

Slightly sore I trudged from the bathroom minutes later. Noah was dressed and on the side of the bed, an unlit cigarette dangling from his lip.

"I'm going out to smoke. Let me know when you're ready for me to take you home."

I could count on one hand the times I'd been genuinely hurt by another person.

My saving grace was that he walked out the door at that moment and didn't see the tears that welled in my eyes. I'd have been double mad if he'd seen me cry.

I fought back the anguish, the pain that licked at my heart. Go figure, the one guy I'd finally let touch me—couldn't give two shits less.

Fully dressed, I shot a text to Isaac who was on his way to get me.

Noah and I met at the door to the tiny apartment.

"You ready?" His voice was cold, no emotion.

I narrowed my gaze. He could call me names, treat me like a child, whatever…but I'd be damned if he would treat me like a whore. I was better than that. I knew it and so did he. *Fuck him.*

"Ready? For what? You to be a douche? Newsflash, you're already doing that and it's not appreciated." I shoved past him and made it as far as the threshold before he snatched me back into the apartment by my arm.

I wasn't my sister. I'd sworn from the moment she'd told me about the college boyfriend who abused her I'd never let a man touch me that way.

I swung. His reflexes were good, and he'd ducked just as my fist went flying. My fist connected with his shoulder. I'd been aiming for his face.

He took a step back and released me with a sigh, fazed not one bit.

"You do *not* get to touch me." Seething rage brought tears to my eyes. Which made my humiliation worse.

I was an angry crier. The madder I got, the hotter the tears.

"I've already done that."

I curled my lip like he smelled like the shit he talked. "I'm sorry screwing me didn't suit your tastes. You might want to reconsider your sucky bedside manner."

He ignored my jabs and crossed the one arm across his chest and hooked it to his elbow. "You should have told me you were a virgin."

I laughed without humor. "Oh my God, seriously? You're being a complete dick because I didn't tell you something that was absolutely none of your business?"

"This isn't a game, Breanna. You act like everything is, like you can just wipe the board clean and move on to your next roll of the dice. Life doesn't work like that; some things are permanent." He sounded—tired. "And it *is* my business, when I'm the one you're sleeping with."

"So you're saying you wouldn't have screwed me if you'd known?"

He balked and pressed his palms to his eyes. "Jesus, Breanna, don't say it like that."

"Why? You made it perfectly clear that's exactly what that was when you booted me from your bed."

He opened his mouth but had nothing to say to that.

"That's what I thought. I hope the bus you threw me under jumps the curb and runs over your ass." I stormed out of the apartment.

I'd built up a good head of mad and was slightly disappointed I didn't get a second shot at decking him. This time he didn't grab me.

I'd made it across the parking lot before he jogged after me.

"Wait, where are you going? I'll damn well take you anywhere you need to go."

I laughed, manically. "Like I'd get in a car with you? Hell no. Fuck off, McKay."

If he was angry, he was doing a good job at holding it back. "Look, I was supposed to protect you, to take care of you. Let me do that now."

"Or what, you run the risk of pissing Aiden off?" I snorted. "Don't worry, he doesn't even know I was with you last night. I responded to his messages for you."

"What? Did you delete that shit off my phone?" It was his turn to get mad.

Pleased that I'd finally got some sort of emotion out of him, I spun in a large circle with my arms out. "Yeah, so don't worry. Our secret is safe with me."

Isaac and Vic didn't live far from the motel, before Noah could respond, my best friend was slowing in front of the buzzing red Vacancy sign.

I climbed in without even looking back at Noah.

Isaac knew me well enough that he didn't say a word on the ride to his house. When I was mad, anyone who crossed my path was open game for my temper.

It had been a very long time since I'd been this angry. Last time, though, the anger had been misplaced on my sister and her now husband. They hadn't deserved it, and I'd done a really good job of keeping my emotions in check since then.

Not this time, Noah deserved every bit of my ire.

"So, I'm guessing you had an epic fight with McKay?" Isaac lay at the bottom of his bed.

I was tucked under the covers, trying to hide the dirty feeling that clung to me. I'd showered and stolen one of Vic's T-shirts and a pair of Isaac's pants, but I could still smell Noah on my skin.

I hated him. "Something like that."

The first rays of sunshine began to fight their way through the thick blinds on Isaac's bedroom window.

The Morales brothers lived in a small, whitewashed house, right at the end of Main Street. It sported two bedrooms, a shared bathroom, kitchen, and living room. For those of us who hadn't yet married off, Vic and Isaac's house was ground zero for most things.

He didn't push it, just tucked a pillow beneath his head and started to doze. For a tomboy, I never played dolls and the like. I wanted to ride bikes and jump ramps. Isaac had been the one to always be ready to go with me. We fished, we played RPG games, and snuck into street races. I wasn't joking when I told people the younger Morales brother was my best friend.

"Did Cara make it home?" I hadn't heard from my other bestie since Hunter took off with her.

I'd been preoccupied after the race spot got busted.

"Yeah, she shot me a text when Hunter dropped her off at home.

"What the hell were you thinking, you could have got in with her, instead of running like a crazy person?"

"There wasn't room." Upset, unable to get comfortable in my own skin, I sat up and smashed the pillow. I was still too worked up over the fight with

Noah, of how my life altering moment had been ruined, to be still. “I figured I could hide out until someone came back for me. It was chaos.”

“Noah turned around and headed straight at the cops,” Isaac said with a touch of awe before yawning. “When we saw him do that, Vic headed back up the street to distract a few of the other cops.”

“We still got chased.” I twisted a lock of dark hair around my finger and watched it slowly uncurl off the digit.

“No shit?” Isaac leaned up on his elbows, excitement brightening his face.

“Yeah.” I played it off like it wasn’t a big deal. When it was. Being reminded of how thrilling being with Noah was did not help the ache in the hollow of my chest.

“Noah a wheel-man?”

I lifted my shoulders and let them drop, not willing to compliment the guy who’d just used me for a piece of ass. I swallowed back the sick feeling churning in my gut. “I guess? We didn’t get caught.”

Isaac didn’t miss the change in my expression, but he didn’t push either. If he pushed, I’d push back, get mad, and lash out. We’d been around this block a time or two, so he held his peace.

Noah needed to learn this sort of thing if he was going to be in my life in any capacity. Not that I wanted him to be. I wished he would go to hell. But if I meant that, why was I sitting here still thinking about him?

“That reminds me, Vic wanted to know who the guys were that fucked with you in the parking lot at the Rooster.”

I rolled my eyes. With everything that had

happened tonight I'd forgotten the Rooster incident. "I don't know who they were. They followed me out, wanted more than a dance. I wasn't having that shit, so I told them to fuck off." When the fear and anger flashing on Isaac's face were chased by what appeared to be guilt, I waved it off. "Don't worry about it. You were there tonight. We're straight."

"He really go all Navy Seal and kick their asses?" Isaac sat up fully and wrapped his arms around his knees.

"Yeah. But he's a Marine, not Navy. Plus, they were drunk, and he wasn't."

"Damn." He shook his head and sat back down. I'd successfully distracted him from what had happened tonight.

I laughed. "No shit, right? Between tonight, last night, and the wedding…I'm done."

Relief flooded me as I snuggled into the bed. I knew better than to tell any of them what happened with Noah. It would get ugly if Isaac or Vic found out.

Not that Noah getting the shit kicked out of him wouldn't serve him right.

Chapter Fourteen

The annoying warmth of the sunlight through the sheet that served as a curtain hanging over the window woke me. Isaac snored lightly at the foot of the bed, his legs dangling on the floor. I crawled carefully from beneath the covers and hauled his legs up onto the mattress. With a groan, he stretched out, never once waking.

I left him that way and considering Vic rarely slept without a girl in his bed, I didn't bother knocking on his door. Instead, I called Cara to come get me.

She now drove a tiny, older model Nissan truck. Two people were about all that could fit in the damn thing, but it was great on gas, and thanks to her mechanic uncle, Rascal, it ran like a champ.

Her strawberry blond hair was piled on top of her head in a messy bun. She wore sweater patterned leggings shoved into the tops of a pair of furry boots and an oversized white T-shirt. Easily she could be on the cover of a teen drama magazine celebrating the coming of fall or holding on to the last vestige of spring.

I peeled my lip back in protest as she got out and walked up the drive.

"Okay so, what the hell happened last night?" She threw her hands out and made a face at me, like I was an eighth grade reject.

I had the door to Isaac and Vic's shop open. Vic had bought an old GTO body and had it covered in the backyard. A new block rested on an engine holder in the middle of the shop. A pile of recently cleaned parts spread out beneath it.

I sat amongst them, with a can of lubricant and a rag, polishing each one individually. The simple task would save Vic a load of time. Between work, the races, and everything else he did he barely had time to work on the car. Isaac and I had taken up the slack.

That's what family did. Plus, the busy work helped me not think about all the things that had happened last night. Which in turn, kept me from getting heartburn.

"I caught a ride with Noah, had Isaac come get me when everything quieted down." Well, that was the night in a nutshell. Sort of.

"Bullshit, what happened between Noah saving your ass and coming back here?" She hopped onto a tall, red shop stool.

"What do you mean?" I averted my gaze. I wasn't going to give her a chance to see the lie in my eyes.

"Look, a guy doesn't take on a redneck wielding a handgun for just anybody. Or take on the cops—yeah, Hunter and I saw him spin around to go after you. The sparks between you and Noah are practically electric. So, what happened after he drove right into the trouble to get you?"

One of the reasons I actually liked Cara—when I didn't care much for other girls our age—was her intelligence. There wasn't much you'd have to tell her twice.

Right now, though, I wished she was an idiot. I dropped a part, hard, and picked up another, but said nothing. Instead made an intense study of rubbing the oily cloth over the metal.

"Spill it, Breezy." My brother had started the nickname when I was a kid. I'd hated it so much, everyone else took it and ran with it.

"I had sex with Noah, he acted like a world class piece of shit, and I had Isaac come get me." I spit the words out through clenched teeth as if that would somehow keep them from tasting so vile.

Too bad I'd quit smoking, I could use a cigarette about now. I'd picked up the habit in high school. Devin had caught me, hated it, and told me as much. I stopped not long after he died; allowing him to win one last time.

"Whoa." Cara's eyes widened. "Like, your first time and everything?"

"Yup." Cara was the only person that knew for a fact I'd been a virgin. One of those drunk secrets girl best friends told each other.

I scrubbed the part with more force than necessary. "Apparently, Noah was less than impressed with that aspect and told me to leave."

Apparent anger turned her cheeks red and her nostrils flared. "Oh hell no! Did you tell Isaac and Vic?"

"No!" I snapped off a vehement shake of my head. "We do *not* tell The Brothers Morales. Doing so would ensure that *my* brothers find out. Jordan and Aiden would go apeshit. I don't need that sort of drama. I can handle Noah myself."

She conceded with a twist of her mouth but didn't look convinced. "Are you sure?"

"Yeah, I got this."

But did I really? Would I? The more things happened, the quicker I was coming to the realization that I needed to get the hell out of Arkadia, Texas. Nothing here was good for me. My world was moving on, changing in a way I didn't want to be a part of.

I wasn't made for a family and kids, for the quaint life my sister and brother had.

There was an entire world out there I hadn't experienced yet. And just once, I wanted a taste of life different from the one I'd always known. What happened with Noah was proof that staying was bad for me. I'd been irrational, chosen poorly, and like always would have to shoulder the burden of my own bad decisions.

The worst part? I had to do so in a world where I faced those decisions every day. Just once, I'd like a chance to escape the fallout.

****

I made the most of every delivery I had for the rest of the week. I drove the speed limit, made small talk with every customer, and stopped for a variety of snacks. Sometimes at two separate stores on the same run.

With Raelynn gone on her honeymoon, Cara covered afternoon deliveries when her classes at the community college were over. That put me in the shop helping Hadley for the remainder of each day.

Noah was also at the shop and there wasn't enough sugar in the world to make a forced proximity with him tolerable. As it was, my pockets were filled with more candy than a Halloween bucket. By the end of the week business was trickling down enough that avoiding him was damn near impossible.

I didn't speak to him. If at all possible, I didn't even look at him. If I acknowledged his presence at all I did so with a blank faced set of rapid blinking.

"Okay, so what's up?" Hadley asked after I pointedly ignored Noah for an entire conversation about the first real weekend of street racing.

To escape the last breath of winter, a group of racers from up north were coming down. It was pretty common for them to chase the warmer weather in Texas to race. We barely got cold enough down here to put the cars up for winter.

Jordan and Raelynn would be home tomorrow. Which meant I got to go back to my regularly scheduled deliveries. No more Noah, score one for me.

"Nothing." I hopped up onto the tall counter and dangled my work boot covered feet. Nothing was up, other than our junior mechanic being a complete prick.

"Breanna." Hadley's voice took on the motherly tone she'd grown good at using since shacking up with my brother and his gaggle of super cute crotch fruit. "Let's be real, this is not normal behavior from either of you." She gestured at Noah through the glass that separated the office from the shop. "Noah is so uncomfortable when he walks in a room with you in it he nearly jumps out of his own skin. You're not even sniping at each other—which is super strange."

"Serves him right," I mumbled before I could stop myself.

She pointed a manicured nail at me. "See. Now, what happened?"

I hefted my shoulders and drummed my heel against the wall of the counter. "Nothing in particular. I just hate him."

I jumped off the counter. We had forty-five minutes before we closed, but her inquisition was driving me nuts. There was no way I was hanging out and answering more questions about McKay. "I'm gone, I can't just sit around and do nothing. Clock me out for four."

Hadley sighed but didn't stop me when I headed through the door, the old bells heralding my exit. I wasn't the type to run from my problems. Confront them head on and end up broken and bloodied—sure. I'd already done that with Noah, and it hadn't done me much good.

Plus, I actually gave a shit about the Speed Shop. This was my family's livelihood. They needed Noah to keep up with demand. If I told everyone I banged Noah and he treated me like shit…that's it. Game over. He'd have his ass kicked *and* lose his job.

As much as the petty part of me wanted that to happen, it would be bad business. *And* it would be my fault. Considering all the bad things my family had been through that I was responsible for, I didn't need culpability for that too.

I wasn't some sort of martyr, but I loved my family.

I drove around for a while, the setting sun fighting for every last second of the day in the horizon. The cloudless sky was stained pink, and the dry brown fields showed flecks of green.

I could blame the nervous twitch in my left eye on the stress of avoiding Noah and the emotional turmoil he'd left in his wake. A long drive should have been what I needed to soothe my mind. Yet, I found myself remembering what being with Noah had been like—

before he'd broken my heart.

Because, that's what he'd done. In the silence, the hum of the truck's engine like white noise, I couldn't get away from that. He'd hurt me, in a way no man ever had. It was a blow to my pride, to my sense of self.

Physically, I didn't feel any different than I had before. I'd lost my virginity, but other than a soreness that lasted a few days, nothing noticeably changed.

I was still me.

I made a sweeping arc around the north end of the county, each mile putting a little more distance between myself and where I couldn't be. My small hometown was like four cement walls closing in around me.

By the time I pulled into my parents' driveway, I was more myself than I had been all week. Next door, my brother-in-law's classic truck was in his driveway.

My heart grew ten pounds lighter by the time I walked in the back door. Raelynn sat at the kitchen table, her face tanned and bright from a week at the beach. My pudgy faced, adorable niece bounced on her knee.

When Rae went away to college, I'd felt like she'd abandoned me. Catching her gaze now, the special something that only we could understand passing between us, I knew that had been false. Distance couldn't change what we meant to each other.

Holding the little girl suited my sister. I leaned down to hug her. "You have no idea how glad I am that you're home."

She laughed. "That bad, huh?"

"Nah, just run of the mill insanity." I plopped down on the chair across from her, stretched out, and crossed my boots on the table. "Guns were pulled, asses were kicked, I was in a high speed chase. Ya know, the usual."

Raelynn's mouth dropped open as Jordan came in the kitchen. It was him, not my mom, who smacked my feet from the table. Had Mom been in the room, I wouldn't have said anything about my weekend.

A Beth Casey freak out was something I did not need. *Ever*. I didn't get my temper and undeniable ability to fuck shit up from Dad.

"I just heard." He leaned down to kiss my sister before crossing the kitchen to the fridge. His large form seemed to take up the entire room. "So tell me why you weren't with Aiden or Vic when shit went down? Or maybe tell me how you ended up with a gun pulled on you at the Rooster?"

Fucking Isaac. This was why I didn't tell him about having sex with Noah. Once Jordan knew about something, he wouldn't let it go. Dude thought he was superman. I'd rather Aiden find out than Jordan.

I rolled my eyes with dramatic emphasis. And stuck my tongue out at Jordan's back when he ducked into the fridge to pull out leftovers.

Raelynn gave me a patient glare as she waited for me to elaborate.

"You know, you have a house *and* a wife that can make food for you." I propped my feet back on the table.

"We just got back, there's no food," he said simply as he dug a fork into cold goulash. "Now, what kinda shit did you get yourself into?"

"Nothing. Noah gave me a ride when the cops busted up the race spot. I stayed over at Isaac's, came home the next day. No harm, no foul." Yup. Didn't need to elaborate any further on that one.

"And at the Rooster?" This from my sister.

I shook that off. "That wasn't me, that was Noah. He works down there. Some guys where hassling me, he stepped in. Dude pulled a gun on him, Noah took it away from him and kicked the shit out of him. Then, I came home and you got married. Old news."

"You didn't tell me when you came home." Raelynn, gave me the big sister look.

I shrugged that off too. "You sidetracked me with the crotch-fruit revelation."

Jordan choked on his goulash and my sister swatted me. "Ssh, don't let Mom hear you. We aren't telling them yet."

"Eesh, got it. Jesus."

Shaking his head, Jordan ignored us. "Sounds like Aiden and I need to buy Noah a beer."

I snorted and jumped from the table. "I wouldn't waste my time."

No reason to reward him for being a prick.

"What's that?" Jordan's left eyebrow disappeared beneath the brim of his ballcap.

And just how was I going to explain that?

Chapter Fifteen

There were times where my sister and I were so eerily similar, it was ridiculous. Then there were times where I wondered if she was the milk man's baby. Like today. Raelynn and her new husband had only been home a few weeks and I was already contemplating buying her a ticket back to honeymoon land.

"This is *ridiculous*." I sat on my bed and made a valiant attempt to neatly wrap one of two packages.

She stuck her tongue out at me, snatched the finished product from my hand, and scrawled *Dad* on the wrapping. I continued the process and my bitching with the second parcel. "Seriously, can't you just go *Hey Mom, Dad, I'm having a baby*? It's not like they're new to this grandparent schtick."

The barb might have offended some and certainly would have hurt the feelings of most. Not Raelynn, she sent me a look that told me exactly how little she thought of my remarks.

"Don't be an ass, Bree." She slapped tape on the next package. "It's important to make a big deal out of this baby—for Jordan."

Why would a giant gearhead want a big deal made out of a baby? Any attention aimed in his direction that wasn't about racing seemed to make him uncomfortable. I made a confused face and she sighed.

"He doesn't have family to make a fuss over him,

not of his own. This is a big deal, it's the first time since the old man died that he'll have blood family. That matters, Breanna."

She was right, of course. I studied my sister for a long moment. Since as far back as I could remember, I had a blood connection to at least four people. My brother and my sister were like copies of me, different but the same blood ran in our veins. Jordan deserved something similar.

But still, the pomp and circumstance was beyond me. "But do I have to be here? I already know. I even went to a doctor's appointment with you." I'd done a great many things over the past few weeks and nothing would ever erase the term vaginal ultrasound from my mind.

I'd done most of it in an effort to avoid Noah McKay. It wasn't often I was a big ole chicken. But it was hard to function when you wanted to rip a guy's face off and hump his leg all at the same time.

"And I appreciate that." Her tone softened and she batted those baby blues at me. "You're his sister too, in all the ways that count. Jordan will want you here, to be a part of it."

Jordan loved Raelynn enough to let her make a big deal out of the pregnancy. The only reason he'd want me here would be to commiserate over the weepy women folk. But I let a big breath out and relented.

The idea of a love like theirs was smothering, but I could stomach it for one evening to make her happy.

The overwhelming weight of the idea of being stuck in Arkadia, nailed down by a husband and a family, sank down on me. I scratched my left arm and my eye began to twitch.

"You okay, Breanna? You look sick."

There was a distinct possibility I would vomit on the floor if I stayed in the spot. I got up and prowled my room. "It just occurred to me how much you and Jordan love each other. While that's great and all, it makes me all funny feeling. Like, the idea is so scary I want to run far away."

Raelynn smiled warmly and shrugged. Only a few months into her pregnancy, but she would have a small bump in her middle soon. "Because, you're not like me. You need to experience life first."

I stopped and gave her a funny look.

"I did that already, it didn't work out so well for me. But you're different…you need more. Everything I need is right here." She spread her hand out over her belly and smiled. The darkness that had once haunted her gaze was gone.

She wasn't lying about things not working out. The abuse my sister had endured I wouldn't wish on anyone. But now, she was happy and I was glad for her.

"But you're vibrant and wild, smart and ambitious. You need more. It's okay to need more, to not want to be me, or Mom, or Hadley. Do you, Breanna. You'll be happier that way."

She was right.

I stooped and kissed the top of her head as the doorbell rang. "That's the pizza. Text your husband. Everyone will be here soon."

I left her to it and went to the door. When we were kids, the three of us would rush to answer it—especially when pizza delivery was on its way. Ever since, neither Mom nor Dad even tried to walk to the foyer.

Expecting a pimply-faced teenaged delivery kid, I

jerked open the door and froze. Instead, there stood a tall, narrow hipped, sexy as all hell man with no pizza. And still my stomach did a funny little dance.

"What are you doing here?" I demanded.

One eyebrow hiked up and the scar on his lip stretched thin when he smiled. "I was invited."

The hell he was.

"Breanna, let him in, don't stand there like a putz." Leave it to my father to absolutely humiliate me.

I closed my eyes, took a deep breath and one step backward.

"It's not that bad," Noah whispered with a touch of amusement as he walked by me.

Everything in me shouted that I should walk right out the door I'd just opened, straight to my truck, and take off without ever looking back. They probably wouldn't notice I was gone. Hell, they apparently hadn't noticed all I'd done was avoid Noah McKay for the better part of three weeks.

Or that he'd broken my heart.

Okay that was a bit dramatic, admittedly. But he had been an epic prick and I couldn't exactly tell any of them about it. Jordan would probably kill him. And he was Aiden's friend. Old Breanna would have stewed, waited until there was a full house, and informed them all about what Noah had done.

That was before Devin had died, before I'd seen the sort of pain that came from blowing up everyone's secrets.

With a trembling breath I opened my eyes and cast a longing glance at my truck in the front driveway. *Escape.*

"Bree?"

I turned to where Raelynn watched me from the hallway. Her brow was knitted with worry. I could run away, but it would hurt her. I'd done that enough already.

The door closed with a click. My movements stiff and jerky as I fought against my natural instinct to beat feet and get the hell out of there.

Pizza night was a Casey family tradition, that over the years expanded to include my brother's friends and my own. As Aiden's own family now came with two high chairs and a booster seat, the rest of us were relegated to eating in the living room on TV trays.

Aiden, Hadley, and my parents in the kitchen. Me, Raelynn, Jordan, Vic, Isaac, Cara, and Noah spread out through the living room.

My sister barely touched her food.

"It's not nerves," she assured me in a hushed whisper.

"Sure, it's not."

She scowled at me and pointed at the now cold slice of pizza on my plate. "What about you?"

Noah. Each time I looked across the living room and saw him, sickness churned and acid burned its way up my chest. There would be no eating for me tonight. "Maybe I'm nervous for you?"

Her lips twisted and her eyes narrowed. She obviously wasn't buying it, but I really couldn't tell her anything else. I made a show of taking a giant bite. Chewed with a smile that was probably more like a grimace, swallowed, and tried to keep the cheesy, greasy ball of lead down.

The conversation was so loud around us, nobody heard a word that passed between us. Three people in the house knew what was about to happen. I tried to focus on the positives. It was cool to be one of the only people who knew what was coming.

At least until I glanced up and was caught in Noah's steel blue gaze. I'd seen those eyes, hazy with arousal. Worse, my body responded even now, when all he did was shoot me a questioning look. Almost like he was willing me to forgive him.

Which was ludicrous. Guys like Noah didn't apologize twice. Not to mention, what had happened between us wasn't something that he could easily fix. Not that I wanted him to.

I whipped my gaze from his and trained my attention where Vic and Jordan discussed optional components for the GTO. Vic's Mustang wasn't the sort of car that could compete with the big boys, though it would smoke most wanna-bes on small tires. The Pontiac was his swan song, so to speak, if we ever managed to get it put together.

When the discussion turned to roll cages, Aiden stepped into the doorway between rooms and added his two cents. No matter how much I loved them, tossing insults across the room at Isaac, teasing Cara about her enjoyment of the mad dash from the cops with Hunter, all of it was suffocating. Add Noah to the mix and I was forced to dig a butterscotch candy from my pocket, unwrap it, and toss it in my mouth.

As the seconds clicked down closer and closer to the big reveal, the walls crept in on me. I scratched my arm and massaged the impending twitch from my eye. I caught Isaac's gaze. Judging by the amused way his mouth turned, my eyes were reflecting the caged animal reaction I had inside. I *needed* to get out of there.

As we cleaned up after dinner, Raelynn nudged me with her shoulder.

That was my cue and I left the room to retrieve the packages. Though it was a small reprieve, I took my time with it. Anything to get away from Noah and the memory of my night with him. As angry and as humiliated as I felt, I couldn't stop watching him. It was maddening. I'd had sex one time and suddenly couldn't think of anything else.

This was how girls ended up chasing after assholes for years. Nope, not me. No way.

My sister's voice floated from the kitchen as I made my way back through. "Okay you guys, it's my parents' anniversary in a few weeks and we got them special presents on our honeymoon."

I walked into the kitchen, brushing against Noah in the doorway as I did. Ignoring the tingle from the contact, I handed Raelynn the two gifts.

Across the kitchen, near the back door as if he might cut and run, her husband leaned against the wall, arms across his chest. That was amusing enough to make me smile. At least I wasn't the only one who wanted to bug out. Though, for vastly different reasons.

Everyone crowded in the room, the babies reaching for the paper that Mom and Dad tore from the packages. Dad opened his first, to find a three quarter sleeve crew shirt. White with red sleeves and sporting the Casey Speed and Performance logo on the front right chest. The back read *PAPA*. Mom's was the same, save for the back of her shirt read *GRANNA*.

Mom wasn't looking at the shirts. Instead, she gazed down at the tissue paper in the box. There, lying neatly upon it, was an ultrasound photo. I had gone with

Jordan and Raelynn to that visit. And while the memory had burned terrifying images in my head, watching Mom's face transform now was worth it.

In red Sharpie I'd circled a little blobby peanut looking thing. My newest niece or nephew.

"Oh, Rae," Mom's voice was thick with emotion as she showed the image to my dad.

His gaze landed on Jordan with a sort of pride I hadn't expected. Judging by the way the big guy ducked his head and hid beneath the bill of his cap…my sister was right.

This wasn't about her or the baby, it was about Jordan.

My mom leapt from the table to embrace my sister and then her husband. I watched as amused realization dawned on everyone else in the room. Yeah, I needed out of Arkadia. But I was glad I stuck around long enough that I didn't miss this.

"Wait, Rae's pregnant?" My brother jumped from the table, a smile as wide as Texas. "No shit, bro?"

I'd never seen Jordan sheepish before, but he was and it was for lack of a better term—adorable. Blush on his cheeks, watery eyes, and all.

I waited for Cara to hug my sister and Jordan, before nodding toward the back door. Escape was close at hand.

Jordan was the only thing my sister had been right about. I needed to get out of here. Not my parents' crowded, happy kitchen. But Arkadia. I needed more, there had to be more. I'd just finally found the courage to go after it. Maybe, that was, if things would swing my way just once.

"Where we going?" Cara asked as she jumped into

my truck.

“To see a man about a horse.”

And to get the hell away from Noah McKay.

Chapter Sixteen

"So by horse, you mean car, right?" Cara knew I'd been saving to buy my own race car, house, or a plane ticket to Timbuktu and obviously wasn't surprised by my desire to leave. "Or are we just escaping Noah?"

I grunted. There was no sarcasm or judgment in her tone. Hell, she was the least likely person to cast stones. One of the reasons I liked having her around.

"Sort of, but not necessarily in the way you're thinking." I steered the truck through Arkadia and into the south side of town. I'd spent most of my brother's racing career making friends. Talking to people, saying the things they wanted to hear.

Marcus Calloway was one of those friends—was one of Devin's friends from way back. His family was to professional drag racing what mine was to street racing. He'd seen me drive for Isaac a time or two. And I'd heard he was looking for a new driver.

"Really? The Calloways?" She perked up in her seat when I turned down a familiar road.

I'd texted Marcus before I left home. His familiar truck was out front when I pulled in the driveway of a huge, white walled building. A giant sign hung above the four, large bay doors, boasting Calloway Racing.

Cara cast a curious expression my way.

"Ed's hanging it up, retiring from behind the wheel. Marcus and I have tossed around the idea of me driving for him next season."

If she'd been surprised when Raelynn's pregnancy was announced, she was downright shocked as I opened the door to the truck.

Impatiently, I waved with my hand. "Come on."

"Why am I here?" she whispered harshly as she fell in step beside me.

"Because you think Marcus is cute?" I got a big ole dose of Cara side eye for that one. "Because you're friends with Ava?" She wasn't buying that either.

In reality I was too nervous to come alone, to answer questions from my family about my hasty disappearance. "Nobody was going to think anything about me leaving with you."

That and I had moral support. It grated knowing I needed it.

"Hey, girl." Marcus wrapped me in a hug and then offered Cara the same treatment. She blushed, because like every other chick in Arkadia…she thought he was cute.

The bay doors were up, an open wheeled dragster and pro-modified new model Mustang sat on the concrete floor beneath the bright fluorescent lighting. Both cars were decked out in the Calloway gold and blue.

Ed Calloway stepped around the car, our arrival having drawn his attention. He wore an expression of bemused interest. No doubt he was used to girls showing up to see his son.

The princess to this racing empire, Ava, wasn't far behind her father. She waved happily at us. I liked the girl, she was still in high school and nice enough. We just hadn't ever run in the same circles.

"Breanna." Ed nodded and extended his hand.

As my daddy had taught all of us, I gave the older man's hand a firm shake, ignoring the jumpiness of my nerves. "Hey, Ed."

He looked past me to his son and raised a brow.

"You said you wanted Casey, Dad. Ain't no way Aiden is going to walk away from his street car or his family."

Ed laughed and shook his head.

I didn't let him finish whatever he was going to say. "I can drive, I'm younger, and I'm better looking."

"It's been a while, but I've seen you drive," the older man grumbled.

Ed caught Marcus watching me drive on the street for Devin once. And had turned us all over to my dad, who forbade me to ever do it again and tore Devin a new ass over the ordeal.

Not that any of that stopped me from doing the same thing, several other times.

"She's good, Dad. Her reaction times are on point. A few practice runs on a pro tree and she'd kill it." Marcus was insistent.

I got the feeling they'd had the conversation about me driving for them before.

Ed's steely gaze settled on me. "What would your dad think about me letting you make a few test passes in my ProMod?"

"He'd probably shit a gold brick." No sense lying about it. "But, I'm grown."

"And pissing off a friend and man I respect and do business with is a good idea, how?"

Thankfully Marcus fielded that ball. "Because *your* business partner thinks it's a great idea. Breanna's a better driver than most people I know. Hell, she's been hustling cash off Grudge Night for years wearing Isaac Morales' race suit and pretending to be him."

Behind him, Cara's mouth fell open.

I shot him a look and Marcus grinned. "I don't see how the entire world didn't figure that one out, you ain't exactly built like a dude."

Cara was still staring at me, in a sort of dumbstruck awe.

"I know the people, the scene, it's not like I'm new to the circuit—"

"And she'd look great on camera." Marcus cut me off. "Sponsors would be all over that."

I snorted.

Ed laughed.

"I can drive, Ed. You even said it was a shame Dad was all about Aiden when he had me to drive the 'Vette."

The older man sighed, but we were wearing him down.

Marcus continued. "She's right, Dad. I say we give her a shot. Hometown girl, racing a limited schedule, maybe pick up a sponsor or two. At least let her make a few passes before you shoot it down completely."

"How 'bout a tryout," I interjected before Marcus got too eager and cost me a ride. "Let me run a few laps in it, see if you like my times."

Ed chewed on that. "We'll make a few hits out in Dallas in a few weeks, get some kinks worked out, before the season starts. Come with us, make a few hits in the car. We'll see how it goes."

I was so excited, I couldn't react at first.

"Just remember, kid, this ain't no eighth of a mile

street race. This is the real deal."

"Yes, sir." I gave an eager nod of my head.

It was a miracle I managed to shake Ed's hand, gesture for Cara to follow me out, and walk numbly to my truck without peeing on myself or falling to the ground.

Marcus followed us out with a smug grin. "I'll give you a call tomorrow, work out all the details."

I hugged him, hard. "Thanks, Marcus. I won't let you down."

"I know you won't. Let me know how your dad takes the news."

I had no idea how I was going to tell Dad. Much less how he was going to react. This all happened so fast, so suddenly, that something was bound to go wrong. Or at least, that's what the niggling feeling in my chest told me.

****

The first official race night of the season was always special. After the incident with the cops the weekend of the wedding, Vic had the street by the old canning factory blocked off and the local cops in his pockets. This was like dancing with an old friend.

After the disaster the past month had been for me, I needed this.

Loud bass beats dropped from Vic's stereo by Jordan's trailer. The Malibu sat glistening in front of my brother's Camaro. A few dozen yards behind us, Hunter's truck sat with a group of others. Much like the last race, this time we were all on the same side.

Guys from out of town only came down every so often. When they did, we put up a united front. This week, the Street Kings would reign.

Noah knelt at my brother's car, checking the tire pressure. I tried not to notice him. Easier said than done when he walked by me every few seconds. Since his appearance at pizza night, this odd sort of tension began to build between us.

I couldn't explain it, but even thinking about it made me anxious. I glanced back to where he'd bent by the tires and he was gone. I exhaled with a rush of relief. Then turned to find him standing directly behind me.

"Jesus!" I yelped and stumbled backward, nearly tripping over the trailer's ramp.

He steadied me with a hand on my arm. "Can we talk?"

No. I had zero to say to Noah McKay, today or tomorrow, or any other day. Hell, he was the driving factor in why I finally went to talk to the Calloways. Getting out of Arkadia was necessary, escaping Noah added the urgency I'd needed before.

Still, he left me little room to argue and tugged me around the trailer until the music died off behind us. With a red shop rag hanging from his back pocket, in nothing more than a red T-shirt and a faded pair of jeans he looked good enough to eat.

Another reason to want to throttle him.

"I'm sorry. When I fuck up, I admit it. I royally fucked up where you were concerned and I apologize for that."

Tears threatened, tingling up the back of my throat, past my sinuses, and into my eyes. I bit back the emotion as the tension that had hovered between us reached its climax. I couldn't breathe, he was suddenly too close and the night air too thick around us.

"I can't—" I wasn't the type to be speechless, but in that moment I couldn't think of a single thing to say to him.

Noah reached up and stroked his thumb across my bottom lip. "You don't have to."

He saved me an undignified escape, by shrugging once and walking away. I took several deep breaths to compose myself before diving back into the fray.

The first races went off without a hitch. The cars that ran on smaller tires, true street vehicles, always made their passes before the guys like Jordan and Aiden did.

Before the big dogs ran, we all walked the eighth of a mile stretch of road to check for debris or leaked fluid. I was quiet then, mainly because Noah walked with Aiden. I no longer wanted to scream that he'd slept with me and been a dick afterward. But, I couldn't exactly act as if all was right in the world.

Apologies didn't fix a damn thing, never had. That was a lesson I'd been taught more than a few times. Or maybe I was putting too much thought into it. Noah had always been a dick to me, maybe this was his way of shoving it in my face.

If that was the case, I wanted to claw his eyes out.

On the reverse trip, Aiden and Jordan had their heads together and everyone else dropped back, I stole a glance at the man in question. He didn't offer me a smile, but his face was soft—forgiving almost. Avoiding him had left me battling a strong case of self loathing. I wasn't the girl who got burned by a guy and whined about it, who made a big deal out of her own stupidity, and yet here we were.

I refused to play the victim, it was easier to forget

it ever happened.

I forgot all about Noah in truth, about all the things that weighed so heavily on my spirit, when I saw Marcus Calloway and a group of track racers lined the side of the road.

On a shout, I jogged across the road and threw myself at him. A lifeline, my ticket out of all this mess.

He was tall, dark, and every bit as handsome. The sort of guy you see on the cover of a romance novel. Or, as was the case most of the time, on the cover of a racing magazine. He was the small-town driver gone big and more—a good friend and the reason I had a shot at making all my dreams come true.

He scooped me up and held tight. We'd dated, off and on, quietly through high school. It had never gone very far, though. No matter how gorgeous, his edges had been too smooth.

"What's up, Casey?"

"Not much. I can't believe you guys are here." When he put me down my cheeks were happily flushed. I gave a few more hugs and a fist bump or two.

When I turned to see if it was time to bring my brother to the line, Noah caught my gaze and held it. A street could have been an ocean, so big was the divide between the two of us. Yet, it would be far too easy to forget what had happened, to allow it to happen again.

"Did you hear me, Breanna?" Marcus nudged my shoulder.

"No, sorry, I was checking on my crew. What's up?"

"You've got two weeks to let your old man know about your new gig. That's when we head out."

My gut clenched. Two weeks to tell Dad. I couldn't

just bail and keep this a secret, the way I'd done with so many other aspects of my life. I'd have to tell him and he'd be pissed.

"Look, I'm going to go find Vic and throw down some money on the races. I'll see you later."

I hugged him one last time, thankful for the momentary reprieve. By the time I made it back to Aiden's trailer, Noah was there and rounded on me, his gaze over my shoulder and aimed to where Marcus and his crew had found Vic.

Who I spoke to, spent my time with, was *not* his business. Apologizing hadn't given him some sort of say so over who I associated with.

"Down boy," I all but growled.

"At least he had the decency to act like he liked it when he touched me." I couldn't help but pop off. I was angry and knew exactly where to focus that anger. It wasn't that he was an asshole. He was a caveman asshole.

Noah went rigid, his knuckles white on the nozzle of the air hose in his hand. "It wasn't like that, Breanna."

"It wasn't?" I stepped back in mock surprise, my hand on my chest. "I'm sorry, the banging me and telling me to leave was pretty self explanatory. Apologies don't fix that."

"You should have told me."

I snorted. "Why, because experience matters when all I did was lay there?"

"Baby, you did more than lay there."

I stood there with my mouth open, as the Neanderthal went back to work, a cocky half-grin spread on his lips.

Chapter Seventeen

Two weeks went by and I still didn't tell Dad about my new gig. I didn't tell anyone. Aside from Cara, who was like a vault, and the Calloways—no one knew. This was my dream, everything I'd ever wanted, and none of my family was there to share it with me.

Because I was too big of a chicken to tell my dad.

I drove Cara and myself to the track. Driving in through the open gates with the scoring tower looming in the distance was one of the most surreal experiences in my life. Yes, I'd been to large tracks. Yes, I'd arrived well before the fans. But, never had I arrived to find the track deserted save for two or three large rigs.

I stepped out of the truck and shook off the eerie feeling of the almost empty drag strip.

"Whoa, this is crazy."

The rapid beat of my heart matched the awe in Cara's voice.

"Dad and a few other teams rent it out for the weekend a few times during the off season to make sure they've got all the kinks worked out in the cars." Marcus met us at the truck with a ready grin. He wore a blue and gold shop shirt and navy work pants.

"Do most teams do it?" My voice sounded strange to my ears. My entire life the Casey family were the racing big shots. Here, I was out of my league and barely treading water. Never had anything been more motivating.

"If they've got the money, yeah. It ain't cheap, that's why we go in and pool our resources." He grinned at Cara and gave her a once over. "Hey there."

"Down boy." I shoved him in the shoulder. Cara didn't need any more guy issues. Her love life was confusing enough as it was.

"Hey, there's plenty to go around." He held his hands out wide.

Cara's eye roll spoke to my kindred soul.

The day was a rush of insanity. I shook more hands and met more people than I imagined I could considering how empty the large track was. From the lowest mechanic to the richest investor, everyone milled about and spoke to each other as if they were on the same level. Because they were, they all sported the same colors and the same dream. They were a team.

By lunch, I stood in the wide, well paved staging lane in a blue and gold Calloway race suit. I was part of this team and had no intention of going anywhere. I was going to prove my worth. Anticipation crept up my spine, hot and ready. This, the thrill of knowing I was about to make a lick, was *almost* better than sex had been.

I wondered what a guy like Noah would think, if he could see me now. Would he take me seriously? And more—why should it matter?

Angry at myself for even thinking about him, I methodically pulled my hair back at the base of my neck with a black hair band. Cara moved around behind me, shoving the long tail of chocolate locks down the back of my race suit.

"I don't want your pretty hair catching fire if you

crash and burn." She sang out in an almost melodious voice. The high pitched sound she used when she was nervous.

"Are you fucking serious, Cara?" I squawked.

She laughed and dodged the helmet I swung at her. Then turned serious. "Break a leg, Breezy. You got this."

"Don't jump." Marcus gave me a wry smile.

Jerk. I glared at him. The teasing pissed me off but served a purpose. I shoved the tiny speakers into my ears, and smashed the helmet down on my head. I wasn't nervous anymore, I was too annoyed to pay any heed to the eager twitch in my gut.

I climbed into the car. Time to prove I deserved to be here.

My entire life had led me to this place, *this* moment. Dreams couldn't compare to the rush of adrenaline that flowed through me. My hands were steady as I flicked the first switch, then the second, and the engine roared to life around me. I strapped myself into the seat, tightened the belts, and pulled on the dark blue driving gloves.

Ed's voice crackled through the earbuds and over the scream of the engine, drowning out the rumble for a few seconds at a time. "Pull up to the line, bump in how you feel most comfortable, the tree will go on you this time. Make sure you're ready."

Don't jump. *Yeah, fuck you, Marcus.*

There was no Vic and a flashlight here. Instead, the starting line t-shaped tree taunted me.

With my right hand, I put the car in gear and rolled forward, stopping a few feet from the start line in the left lane.

Before me, sticky asphalt stretched out for more than a quarter mile. This wasn't the eighth mile stretch at our local track. Huge stands towered high enough to block out the sun. How many times had my brother pulled to the line at a track like this? Did he get the same rush I did; as the muscles tightened in my body and the boost built, numbers flipping faster and faster on the digital meter on the dash? It wasn't the Vette, and family wasn't behind me, but this was as close as it would ever get.

I bumped in and held the button on the steering wheel, the car roared and shook beneath me, barely controlled attitude and torque.

The lights came down fast, lighting up like Christmas.

I let go of the button a breath before that final light, the car launching beneath me like a rocket on wheels. The eighth of a mile came and went, the rocket ship steadily building speed, the steering wheel shaking in my hand.

When I grabbed for the chutes and let off the gas, the car shook, barely attached to the asphalt beneath us. Everything happened so fast, my first instinct was a desperate desire to do it again.

Static popped in my ear as I coasted the car to a stop. "Nice run, kid, Marcus's grabbing your time slip. Let's pull her around and see if we can do it again, only faster."

That's how our day went. A few passes in the car to see if I could handle her turned into eight runs. Each one faster than the one before. Followed by a side by side pass with Marcus. I left first, but the much faster funny car beat me to the other end.

"I want to drive *that*," I shouted, flushed and happy as we climbed from our race cars. The precision-built dragster was terrifying and amazing.

"Down, girl, you ain't ready for all this yet." He laughed.

Ed walked up, time slips in his hand. "I don't know about that, son. I'd say she's pretty damn close."

He handed me the piece of paper with my speed on it and grinned. "I can have a contract for a limited schedule drawn up for you to sign sometime this week. A handful of races to start out, with an option to add more depending on sponsorship and how well you do."

I gave a whoop and jumped on Ed, hugging him tighter than I'd been belted into the car. "Thank you so much, I won't let you down, I swear it." It wasn't that I'd gotten a ride, it was that I'd proved myself. For once, someone was taking me seriously. I didn't have to be stuck delivering parts for my family my entire life.

"You better not, kid."

****

I wasn't putting off telling my dad, I was holding on to my celebration. Privately. And I ached because of it. I couldn't share my joy, my overwhelming excitement with anyone. Doing so might risk watching disappointment flash in my father's eyes.

My happiness always seemed to come at a great cost, which really pissed me off. All I wanted was something that was mine, to do something for me, and have the people I loved be happy and support my decisions.

So, I celebrated in silence, daydreaming of that first race when I'd be living my dream. Maybe I *was* being a coward, but at least I had something to look forward to for once. At least I was being nice to Noah and wasn't outright avoiding him. Right then I was leaned against the counter, staring dreamily out the front glass as he stacked service orders beside me.

When Dad came back to work from lunch and climbed from his truck, his brow furrowed in a way I hadn't seen since Aiden told him he'd knocked up Wendy. The air in my festive mood deflated.

"Shit." I spat the curse when he slammed the door to his office.

Through the glass and across the bay my brother caught my gaze, a question I couldn't answer posed on his face. I turned from my brother. Noah's keen blue eyes laser focused on me. I couldn't bear being caught between their questions and fidgeted as my stomach plunged to my feet.

"Breanna?" Noah dropped the papers and rounded the counter to me.

Fear threatened to buckle my knees. I was reverted back to that little girl that just wanted her daddy to love her as much as he did her brother. "He knows," I whispered.

"Knows what?" Was that concern that creased his features, worry in his voice?

There wasn't time to analyze Noah's reaction, not when I squeezed my eyes shut tight against the reality of my situation. No avoiding it now, I had to tell them.

"I took a job driving for Ed Calloway?"

When a customer came in, I moved away near the glass, Noah followed.

His fingertips were warm, anchoring me to where I stood. Emotionally, I needed the centering presence more than I would have ever admitted.

"You're kidding? You don't drive." Noah studied me but kept silent. As if he could see the war being waged inside of me, he reached for me. As if he could understand that war, he let his hand drop to his side.

"I do," I whispered again, watching as Aiden disappeared into my dad's office.

Hearing me, Raelynn came out of Hadley's office as the other woman finished up with a customer. My sister's small belly had finally begun peeking through her red shop polo. "Are you serious? Oh you are, you look like you're going to pass out."

I snorted. But I was lightheaded and a bit shaky. Not because Dad knew, but maybe somehow he'd stopped the Calloways from hiring me. Maybe I wouldn't get my dream at all? I could deal with my dad being angry and even disappointed. As long as I was out of here.

Hadley had appeared at my sister's side. "Driving what? They delivering parts or something?"

My gaze danced between the two other women and my dad's door. I refused to look at Noah. His fingers had fallen away, and I could practically feel the tension radiating off him.

"Wrong sort of driving, Hadley," Raelynn's voice was filled with realization.

I finally took a chance and peered at Noah. No condemnation, only confusion.

"Whoa." Hadley's comment gave voice to his reaction.

"Dad must be losing his shit," Raelynn said as the bells on the door trumpeted the customer's exit.

Noah shook his head and peered at me. "Maybe you should head out?"

"No, I need to do this now, get it over with."

As Dad's office door opened and Aiden stepped out into the bay, I did the same across from him. I met my brother in the middle of the shop. He grabbed my face and placed his forehead to mine. Unlike Raelynn, I wasn't much shorter than our brother. Tall and lanky, like him and Dad.

"Why didn't you tell me, punk?"

I shrugged and stared at the scuffed toes of his boots. Aiden wasn't angry or really surprised, of that I was grateful.

He chuckled and pulled away enough to kiss the top of my head. "He's beyond pissed."

"I figured."

"He couldn't talk Ed out of hiring you. Seems like you made quite an impression on the Calloways," he said full of pride and a touch of awe.

I brought my gaze to my brother's face, searching to ensure his words were true. The seed of dread, the tiny voice I'd ignored the moment my dad came back from lunch, silenced completely. Ed hadn't let me go. I was still racing, no matter what Dad had to say.

"Good."

He laughed and gave me a hard hug. "You need back up?"

I shook my head and started the slow walk to my father's office door. I arrived at my destination far too quickly, as if each lead weighted step hadn't taken an eternity.

My heart throbbed violently, pounding so hard against my chest I figured someone could see it. I hated that my fingers trembled as I turned the knob and stepped through.

One look at Rick Casey and I felt two inches shorter and ten years younger. I shrank before the disapproval and betrayal in his eyes.

"Were you going to tell me or just disappear this weekend?" The chair creaked as he leaned back, and my heart crumbled as he stared angrily at me.

"I was going to tell you," I whispered, still so much Daddy's little girl.

"You lied to us." His face and neck grew a darker shade of scarlet with each word.

"Yes." I had.

"You went behind my back."

Couldn't deny that one either.

But still my head snapped up, defiance steeling my resolve. "You wouldn't let me race. If you had, I wouldn't have had to lie or go behind your back. We have a perfectly good race car sitting in Aiden's garage not being used."

"And I'm just supposed to let you drive it, just like that?"

I stopped short of stamping my foot. "Yes, for the same reason you let Aiden drive it."

"That's different, Breanna."

"Because I'm a girl?"

"No, not just because you're a girl. Because you're *my* girl."

Chapter Eighteen

My mouth fell open and for several seconds we just glared at each other. This was my father saying these things, the man I'd looked up to my entire life—against whom I'd measured every other man on the planet.

Maybe this was why I hadn't told him yet, because hearing the things I knew he'd say would rip a divide in us so big it couldn't be repaired.

"So because I was born with a vagina, that makes me unable to drive a race car?"

"No, it doesn't. But you don't have the experience or the ability to perform at that level, you can barely keep your mouth shut, what does that say about your judgment?" He'd stood behind the desk now, his hands fisted atop it. The permanent grease stains in the lines of his knuckles a reminder of all I'd never be to him.

I loved my daddy, been his biggest fan for as long as I could remember. Until this moment the two worst days of my life were when Devin died and the day Dad quit racing.

"Says who?" I was shouting now, adamant and full of seething resentment. "You? I'm sorry, Daddy, but Ed Calloway and his team think otherwise."

With a sweeping arc of his arm, he slapped everything from his desk. Pens, a stapler, and various other office supplies crashed violently against the wall.

I didn't so much as blink. Dad didn't get mad

often, but when he did it was epic. The youngest, most stubborn, most hell raising of his children…I'd seen this side of him a few times more than my siblings.

"Calloway doesn't know as much as he thinks he does. To him you're a spot filler, someone to make enough noise to get him noticed." He stood and shouted, his voice thundering off the walls around me.

"He sure as hell knows racing, and he's not the only one trying to get noticed."

"But he doesn't know you, how easily you fly off the handle, how little you listen—you're not mature enough to drive a race car. That's why I've never let you behind the wheel, because at the end of the day Breanna you still need to grow the hell up."

I took the verbal punch and a deep breath at the same time. Before speaking softly. "You should know me well enough, then, to know that the only thing in my life I've ever wanted…was this."

"You're better than that life, Breanna. You could do so many things, be so much more. You're smart."

"It was good enough for Aiden when you wanted him to chase your dream for you. But if it's me, suddenly racing *isn't* good enough? Or is it that you're afraid I'm not good enough to race?"

Emotion clogged in my throat, threatening to suffocate me. "Afraid I'll embarrass you, Daddy?"

When he stood there with his nostrils flaring and said nothing, it was all the answer I needed.

I turned and walked out, angry tears streaming down my face. I hated those tears, the weakness they signified. By the time I made it halfway across the parking lot I was in a dead run. No looking back—not when I climbed in my truck, nor as I drove away.

****

I didn't work for the rest of the week, I didn't even go home. Dad and I existed in a place where we didn't speak. Even Mom gave him the cold shoulder, when I stopped at home for clothes.

She treated me with a solemn grace. Home was uncomfortable to say the least, so I didn't hang around. I survived on a steady diet of my smoldering anger and late nights helping Vic with the GTO.

"Listen, it's cool and all that you're doing this DRAA thing. But, you need to make peace with your old man before you take off." Isaac stood across from me; a huge, chromed out engine swung between us as Vic centered it.

"He's right, Breezy," Vic agreed with a grunt.

I did my best not to pout. I'd like nothing more than to hug my dad goodbye, to spend one last family dinner at home before I was gone. "It's not me, it's him."

Isaac shook his head and took a swig from a dark bottle. Even his beer was an import. "You're his baby, go home, tell him you love him. That's all that matters."

"But"—Vic grunted again and hefted the cherry picker, pushing the engine a few inches closer to the front glass—"*after* you help us lower this."

I was too uncomfortable in my own skin to face my family. The fight with Dad had destroyed my confidence in such a way so that I didn't know who I was anymore. I had a chance to do what most drivers never get a shot at. All that work, all the time, all the drive and desire—and the person I needed to believe in me the most…didn't.

He was supposed to love me, support me, and this was where we'd ended up.

My stomach churned and something inside my chest ached. I needed to forget who I was, where I came from—to exist on a level where nothing that happened mattered much.

There were two ways I knew to do that. One was racing. The other—Noah McKay.

We settled the engine in the bay; got it mostly bolted in before calling it a night. It was the Morales equivalent of a Saturday night at home. Which meant, by the time I got out of the shower the small house was full of people, voices, and the grill was going.

Not the sort of night I had in mind.

Vic watched me through a narrow gaze when I stepped from the bathroom. It wasn't the outfit, so much as me. The Brothers Morales could read me, had to know I was set to self-destruct.

Isaac choked on a beer and moved to intercept me. Other heads in the room turned, gazes landed on me, and quickly averted when Vic gave the *big brother will kill you* look.

Well after midnight, the party had been enveloped in a cloud of marijuana smoke and thunderous rap music. I shrugged Isaac off, gestured to his other friends, but didn't bother talking. He could barely hear me.

My shirt was a small knit halter that tied behind my neck and was cut low between my breasts with two skinny straps that tied around the back. The faded, worn cutoffs were cut plum up to the back pocket leaving basically every inch of my tanned legs exposed and my ass half hanging out.

I'd shoved my feet into a pair of well worn cowboy boots, thrown on a dangling pair of hoop earrings, coated my long lashes in mascara, and wiped gloss across my lips. This was as gussied up as I got. *Ever.*

"Jesus, Breanna," Vic yelled in my ear. "You need an escort to leave the house like that."

"I'll have one." If I lied to him, I'd end up chained to Isaac all night.

"Who's that?" He propped against the kitchen counter that separated that room from the living area.

I kissed his handsome cheek and was rewarded with a quick, sly grin. As I knew I would be. "Noah."

Black eyebrows shot straight up, the cute creases of his forehead raised. "Really now? It's like that?"

I shrugged. "If I want it to be."

****

I sat in the parking lot of the Rooster and toyed with the idea of going in, taking a few shots for fortification. Instead, I waited until the last of the patrons were booted from the bar, before slipping out and walking to Noah's car.

There were cat calls and lewd comments as I waited, but nothing that couldn't be handled with a well placed middle finger salute.

All of it was worth it for the look on Noah's face as he walked out of the bar, headed toward his car. Before he caught himself, there was a flash of pure, unadulterated lust in his eyes. My core warmed and my body responded.

The night was cool and I'd dressed for a purpose, not the weather, and yet the warmth flooded across my body and through my extremities. My mouth watered and gooseflesh covered my skin. When he watched me like that, I could forget all the smart ass retorts and self-righteous accusations. I could put away the times he'd hurt my feelings or made me feel like nothing.

"You know what's on the last page of a Camaro manual?" I asked with a grin in an attempt to hide my anticipation as he got closer.

"What's that?" He hovered over me now, one arm braced on the car over my shoulder.

He was warm and smelled faintly of cigarettes and whiskey.

"A bus pass." I sucked on my bottom lip.

He laughed. I hadn't expected the way the sound rolled from his chest and straight to my middle, turning everything inside me into melted chocolate.

"What are you doing here, Breanna?" He was so close, his breath kissed across my cheek.

"I came to see you."

He arched one eyebrow, the one with the scar, but didn't say a word. We both stood suspended as the parking lot emptied for the night.

When he finally spoke, his voice was husky in a way that shook me with heated memories. "Why's that?"

I trailed the tips of my fingers up his chest to his shoulders. My breath came between my lips, broken and trembling. I brushed my mouth across the sharp line of his jaw. "Because, you make it easy to forget who I am."

He kissed me, slowly at first, giving me time to memorize the taste of his lips and the texture of his tongue. I clung to him. This wasn't just making out like I'd done countless times. Noah kissed me with a purpose. The intent for *more* was clear with every responding beat of my heart.

His hands found their way to my bare sides and stroked up and down, leaving shivers in their wake.

I took the kiss deeper with an angle of my head, pressing myself fully against him. Each second that passed, his kiss sent me further into the sort of passion driven peace I sought. Nothing else mattered.

"You drive me crazy," he whispered huskily as he trailed wet lips down the side of my neck.

"Good." I threw my head back and gazed up at the stars, twinkling in the early morning sky.

"Hey! You two, don't give the show away for free. Get the hell out of here." Kevin the doorman's voice boomed across the lot.

Noah pulled away, his face strained.

"That bad?" I teased.

"That good. Get in." He tugged me from the door and jerked it open. I barely had time to grab my bag from the ground beside me, and toss it through the car, before he was shoving me across the driver's seat.

I couldn't keep my hands off him on the drive to his place. His body was tense, coiled tightly like a snake about to strike. I kissed his neck, the hollow of his throat where his pulse beat as fast as my own. I nibbled his ear as my fingers dragged across his chest, his stomach, and stroked lower, and earned a throaty moan as he drove hell bent for leather.

"Breanna."

No, no talking. If he spoke, he'd ruin it, say something that would make me remember everything.

But when he touched me, when he kissed me, the world around me disappeared.

The souped up Camaro lurched to a stop in front of

his apartment, and I crawled over the console and kissed him in such a way that left little doubt what I needed, what I wanted.

With rough, frantic motions Noah tugged me from the car. He picked me up, my legs instinctively wrapping around his middle and kissed me like a man half-crazed and starving. We hit the car, hard, slamming the drivers' door shut. The impact almost stole my breath, but I never took my lips from his.

He jerked free, gasping, panting, his eyes bright and alive. "Breanna—"

"No," I placed my finger against his lips. "Don't talk, just touch me. Please, Noah."

He dropped me then, my booted feet clicking on the pavement, took my hand, and pulled me into the apartment with him.

"You got it, no talking." The door shut with a resounding thud.

****

I didn't see Noah again after he dropped me off at my truck the next day. Over the first part of the week my nervous energy built to the point it was nearly bursting through my skin. Still I avoided work, my dad, and as many people as possible.

By Wednesday I was anxious and enlivened, unable to stand still. I stood between the Calloway's big garage and the two giant car haulers and bounced on the balls of my feet as my heart hammered in my chest. Nearly my entire life shoved into the bag slung across my shoulder.

Across the side of one trailer, my name was spelled out in large letters. Everything I'd ever wanted was inside. The car I'd drive, my shot at doing something other than deliver parts for the rest of my life.

The Calloway crew scurried around, getting loaded up and race ready.

"That your stuff?" a little guy, older, hair once red now gray mixed with a faded rust color covered by a blue trucker hat with gold trim said.

I glanced from him to my bag and back again. "Eh, I occasionally carry around random people's bags."

His quick guffaw was endearing and his weathered face brightened as he lit the cigarette dangling from his mouth. "Name's Pete, you must be the Casey girl."

"Guilty."

Ol' Pete looked a lot like a little redneck gnome with his rust flaked goatee, big ears, and faded freckles.

"Go on and stash it in the black Denali, you'll be riding in that to the track."

I did so, then followed the sounds of familiar voices.

And froze.

There, in a blue and gold Calloway racing shirt—was Noah.

Unsure how I felt about that, I could only stare.

"What's he doing here?" I asked Ed, as Noah glanced my direction before disappearing in the direction Pete had moments before.

"My peace offering to your dad." Ed tossed a companionable arm around my shoulder. "He wanted someone he trusted around to keep an eye on you. I was all right, so long as it wasn't one of those scum bag street racers."

"Huh." I made a valiant effort to seem unaffected. Not that I thought any of our street racing friends was a scum bag, but men like Ed Calloway thought most of us outlaws were. But, I wasn't going to rat Noah out.

Not yet.

I went in search of Noah, as much confused as anything else. He was irksome, annoying, and hot. I didn't know where to place him, what to do about him being here. And yet, he was like a tether to a time when my dad gave a shit about me.

"Are you kidding me?" I hissed when I found him tossing his bag by mine.

He hitched a shoulder in what I interpreted as lazy curiosity. "Your brother asked me to."

"And you always do what my brother says?" Not that it mattered. As much as he was a link to happier times, Noah was also a spy of sorts. Probably here to report back to my dad and Aiden.

"When someone doesn't delete texts, yeah." There was a spark of challenge in his eyes.

"Oh please. He was being nosy then, just like he is now. They just sent you here to report back on every little thing I do."

"And you really think they'd like the reports I have to give?"

I ground my teeth. Now he was messing with me and it was pissing me off.

He grinned. "You're cute when you're mad."

I smacked him in the chest, none to gently. "You need to go."

"Can't."

I tossed my arms out. "Why not? It's as simple as grabbing your bag and heading back the way you came."

He leaned forward, hitched a thumb in the front of my jeans, and jerked me to him. "Nope."

I shoved off, angrier at the sparkle of amusement in his eyes.

"Seriously."

"Aiden and Rick asked me to do this. I show up, not seeing it through, I can kiss my job goodbye. They feel better knowing you aren't jumping into this without someone to watch your back." He pulled the back hatch shut with a tattoo covered arm.

Then it hit me. "You knew, didn't you? When we were together the other night."

He stepped back, lit a cigarette, and took a long draw. I grew angrier when I had to fight the urge to take it from him and smoke it myself.

"You told me not to talk."

Chapter Nineteen

My first taste of the big show came at an event near El Paso. Which meant a cramped ride across the state with Noah and no ability to escape. Not that I complained. I still had no idea what sort of ground we stood on and whose side he was playing for—mine or Dad's. But this was about me and the life I always wanted.

I was getting the hell out of Arkadia.

Since I was running a limited schedule, I'd only race at the events Ed and Marcus thought I'd do well at. If I gained enough points and sponsors, he'd put me on for the full run next season. I wasn't fully gone yet, but I was closer than I'd ever been.

Each test pass in the sweltering, vibrating, behemoth car parading as a rocket ship was faster than the one before. I could practically taste the speed that left my limbs numb and trembling. Whatever nerves I'd had disappeared—I'd found my Mecca.

Here, I had a new home where opening your mouth at the wrong time meant a ten-minute diatribe by the diminutive Pete on knowing your roll, while the steady chirp of compressed air propelled torque wrenches sang out between shouted obscenities.

Noah slid into his role as seamlessly on the crew as he had at the shop. He was quiet but not overly so. Did what he was told, as soon as he was told, and knew his way around a race car. Which, admittedly, was stupid sexy.

I found myself sneaking glances, watching him work, especially in those times when I started feeling overwhelmed. Yet when I should be happy, excited—I was alone in a sea of people. Except when Noah was close by. I owed him for keeping the homesickness at bay.

My second qualifying pass Saturday morning left me filled with an eager hope. I'd felt it, that moment of speed so fierce it was as if the car was airborne. The loss of control, the sheer indulgence of the moment was so great I was still reeling when I climbed from the car.

My left foot caught on the roll cage, right as a cute, too much makeup wearing reporter waltzed up with her camera guy. It would have ended badly, had Noah not caught me before I fell.

"Easy, Breezy," he whispered with a devilish grin.

Now I had two reasons to be all wobbly legged.

"Breanna Casey?" The reporter thrust her microphone right into my face and didn't bother waiting for a response. "I'm Lainey Thomas from Drag Race Today, our readers and podcast listeners are all eager to hear how you feel about laying down the fastest qualifying time this track has seen in a ProModified door car?"

"Most fun I've ever had in a car." She asked, I answered.

I pushed the mic back with a half sneer and popped a piece of cinnamon candy into my mouth. It wasn't a lie, the most fun I'd had in my life was on that pass. Eagerness to do it all over again bubbled up inside of me. I could only think of one other situation where I'd felt like that.

I took the small slip of paper from Noah's fingertips and whistled as I read my time.

"That's an unbelievable time for a rookie and untested driver." The reporter hadn't taken my hint and gone away.

"Not completely untested," I quipped through the lazy melt of sugary covered cinnamon.

Something glinted in her eyes and her upper lip curved in a predatory fashion. "That's right. You're an Arkadia Casey, correct? Known for a more dangerous and illegal brand of racing. Not exactly DRAA standards."

It wasn't so much her words that held the knife's edge but her tone. She might as well have straight up called me trash. Something inside me twisted and turned ugly. "And still have better racers than half those here today. The proof is in the time slip."

I tossed it at her and stalked back to the pits, leaving Noah and the crew to push the car to tech inspection.

I didn't sulk, instead threw myself into the job. As the final passes were made and qualifying order was announced, I made my way to the driver's meeting—lighter than air.

With Marcus Calloway at my side I pushed open the large, metal door and was immediately hit with a blast of cool air. One by one every head in the room turned to us. Some openly stared as if I was a sideshow freak, others whispered amongst themselves.

"What the hell?"

Marcus shrugged with a snicker of amusement. "I think they all heard your interview. Might have pissed them off."

"Yeah?" I almost laughed. Didn't take much to get this group's panties in a twist.

"Seems like it."

"Well, you know what I think about that?"

He leaned against the wall and raised his brow.

"See that parking lot out there?" Over his shoulder was a barren, empty asphalt lot with two-foot weeds growing sporadically from the cracks.

"Yeah?"

"That's the garden where I grow all the fucks I give about what they think." And with that, I marched all the way to the front row, head high, and took a seat. I stopped a breath from giving them all a middle-fingered salute.

Knowing that Marcus was behind me, that he had my back, made having all eyes on me a lot easier.

Zero fucks given. This was *my* time.

****

I ignored the whispers and stares as I marched back to the pits, head held high. Damn right I was one of those Arkadia Caseys and proud of it. This unknown and *untested* driver who was the gossip of the pits had graduated to the buzz surrounding the race.

And I'd busted all their asses in qualifying.

Ed Calloway didn't appear to share in my confidence. His eyes narrowed and his mouth twisted as I approached. I didn't wilt as I might have were it my dad, but I held my tongue. Which was a big deal for me.

"You're out here to get sponsors, not strut around like a puffed up wise ass and piss everyone off."

I wasn't getting dressed down in front of a crowd,

so I stepped around him and into the trailer where gossips weren't listening in. If they were, they couldn't hear over the steady beat of the shop fan in the corner.

Thinking I was ignoring him, the boss man cursed under his breath and stalked after me. "Now listen here, Breanna. This ain't some country road with a bunch of piece of shit street racers. You can't act like that here, and you damn sure can't walk away from me like that when I'm trying to talk to you. You work for me, understand?"

"Yes, sir," I mumbled and leaned against a toolbox. That took a lot, because I really wanted to tell him to bug off. I hadn't acted that bad, in truth I hadn't said anything bad or untrue. I'd only drawn attention to who I was.

Hell, it was like Ed had been waiting for me to do something so he could chew me out. And none of the street racers I knew were pieces of shit. That was a severe miscalculation on his part. A seed of dislike sowed its way through my middle where it would fester.

His nostrils flared and if we'd had more space he'd have been pacing by this point. I waited in silence, with my gaze focused over his shoulder at the wall. I didn't argue, though I wanted to.

After a few minutes of the awkward stalemate, he huffed a sigh. "That was one hell of a pass, kid. Let's see what you do in the opening rounds."

I stayed in the trailer, alone, until the staging call came over the loudspeaker. I stepped out and immediately caught Noah's gaze. He stood by the car, Calloway shop shirt unbuttoned at the collar, and a cigarette dangling from his lips. All of that, normal.

But the glossy look in his eyes was not. Worry lurched in my chest, propelling me to him.

Then Marcus was beside me, talking about the driver lining up beside me first round. "You'll race the last place qualifier, should be an easy win. They're having problems out of the car."

My first race at the big show—none of that would be easy. But I kept those words to myself and let Marcus's faith in me replace the confidence Ed had fielded out of the park.

He was right. As I tucked myself into the car, the scented burn of race fuel and the throb of the engine's revs consumed me.

A breath later I was lighter than air, the argument with Ed, the stupid reporter, and the strangeness in Noah's eyes disappeared.

Just me and speed.

****

Exciting, terrifying, exhausting…were all three words I typed into the text message on the group chat I was sending to everyone back home. If I only admitted it to myself, it was gratifying to know they were all watching and supporting me.

Thank God they'd stayed in Arkadia for this first weekend. Though, I think my dad's anger was what kept Aiden away. I was okay with that.

Maybe I missed the car ride from the track to the hotel with my brother, discussing each run and what we could do differently. Instead, this time I'd sat quietly in the backseat of a rented sedan while a crew member took me back.

In truth, I needed the space to unwind, recharge, right up until I started up the steps of the hotel.

The noise, the excitement, had all gone away. It was after midnight, my body was sore all over, and I smelled of brake dust and exhaust. And for the first time in my entire life, I was swamped by the overwhelming feeling of alone.

The parking lot was suddenly thrust into an eerie darkness, the crew that I'd ridden with had gone their various ways and their friendly chatter followed before disappearing.

I stood on the warm pavement, my phone buzzing in my hand, and felt like I was a million miles from home. In a lot of ways I was on a completely different planet.

The flickering yellow light on the stairwell winked out as I mounted the first step. "That's just fantastic." My voice bounced off the painted concrete walls and echoed through the landing. I thought about saying something else, just to hear the echo as I had when I was a kid. But stopped when I heard something else—almost a human like mewling.

I don't scare easily. When Aiden hid behind doors and jumped out at us it was always Raelynn who screamed. Not me. So I took the steps in a calm manner, curiosity propelling me forward. I glanced down at my phone when it buzzed again and almost ran over Noah.

He was sitting on the steps, partially hidden from the path lights on our floor's outdoor walkway. Shadows were tucked around him, as if he'd shrouded himself on purpose.

When I would have snarled out some sort of annoyed reply, I shoved my phone in my pocket and approached him as I would a stray dog. "Hey there."

I stopped short of reaching out to him. Something was slightly off kilter about him. Not quite drunk, but something else. What I'd seen in his eyes at the track had spread all over his face in the dim light cast by my phone.

He didn't say anything, but the ember at the end of his cigarette grew momentarily brighter as he took a drag, illuminating his face and hand.

"Noah?"

He'd chewed his nails down to the quick. I almost flinched at the pale traces of blood that coated the tips of his fingers from the act. Yet, I wasn't afraid. Not even as I realized the strange mewling sound had come from him.

His foot beat a rapid rhythm on the step in a nervous motion, and his fingers trembled around the butt of the cigarette. His eyes were focused on something past me, across the landing and over the rail into the parking lot. At the same time I figured he saw nothing at all.

"Noah," I said more firmly now.

He was so tense, the veins in his neck protruded, throbbing with the rapid beat of his pulse. Something was very wrong here, and I finally felt the first tingles of fear slip under my skin—for Noah.

"Hey." I slipped my fingers into his hand that was clammy and cool, despite the warm air.

He blinked once before peering up at me from the step. He jumped a bit, startled, when he finally saw me.

"Breanna?"

"Yeah, I just got back." I noticed the hand with the cigarette now, wrapped with a makeshift bandage. There was blood too on his T-shirt. So not from biting his nails.

"What happened?"

He shook his head as if to clear it and made a valiant effort to act normal.

Not that I was buying it. His voice was too strained, too high pitched as he flicked the cigarette out into the night. "Oh yeah, I'm good. It wasn't much, just caught the skin on my knuckle between a hammer swing and a caliper on the car. Tiny cut really, bled like a mother."

So he hadn't been in a fight, and I wouldn't find a body stashed around the corner. I relaxed a good bit.

"Come inside, let me take a look at it. I've tended my share of shop injuries around our crew." With his hand still in mine, I tugged him from the stairs. He was putting on a good show, but something inside me was telling me not to let him go, that he shouldn't be alone. In truth, I didn't want to be either.

I was compelled by an imperative desire to have him stay with me.

"Nah, I'm good. Thanks. I'm going to go crash." He still didn't sound okay.

At the top of the stairs, he moved to pull his hand from mine and take off toward his room. A room he shared with one of the other crew guys.

"Humor me, please?"

After several moment's hesitation, he relented and followed me toward my room. I had a king size bed, mini fridge, and a full bathroom. I snatched my first aid kit that Raelynn had made me pack, and Noah followed me to the sink.

"What's really going on?" I asked as I slowly unraveled the black tape and took off the shop rag bandage he'd made.

His hand was warming up now, but one glance in the mirror where his reflection watched mine work, and I could see the demons still in his eyes.

"Tell me, Noah."

"I shouldn't be here right now," he grumbled and tugged his hand back.

I didn't let go, wouldn't. "No. You *should.*"

"Breanna." My name was a plea on his lips.

Caring about people came easy for me—except where he was concerned. At every corner something about him called to me and I fought it. I was done fighting now. I didn't want to experience this by myself, and I didn't want to leave him alone. Not after finding him in the midst of some sort of panic attack.

I peeked behind the veil of my lashes and saw a man struggling, on the verge of something dangerous that he wanted to save me from. He was dirty, appeared as if he hadn't slept in days, and was utterly beautiful despite all of those things.

With a resolute decision I pulled him with me from the sink and into the bathroom. He'd stopped fighting me. His stance was passive, like if he moved he might hurt me. It was work to ignore that, to point out that he'd saved my damn life. But I did and turned on the water in the shower.

His body grew even more tense when I jerked his bloodied shirt over his head and tossed it to the floor.

"Your shoes, kick them off."

He obeyed, silently, while not for the first time I undressed in front of him. Naked, completely, I rid him of his jeans. I pulled him into the stone shower, and shut the glass door behind us.

Chapter Twenty

Warm beneath the water, its soothing cascade rushing across both of us, I took my time. My fingers worked a lather in his hair, across his skin. I massaged my way across his body until he relaxed against the stone, eyes closed.

I tried my best to literally wash the pain from Noah. Beneath my touch his muscles softened, the color gradually returned to his skin. He'd saved me once; it was only fair I return the favor.

His body was warm beneath my fingers, the muscles rigid and at times they trembled and spasmed. His breathing mellowed. His pulse slowed to a more manageable rhythm. And as I leaned against him, to tilt his head back beneath the spray, his body responded to mine.

As inexperienced as I was, I hadn't expected that. Not every part of him was relaxed.

Water cascaded off him, carrying with it the woodsy scented lather, the grime, and whatever it was that haunted him. His eyes, droplets trapped on the ends of his lashes, fluttered open.

"I don't trust myself to touch you right now," he growled.

I took his hand, the one he'd had wrapped before, and brought it to my chest. Flat palmed against the beat of my heart. For the longest time we stared at each other, steam filling the stall around us.

"You aren't alone, Noah." I brought his other hand to my waist and kissed him gently once. "And I know you won't hurt me. You'd never hurt me."

This time when I kissed him, I pushed my tongue past his lips. He tasted of heat and longing, of all the delicious things you shouldn't have. Yet, you keep going back for more. A gradual build of heat undulated between us, a mix of desire and hot water. Until we were both wet and gasping.

In a swift, easy motion, Noah turned us so that I faced the wall beneath the spray. From behind me, he kissed the back of my neck, between my shoulders.

"I can't bear to look at you, not now, not when my mind is filled with so much chaos. Let me have this."

The way he said it, so sorrowful, my heart ached for him even as my body wanted. I nodded my assent. I'd give him just about anything to erase the hollow, lost look in his eyes.

He took me like that, his hands braced on either side of my head, murmuring words I couldn't understand against my shoulder. I let him have his anonymity, let him love me without touch. Because he needed it.

Because I was in love with him.

Later, we lay wrapped in a towel, beneath the white cotton sheets on the king size bed. The no vacancy sign cast a dim red glow behind the thick curtain. Per Noah's request, the lights were off and the room stone quiet.

"Stay," I whispered, fearful the sound of my voice might spook him.

Warm and strong, spooned against my back, Noah

stroked down the length of my arm. He still hadn't looked at me, not since he'd turned me around in the shower. "Aren't you worried about what the crew will say?"

I snorted. "No. Did you really ask me that? When have I given two shits what anyone thinks?"

He chuckled. I was so happy to hear that sound, I almost jumped from the bed and kissed him.

"Thank you."

I sat up and turned to him. "For wh—" I caught myself and pulled the sheet up to my chest. "You're welcome."

"For tonight, for everything." In the dark, he reached out and pulled me to him. "I've never met anyone like you."

"That's because I'm one of a kind."

Another laugh. "Truer words."

We lay in silence for a long time, which I was grateful for. All the noise of the weekend, from the squawking of fans, shouted orders, the loud speakers, the engines, it was nice to decompress in the silence and warmth of Noah.

I'd never been held before, not like this. More than a few times I'd made fun of the girls who said how much they loved it. Here I was, loving it.

But this was Noah, and he was different from every guy I'd ever known. He made me angry, he defied my judgment at every turn—he was an impenetrable force.

He hadn't been unbreakable when I'd found him tonight. The spell I'd pulled him from came from a damaged place. With his arms around me, I nestled my face against his neck and put two and two together with what little I knew about his past.

"PTSD?" I asked, unimpressed with how mousy my voice sounded in that moment. "From when you were a Marine?"

"Always a Marine, Breanna." He no longer sounded lost but had taken on the brusque confidence I'd grown so used to.

But that wasn't an answer.

After several long seconds of me staring at him in the dark, he sighed. "Sometimes when it gets too much, when things that have been loud for a long time go quiet…I start to remember, to think back to things I'd rather forget. Then I do something stupid, like make a mistake and bleed all over the pavement. I can't stop the flow fast enough and I can smell it, thick and metallic. Those things stay with you. Sights, scents, tastes…And then, it all comes back.

"Those aren't the sort of things you want to remember."

I wrapped my arm around him, slid my leg between his; using touch to comfort myself as much as him. I'd never thought about what it must be like, to live a life like that, to keep all those memories bottled up inside you.

"Do they give you anything for it?"

"Besides a pink slip?"

I flinched. Not from his words as the painful truth in them.

"They give me lots of shit. Anti-depressants, anti-psychotics, pills that make me drool on myself until the episode passes." He nuzzled my hair from my forehead and pressed his lips there.

"I can't live like that. I've been spinning my wheels for a year, running from this—the flashbacks."

And then the dam closed back up and Noah was quiet again. I felt like I'd touched the real man behind the wall he put up. I'd known him for an instant before the door slammed shut.

"Do you want to talk about them?" Well I could beat down walls and kick open doors. I'd been doing that my entire life.

He kissed my hair, my cheek. "No. I can't. What happened in that desert isn't something you need to hear. I can't change it."

"Was it that bad?" I'd watched the news, practiced active shooter drills at school. I knew enough to know that whatever he'd done was done for the right reasons. That didn't change who he was.

"We had a job. We did it. It's done," he said with a gravelly undercurrent in his voice.

It wasn't done. Whatever had been there had left a visible, emotional mark on Noah. How had I missed it before?

"That doesn't change who you are, what makes you a good person. In fact, I'm betting some of the reasons you signed up was what makes you that guy."

"You sound like my mom. When I couldn't stand being at home, she understood. I left, quit taking all the pills, and drove until I couldn't anymore. I stopped at a gas station and saw a delivery girl dropping off parts to the exhaust shop in the back."

"Jessup's?" There was only one exhaust shop that Dad did custom welding for.

"Yeah."

And only one delivery girl. "Me?"

"Yup."

He was full of surprises.

****

By time we got to the track on race day, my nerves were gone. The stares, the whispers, none of it mattered. I had Noah with me. I didn't need to know what he'd seen, what he'd done, to know the strength that made it possible for him to get up every day.

I was grateful for his service and more, that we had each other here. I wasn't the sort of girl who knew the right things to say. Hell, mostly I always said the *wrong* things. So, I did the opposite. Behind the wheel of a car, I found peace and solitude I'd never known before—I'd tried to give Noah the same.

But most of my time on race day was spent sitting in the driver's seat while my crew fanned the doors and checked tire pressure repeatedly. With too much time on my hands, my mind naturally wandered. Why did I care so much about helping Noah? Why should I want to? He'd been a dick to me eighty percent of the time I'd known him.

I deserved most of it. I wasn't the easiest person to get along with on the best of days. But I was growing, I was changing—evolving much like our relationship. And out here under the bright lights and surrounded by all the noise? Noah was home for me.

Being his port in the storm as well was the natural thing to do. That would mean a relationship. Something between the two of us that wasn't just sex. I'd never put much thought into that. I was too independent, too used to doing my own thing.

But when he caught my eye through the windshield and his lips curled just a little—a moment passing between just the two of us—I was hooked. No sense lying to myself.

Round after round came and went. Each time the engine growled behind the line and I stared down the start tree as the lights flashed down—my confidence grew. Who was in the lane beside me didn't matter. I was racing myself—my reaction times.

I found myself in the semifinals of my first major race. Hell, the first real race of my professional career. The staging lanes were clear now, as the rest of the field had been weeded out until only four drivers remained.

I was so nervous I couldn't wait in the car as other drivers did. I leaned against the front fender, arms crossed, and chewed on my lip.

"You look like a caged tiger, as I imagine the sort the Romans used in their Colosseum would appear."

I whipped my head in the direction of the slightly accented voice. The man who approached was the epitome of exotic, handsome rich guy. His black hair was slicked from his face in a triple digit haircut and his white polo shirt was a stark contrast to the mocha color of his skin.

If Aladdin's genie was a race fan's wet dream—he'd be this guy. Having done my homework with Ed on who the big sponsors were, I knew this was Rasheed al-Nazir. A smaller-younger version of the man flanked him. Younger brother, Kaliq al-Nazir.

"I doubt I'm the man-eating animal in this conversation."

I slid my sunglasses off and shoved them in the collar of my Calloway T-shirt. I'd tied the top of my race suit around my waist in a futile attempt to battle the heat of the day.

Under al-Nazir's scrutiny, I twitched to keep from pulling it back on.

He laughed, a brilliant flash of white teeth beneath a dark goatee. Beautiful and intimidating—the sort of man who could make or break a racer's career. A sponsor like al-Nazir could fund my race team for the entire year and then some.

He was gorgeous, in spite of the strangely symmetrical face. Little brother hadn't inherited that part of the wolfish smile. As if bored, he meandered around the car. From the corner of my gaze, Ed had begun to make his way down the staging lanes. Oh yeah, this was a big deal.

"They said you were…audacious. I'm impressed." The elder al-Nazir took a step closer, paying little heed to my personal space.

Though my heart tried to frantically pound its way out of my chest I flashed a winning smile. "That's a nice way to say I'm mouthy."

"Well, I do try to be polite."

Beside me, Noah leaned flippantly against the race car. When the younger wanna-be Sultan tried to look around him and into the car, he didn't so much as budge. It wouldn't take a rocket scientist to see Noah was a coiled rattler ready to strike.

I twisted my body between them. But kept my attention on the elder al-Nazir. "You do well." I extended my hand. "Breanna Casey."

"Rasheed al-Nazir." His hand was warm, smooth, not calloused and rough like Noah's. Odd that I would compare the two, but I was. Noah was fast becoming the yardstick against which I'd measure every man.

I swallowed hard.

"I like fast cars and beautiful women, it's not often they come in the same package." Easily twenty years older than me, Rasheed appeared barely over thirty.

I snorted but held back my usual smart-ass retort. When he held my hand too long, I had the uncomfortable urge to prance in place.

Noah edged close enough so that he brushed against my back. I didn't need to steal a glance to know he was about to rip this guy's head off.

I stomped his toe, hard. His grunt against the back of my neck earned a chuckle from Kaliq that Rasheed ignored.

"The car's fast, I just drive it. I can't help it if everyone else is slower and bitching about it."

"And bitch they should, not many first-time drivers would come in and do what you've done this weekend, Breanna. That's something to be commended." If it was possible he moved closer.

Noah's fingers wrapped around my left hip. Rasheed didn't miss it. As if an unspoken challenge had been issued, he brought my knuckles to his lips.

Two tigers, both on short leashes, and there I was stuck between them.

Chapter Twenty-One

My career hung in the balance, tethered by my ability to keep Noah from ripping out al-Nazir's throat. "Thanks." I faked a smile and barely kept my gaze from shooting heavenward. "The Calloways put together such a fast bitch of a race car. I'm proud to drive it for them."

The annoying twitch in my left eye was back, but I wasn't going to give either man the satisfaction of seeing me rub it away.

Missing my reaction, but not Noah's, al-Nazir leaned close and twisted a lock of my ponytail around a long, nimble finger. Pretty sure Noah was growling. Like a true, alpha predator, the older man was egging it on; arrogant and amused by the entire situation.

I'd have sold my soul for a peppermint right then. Maybe a chunk of peanut butter candy. Anything sweet to calm down the systematic rise of my blood pressure.

"It is not often we're graced with such boldness and fearlessness, at least not in such an attractive package."

My hair uncoiled from his finger and his hand dropped, almost brushing against my chest as he seemed to reach for the shades tucked in my collar.

Noah's hand shot out, gripped al-Nazir by the wrist before he could touch me. Fingers tinged around the edges with grease wound around al-Nazir's darker digits.

Everything stopped. My breath hitched in my chest and I froze. Both men held me captive; Noah's free hand on my waist and Rasheed's holding my hand. I wasn't just stuck between two dangerous men attempting to assert their dominance over me, I was torn between two worlds. The one I knew intimately and the one I'd only dreamed about.

Submissive little female, I was not. I'd be damned.

I took a bold step to my right, simultaneously jerking my hand from al-Nazir's grasp and sliding away from Noah's touch. I opened my mouth, a burning condemnation for both testosterone filled asshats poised on my tongue, but one look from Ed Calloway stopped me cold. Our conversation in the car hauler still fresh in my mind.

No reason to make him think of me as a heathen street racer.

"Rasheed, I see you've met my driver." Ed's intervention was like pulling the chutes at the end of the run, everything slowed down to a crawl.

This could have been bad, *very bad.*

"Indeed, I have." Al-Nazir spun on a lazy pivot and massaged the wrist Noah had gripped.

"Homegrown Texas talent, I've known her almost her entire life."

The younger al-Nazir moved near his brother now, a look of boredom on his face. I didn't buy it. The keen awareness in his eyes was too intelligent. Something was going on there that was worth further investigation. He paid too much attention to what big brother was doing. When he caught my probing gaze he grinned. That same, wolfish grin. Only instead of feeling dirty as

I did when his brother did it, I smirked in response.

Beside me again, my staging lane shadow, Noah twisted a shop rag in his fingers, until his knuckles showed white.

I ribbed him with my elbow but stayed close. The tension in his neck and shoulders was too close to what I'd seen that night in the parking lot of the Rooster.

"How many races will she run?" The conversation continued without us as Rasheed and Ed worked their way around the car.

Ed rubbed his jaw. "I was thinking about a limited season—eight races, get her feet wet."

"Even after she's put on such a display this weekend? I'd say she's jumped right into the pool, so to speak."

I strained to hear them over the squawk of the loud speaker, grabbed Noah's arm, and held on tight. Once the tension evaporated, the gravity of the situation descended. A sponsor like al-Nazir could launch my career to the next stratosphere—international races and all other sorts of opportunities. This was the next stage of this crazy dream of mine.

"Yeah well, I'm not putting a full-time crew on the payroll until she does this more than once."

Rasheed shook Ed's hand. "I'll be in touch."

I released my hold on Noah's arm when al-Nazir turned to me. "Wonderful to meet you, Breanna Casey. We'll be seeing more of each other if you continue to compete as you have this weekend. Next time, though, I would suggest you keep your guard dog on a shorter leash. I'd hate to see him put down."

If Noah could have throttled the man, he would have.

Al-Nazir and all the possibilities that dangled before me were my breaking point. The cool, collected race car driver I'd been all weekend let her rookie colors show. I blew the tires off my pass and got beat—finishing fourth overall in my first event.

"Bound to happen." Noah took a lazy drag off his cigarette as I climbed from the car.

I hadn't really thought about his reaction to al-Nazir or how close he'd come to costing me a sponsorship until that moment. No, the deep pocketed Arab hadn't made an offer but his interest had been obvious.

The rich sponsor hadn't been the issue. Noah had. I was surprised Ed hadn't used him to wipe up the grease stains in the pit after that.

The angel on my shoulder popped up then. Al-Nazir's flirtations had made me uncomfortable and Noah had reacted to that. But if the man could fund my ride for an *entire* season, a little discomfort was worth it.

This was my dream soldier-boy was fucking with. "We need to talk."

He raised his brow, dropped his cigarette, and crushed it with the toe of his boot.

I jerked my chin for him to follow me and slammed the door shut when we both stepped into the air-conditioned trailer. The last time I'd been here I was the one getting chewed out. "I wouldn't have blown the tires off on that pass had you not went all Tarzan with al-Nazir."

Noah's nostrils flared, and he leaned back against the wall, hands in his front pockets. "So, your shitty pass is my fault? Baby, I ain't the one behind the wheel."

My fingers curled into my palms to keep from reaching out and throttling him. I took a deep breath in through my nose and out my mouth and counted to ten in my head. "It was your fault my head wasn't in the game. If I'm going to get sponsorships, you can't go around assaulting one of the most influential men at the track."

His eyes were heavy lidded as if he was sleepy. That was deceiving. Anger rolled off him in heated waves I could practically touch. I wasn't scared, I had my own head of steam built up and aimed in his direction.

"So, it's okay for you to sleep with me at night, let my hands all over you, then let some other man do the same thing the very next day?" He sneered and pushed off the wall.

"That was *not* the same thing, Noah," I practically hissed between gritted teeth. "Not remotely close and you know it."

He leaned forward much as al-Nazir had done and twirled my hair around his finger. "Do you know why he did this, Breanna?"

I glowered at him, unable to answer the question, and ill at ease with my ignorance.

"Or this?" He brought my knuckles to his lips.

Even upset, my insides quivered at the contact and the warmth of his breath on my skin.

"A man like that, is thinking about something like this." He wrapped the entire tendril around his hand, made a fist in my hair and jerked my head back. It wasn't painful—it was thrilling down to the core. Especially when Noah dropped my hand and trailed his fingers up my neck to frame my face.

My breath quickened, my heart raced, and my mouth went dry. His touch, the promise of it all, rocketed through me like a freight train right to my gut.

His lips were so close, I could taste his breath on mine. My tongue snaked out and I twisted against him, desperately wanting.

But, he didn't kiss me. Instead he jerked back hard and released me. "That's what he wanted—the reaction he was looking for. He wants to make you feel all of those things. It's right there in his eyes when he looks at you, only a damn fool would miss it."

Noah left me panting and trembling. Worse, humiliated. Hot, painful tears burned past the barriers that should have held them in my eyes. The warmth of lust turned ice cold in an instant. I fought the urge to slap him.

"And I'm sorry, Breanna, I'm not going to stand around and let some other man think he can have what's mine."

His?

"I don't belong to anyone but myself, Noah." Anger morphed into full blown Breanna Casey *rage*.

He shook his head in the way parents do when dealing with an insolent child. Like they know no matter what they say the kid isn't going to get it.

That only pissed me off more. We were closer than we had been but by no means joined at the hip. The feelings I'd found for him had temporarily led me to forget that the two of us mixed about as well as oil and water. "What? Has something happened recently that I missed?"

He balked. "Last night, apparently."

"Sex is sex, Noah." I spoke to his back as he turned to walk away.

He paused long enough to glance at me over his shoulder as he stepped from the trailer. "If you think that's all it was, you aren't half as smart as you think you are."

He left me alone and reeling; no longer sure what I felt for him or why when the night before I'd been so sure.

****

Homecomings weren't easy things. I did my best to avoid mine by leaving Calloway's and heading straight to Vic and Isaac's—where I spent most of the next week hiding out.

I turned a wrench on a bolt in Vic's engine. By spending most of my free time with the Brothers Morales I effectively avoided Noah *and* my father. Since both were currently prickly thorns in my side.

The former was spending his time away from Calloway Racing helping my brother on his street car. I'd almost run right into him when I'd stopped by to see the kids.

I was still angry, still unsure of what we were. *We* hadn't defined our relationship, yet Noah had. I'd dated guys before but never had a boyfriend. The idea of those sorts of ties to someone had always scared me to death. Freedom to do what I wanted, live my dreams in a way Dad and Aiden never had, was something I couldn't just give up.

"What it do, Big Shot?" Vic strolled across the small, box like backyard, the screen door slamming shut behind him. "Why come all the way home just to work on my pile?"

"They don't let me get my hands dirty. Besides, she ain't a pile, she'll be a beast." The headers gleamed, as did everything else. The GTO would run like a scalded dog.

"Ain't she though?" His lips twisted into a proud smile. Jordan, Vic, Isaac, and Aiden…when I looked at them I felt the same inside as Vic did about the car. I was proud of the brothers of my heart. My entire life had been measured by what they accomplished.

Now, it was being gauged by what I could accomplish, and I was letting a boy get in the way.

"What's on your mind, Mama?"

Too much, not enough. How could I not think about Noah when I could still feel him trembling against me…when I could still see the war that had been waged in those dark blue eyes? The secrets he kept would eat him alive and no matter what he said or how he showed his ass—I wanted to save him.

To say I was conflicted with the distance between us was an understatement.

"Everything is different." I put the tools away and wiped my hands on a shop rag. "And Dad barely talks to me. I've got a shot to really be something and it feels like I'm doing it alone."

"Think maybe that's because you pushed everyone away so you could do it yourself?"

I pursed my lips. Leave it to Vic to use logic to point out my flaws. He was absolutely right, though. I'd wanted to do this on my own but hadn't realized how hard that would be. I'd avoided my family—for what?

When I didn't respond, just stared out of the garage, Vic pulled me to him and hugged me tight in the way he and Isaac were known to do. They didn't hug lightly. Every man I'd had contact with while I'd been at the track had wanted something from me. Vic didn't. The reassurance of his love, of family, was what I'd needed the most.

When he released me, he held me at arm's length and spoke somberly. "You are never alone. Not when you have us. Rick will come around, it's just hard for him to see his baby girl doing something that could get her hurt."

"Any of us could get hurt, Vic." The double standard there was going to drive me insane.

He shook his head and hitched a hip on the fender of the car. "Nah, it's not the racing that scares him. It's the world, that sort of life can eat you and spit you out if you don't watch it. Those guys, the ones with the deep pockets, they don't care about a small-town girl like you. Just what you can give them."

And we came full circle, Vic giving voice to the conclusion I'd already come to.

Had I not experienced that moment with al-Nazir I would have blown off Vic's words. Instead, I chewed on that thought. It would be easy to pout and say I could take care of myself. Especially when I'd always been surrounded by people who had my back. My brothers, my friends.

Hadn't I already seen what happened when I got too cocky? That scene in the parking lot of the Rooster had been proof of that. But Noah had been there, he'd had my back—even with al-Nazir.

His. I shivered.

"He sent Noah with me."

Vic nodded. "He's a cool cat. I still can't figure him out, though."

"He was overseas." The words tumbled out of my mouth before I could stop them, propelled by a need to defend Noah. "I think, maybe, he saw a bunch of screwed up shit."

"I can see that." Vic eyed me, like he could see all the things I didn't say. "So, the two of you got something going now?"

"Something like that."

"Well, ain't that some shit."

"Shut up, Vic."

He laughed. "Wait until Aiden hears about this."

Chapter Twenty-Two

My first plane ride was to Florida. Being cooped up in a super-fast, metal death machine I wasn't in control of—was terrifying. I'd plugged in earbuds, stretched out in the seat as much as possible, and tried to zone out until take off. Not that I could remain still. I shook my leg to the beat of an urgent, restless song, and constantly shifted in my seat unable to get comfortable.

I didn't look away from the small window until Noah stowed his carry-on in the overhead and sat in the seat beside me. Even when he said nothing, and I hadn't seen him in days, my body reacted. My skin prickled with an acute awareness, the rest of me tensed with the promise of his proximity.

I closed my eyes and pretended to try to sleep, thanking the good Lord above that Noah was the quiet type.

"Are you ignoring me, Breanna? You're usually more confrontational than this."

I took a deep breath. I was packed in a confined space with dozens of other people and was a direct representation of Calloway Racing—a fact Ed was quick to remind me of. Considering the very idea was to entice sponsors, not incite a riot, I couldn't very well lose my shit on Noah on a plane.

No, I really didn't want to argue with Noah. His tone was teasing and light, it was my tightly wound nerves that were the issue.

I opened my eyes and kept my voice at a whisper. "Something like that." I held my breath and dug around in my purse for a peppermint. Maybe he'd take the hint and if not, I could drown him out with music until we were back on solid ground.

Noah snatched the dangling plastic cord from my hand. "You've been avoiding me for days."

"Observant." The urge to turn toward the window—away from him—was so strong I wanted to punch him in the throat. I hated feeling this way, running headlong into disaster to keep from dealing with the emotions he churned up in me.

When the scenery began to move, I was pretty sure I turned a faint shade of green.

"That I am. Enough to realize you're terrified of flying."

"I'm afraid the first time I do anything." I hissed around the mint, to keep my voice from slipping into the high-pitched screech it took on when I was nervous.

His brow shot up and surprise etched its way across his face only to be quickly replaced by something else, something more knowing. "So, you were afraid that first night you made love to me? You didn't respond like it."

I glanced around to make sure no one had heard him. I pressed two fingers of my left hand to the twitch in my eye. "No. That was different."

"Was it?" he teased.

I checked my seatbelt and swallowed as the plane taxied down the runway. Noah intertwined his fingers with mine, and I held tight to his strong, work roughened hand.

When I ignored him, his tone softened. "This isn't so bad. When I deployed, I was strapped into a seat on a C-130 for nearly twenty hours. It was loud, uncomfortable—sitting straight up. The entire unit, all our gear, jerked and tossed around everywhere. God, I just wanted that trip over." He switched his grip, the rough pad of his thumb stroking rhythmically across my knuckles as his voice trailed off.

"It's funny, because looking back, that plane ride was the smoothest part of the whole fucking thing."

My first instinct was to look away from the shadows that darkened his eyes. I wasn't one to run, even if what I found there was scarier than this plane trip. But the pain that haunted those blue depths for only a few seconds was so intense it stole my breath and I forgot all about my fear.

When I didn't immediately fill the silence, he continued. "I remember focusing on how uncomfortable I was the entire first ride. Then on the ride back, I crashed right after take off. First time I really slept in more than a year."

I wasn't a mushy person. I left the sweetness to Hadley and the understanding to Raelynn. I shoved away the emotion that throbbed in my chest. When I couldn't deal with things, I ignored them. I couldn't do that with Noah touching me. I pulled my hand away and leaned against the window. Though the cabin of the plane was crowded and stuffy, the pane beneath my cheek was cool. I closed my eyes and focused on the hum of the plane's engines, the vibration of my seat, and the gentle rumble of conversation around us.

"I can't control the plane or what happens while I'm in it. It's not really fear. I just don't like it. If I'm going to crash, I'd rather be the one behind the wheel."

I opened my eyes in time to see the corner of his mouth curl.

"You can't control every aspect of life, Breanna."

"Can't I?"

He sighed, the sound filled with obvious irritation.

"I hate it when you do that. Act like I'm too stupid to see what is right in front of me." I waved my hand in front of my face for emphasis.

Leaning back in his seat, he smirked. "Sometimes I think you might be."

My back shot straight and I glared at him. "What the hell is that supposed to mean?"

He shook his head, then pinched the bridge of his nose as the captain announced we were at cruising altitude over the Gulf of Mexico. I didn't have time to shudder at the thought of nothing beneath me but water.

Slowly, he unfolded from the seat and leaned down to whisper against my ear, so only I could hear. "It means, you're dumb enough to keep telling yourself and me that it's just sex. Or that al-Nazir is just a sponsor you'll do anything to get. I know better and so do you. That girl in the hotel, the one that took a shower with me? She ain't like that."

"We had sex and that is all it was, Noah, and all it will ever be. And you're wrong, you don't know what I'll do to make my dreams come true."

They were just words. Silly, stupid, angry words. Yet, they were lies.

****

I'd finished in the top four in my first two races. That sort of performance was enough to warrant me a full season in Ed Calloway's ProMod if we could find sponsors. For the part-time gig, Ed's company backers had put up some of the cash. To run full time? Travel, crew expenses, and maintenance on the car was a lot more than that.

The time had come for ass kissing mode. I was oddly well suited for it. My fake smile was on point and I could schmooze with the best of them. But eventually I'd have to meet up with al-Nazir again and that thought left me with a bad case of indigestion.

The constant flow of racetrack meetings served a dual purpose. I avoided most of Noah's brooding, and I might get my ride fully funded for the entire season.

This should be the most exciting time of my life. My brother, my sister, my friends were proud of me. But the person I needed the most, the one whose opinion truly mattered had nothing to say. I'd moved back into my childhood room and my father still gave me the cold shoulder. And Noah and I weren't really on the best of terms—which bothered me more than I cared to admit.

The only thing I could do was keep one foot in front of the other, smile for the sponsors, get mouthy during interviews, and sign the steady stream of autographs that now followed me.

The last sponsor meeting of the weekend was a big one. Noah knew it too, the tension in his shoulders and the sharp set of his jaw made that obvious. The way he glowered at me as I climbed onto Ed's golf cart shook me. Weak kneed, suddenly apprehensive of what I was doing, I turned away from the only person at the track who might know me better than I knew myself.

No. He couldn't. He was wrong. This was my dream, what I'd wanted since I was a little girl at the racetrack watching my daddy. Noah was wrong, I'd do anything to keep living this dream. *This* was my everything. Even if it meant having Rasheed al-Nazir's paws all over me.

Fortified with my newfound resolve, I stepped out of the elevator into the hallway that led to the skyboxes at the drag strip. Watching any of the races from this vantage point would be ideal for a rich spectator. Unless you'd grown up on burnt rubber and race fuel. My soul needed to be down on the concrete, baking in the sun and freezing at night, with the throbbing roar of the engines echoing through my senses.

My first instinct was to look past the handsome man who stood from a leather chair—the room was more suited for an opulent business environment than a racetrack. Much like the room's main occupants. Kaliq al-Nazir smoothed his suit and nodded to his brother, who stood across the room lazily examining a cigar.

The wall of glass overlooking the racetrack beckoned to me and I crossed the room as Noah and Vic's warnings went unheeded in my memories. Al-Nazir was the fastest path to my dreams, when it came right down to it. He was the biggest fish looking to stock my pond.

"Breanna, lovely to see you." Having followed me, Rasheed took my hand and placed a lingering kiss on my cheek.

Any other time I wouldn't have questioned his affections. I was a badass driver, of course he wanted to sponsor me. His touchy ways were just a cultural thing. I was one of a kind; there wasn't another on the circuit like me.

I glanced back at Ed Calloway, who stood in quiet

conversation with Kaliq and another man in a three-thousand-dollar suit. My skin prickled in an uncomfortable way, like something putrid was sliding over me.

Turning away from al-Nazir and toward the large pane of glass, I squeezed my eyes shut. Noah's face flashed in my mind, twisted with defiance and jealousy. No, he was wrong. This was about driving, my dream job. I'd had a taste; I wasn't going to allow it to be snatched from me now.

"Nice to see you too." The words tasted dry and bitter.

I stared out the windows at the view, down the track to the mountains that sprang up in the distance. In the next few days, the gleaming empty seats would be filled with sweating bodies. The track wouldn't shimmer pristine and unencumbered. Excitement coiled up from my middle, reminding me why I was really here. I turned to Rasheed and smiled.

"I love this track, there is something thrilling when the valley fills with the roar of engines. The mountains keep the sounds from escaping and they build pressure as if they might explode." With obvious reluctance he released my hand.

"That sounds a lot like being in the race car." Or spending ten minutes alone with Noah McKay.

Behind me, Ed and Kaliq were discussing the ins and outs of a contract for the season—negotiating their terms. It was a battle to feign interest in Rasheed while I strained to hear what the other two men were discussing.

"Just so long as your driver understands her responsibilities to the sponsorship." Kaliq spoke quietly but not without me hearing.

"She'll be fine, she'll do whatever I tell her to do." Ed responded as if that was to be expected.

And just like that, everything started spinning out of control. My lips flattened and my eye twitched. The quickening of my pulse sounded in my ears so loud I didn't hear Kaliq's response. I was Ed's driver, but if Rick Casey didn't tell me what to do I'd be damned if Calloway did. No, not gonna happen. I'd always respected Marcus's father but was fast learning he didn't have much for me.

"Will you be attending the banquet tomorrow night?"

I whipped my head around, chin out, to Rasheed. I'd barely heard him and opened my mouth to bow out. I wasn't the banquet sort of girl.

"Oh no, Marcus and I will be there. But I—" Ed broke in.

I cut him off. "Is that an invitation?"

There was a swanky sponsors party that the DRAA held a few times a year. It allowed the car owners, sponsors, and schmucks with money to schmooze in an atmosphere not tainted by race fuel, muscled up gearheads, and the occasional wise-ass driver.

My career hung on this season and my ability to entice sponsors. If I really thought about it, the banquet would be a good thing for me. Despite what Ed thought.

Al-Nazir peered to where the white T-shirt was pulled tight across my chest. I almost laughed, considering that what boobs I had weren't even big enough to be classified as modest. *Skeevy prick.* Noah was right, not that I'd tell him, this guy was a predator.

I wasn't my sister. I could chum the waters and

hunt with sharks. So long as they carried around career changing checkbooks.

"Well then, it seems that I have an extra invitation, if you cared to attend." His words rolled out like they'd been dipped in poisoned honey.

I grinned, though my good humor didn't reach past the twist of my lips or the angry glare of Ed Calloway. The boss's chest puffed out and his nostrils flared.

"Shaking down my driver, Rasheed?"

Both men laughed like something was funny and I missed out. The tension in the room sizzled, as Ed had developed the look of an overstuffed sausage. Across the room, the younger al-Nazir flashed his teeth. Knowledge and humor danced in his dark eyes. This was the man I needed to talk to, let the two rams bash their heads against each other to distract themselves.

This was shaping up to be an interesting weekend at the races.

****

I sat in a big chair in my pit. Unlike if I were racing the 'Vette my job here was just to drive. All the in between times I twiddled my thumbs. It was enough to drive me insane. If we had a sponsorship, I'd be out promoting my team.

Needing something—or someone to scowl at in my boredom, I sought out Noah with my gaze. He wasn't in the pits anymore, instead he stood, chatting amicably with a young couple. They embraced and Noah smiled, his body loose and posture familiar. I'd only ever seen him with my brother or another one of us…

I didn't sit idle and all but leaped from the chair. Noah had friends? Family? It seemed improbable that he invited a buddy here to see him, not if he'd left it all behind. Judging from the guy's super short haircut and ramrod straight spine, he was likely a Marine too. Someone Noah served with.

Someone I *had* to meet. Maybe weasel out a few clues about Noah McKay.

"Hey there." I sidled up and gave my best attempt at a sweet grin.

Noah balked. I couldn't be sure if the tension in his muscles was in response to my arrival or my smile.

His friend didn't miss a beat and extended his hand with smile. "Hey there. So, you're his lady driver."

"Something like that." I practiced polite, happy Breanna. The one Ed wanted me to be, the easily controlled one. I kept the eye roll to myself.

Noah's gaze narrowed, and he did that sexy little jaw clenching thing he did. He wasn't buying it. Amazing that his signs of annoyance turned me on more than any compliment al-Nazir could offer.

Noah's friend smiled brighter. "I bet this is better work than the desert."

My gut clenched for Noah. Though, he showed no reaction.

"Probably. I'm Breanna Casey." I gave a firm shake.

"Jerry Nichols, this is my wife Nikki."

I repeated the gesture with his pretty wife. "Nice to meet you both, swing back by some time and I'll get you a few T-shirts."

"Will do!"

Noah hadn't said a word. I took the hint and sauntered back to my chair.

He'd told me some bad shit had happened to him but never what. Something had ripped him to shreds emotionally, had put the sadness in his eyes that refused to be washed away. The glutton for punishment that I was, I had to know.

When he and his friend separated, and Noah went back to work, I was off to the metaphoric races. I checked the time, snatched two shirts, and took off in the direction I'd seen Jerry and Nikki Nichols take.

If Noah wouldn't tell me things about himself, maybe his friend would.

Chapter Twenty-Three

Al-Nazir had been right about the sound of the cars in the hollow. The scream of the engines on qualifying laps echoed across the surrounding mountains only to slam back into your chest once the run was over. A double whammy of resounding throttle and adrenaline. It was a rush, though I didn't stand at the bottom of the stands long—I was on a mission.

The throng of people that would be here for the races hadn't yet filled the stands. Not in my race suit and still relatively unknown, I maneuvered through the thin crowd with ease.

Jerry and Nikki were in the stands near the top, taking full advantage of the general admission—sit where you want—pre-race setup. Tomorrow those seats would be filled with people who'd paid my entire paycheck from two weeks at the speed shop for one seat.

"Hey, I grabbed you a few T-shirts," I said as I waved and made myself at home on the bench seating beside him and his friends.

His wife smiled once, before launching back into the conversation with the young woman beside her.

"Hell yeah!" He grinned big and took the shirts from me before saluting with his beer. "You didn't have to chase us down for it though."

I sized him up. His brown eyes were sharp and

keen. This wasn't his first rodeo. "I might have had ulterior motives."

Anything else I had to say was drowned out by the dual roar of engines revving into burnouts as two cars lined up for passes.

After the run, it looked like one of the cars leaked fluid onto the track. I took advantage of the precious moments the track crew cleaned up the lane.

"You asked if I was Noah's lady driver—why?" I wasn't known to be one who beat around the bush.

The grin was quick. "His mom still sends most of us care packages, those that kept in touch"—he gestured to a guy a few seats down—"we email. She told me he was dating a lady driver and working on her crew. That's how I knew to look for him while we were out here."

"Huh." I made a face. Noah and I dating? News to me. Hell, that he had a mom—one that sounded pretty damn amazing—was too.

"Yeah." Jerry watched me for a long moment. "McKay, he's had it rough. Makes it hard to get close."

"No shit." I hadn't made it easy, either. "He's never told me about any of his friends." Or his family. Or anything, really.

"He's a good guy, hell he's a god damn hero." He winked. "And *obviously* has good taste in women."

I snorted and his wife elbowed him with a roll of her eyes that told me she wasn't the least bit concerned. Could Noah and I be like that? I couldn't remember why I'd even chased this guy down. I'd been trying to find a tether between Noah and the real world, when everything he gave me made him more of a mystery.

"A couple of us are meeting him for a beer

tomorrow night at the hotel, you should come with him."

I couldn't—the banquet. "Maybe. I think I've got a thing."

"That's right, Big Shot Race Car Driver." He teased but amusement twinkled in his eyes.

"Something like that." I smirked and did my best hair flip and sashayed from the stands.

Noah had friends, a past, things that I wanted to know. Suddenly the banquet wasn't so imperative. I needed to figure out how to be in two places at once.

****

I couldn't for the life of me figure out why Ed would be angry about my going to the banquet. It's not like he wasn't going to muzzle me before I got there. Sure, I owed the guy a lot, but his parental behavior and constant condescension was starting to chafe.

The only way not to rail against Ed's authority was to think of other things. Like my relationship status. There was no clear definition of Noah and me as a couple. Especially not since what he'd said on the plane. It burned me to know he thought I was too stupid to see through al-Nazir.

I was a lot of things, I'd done a lot of fucked up things, but I wasn't going to prostitute myself for a sponsorship. Not fully, anyway. I knew this game. I could play it as good as al-Nazir and still keep my panties on. Noah, most likely, was jealous.

He had to learn I wasn't property. I was my own person.

It would never get that far with al-Nazir. Just the banquet, that Ed and Marcus would attend as well. If the rich Arab wasn't slapping his stickers all over the car by the end of the night, I'd drop it.

Bile rose in my throat and tears pricked my eyes like tiny, evil daggers. My entire life I'd wanted one thing, to make a career out of the dream I was living.

Why couldn't Noah understand that?

I sought solace in the one place I could truly be alone. Sure, voices crackled in through static in my earpiece, but I could drown them out with the roar of the engine. The driver's seat was my zone, my clarity, the one thing I could control completely.

I sat in contemplation as I waited in the staging lanes for my final qualifying pass. Around me, Noah and the rest of the Calloway crew worked in a rhythm of clanging parts and inaudible shouts. They checked tire pressure, pulled me forward, and wiped my windshield at least a hundred times. And still I sat, gloved fingers wrapped around the steering wheel, refusing to think of home, of Arkadia, of my family.

Then, finally, I was rolled under the bridge and released from the cart that pulled me. In my ear, Ed's voice crackled to fire it up. Before he finished, I had flipped the switches and jabbed my thumb against the start button. She rolled over immediately, a rumbling purr as the pistons steadily worked up and down.

The vibrations from the motor tickled the bottom of my foot as I gently worked the gas pedal. The first time I'd sat in this car, at a large track, nervous energy had practically leaked from my pores. Now, *this* was home. For the first time I wished I was sitting in a Casey car—not a Calloway.

I flinched when that old wound tore open and began to fester. The 'Vette sat in my brother's garage collecting dust rather than winning races for me. All because I was a girl.

Anger swelled higher and higher as did the RPMs on the two-step staging system. My frustration with all the things holding me back and all the things I couldn't explain expanded. By the time the lights on the tree flashed and I released my hold on the red button, my foot was on the gas pedal as if the hounds of hell were gnawing at my rear bumper.

Everything flashed by in a Technicolor blur of adrenaline and race fuel. The car roared so loud the vibrations pounded in my chest and stole my breath. It was in those moments I found clarity, everything made sense. It wasn't about pleasing someone else or being something I wasn't.

In these moments, I was the truest, best form of myself. Life breathed here in a swirling mass of speed, on the edge of reason and control.

I took my foot off the pedal and jerked down on the lever that released the chutes as I crossed the quarter mile stripe. The pass was good, better than most. I didn't need a time slip to know it was fast, I'd practically felt the tires blistering the concrete. No tire shake, no slipping, a straight line to the finish—full tilt boogie.

I brought the car to the turn off the track and waited on the guys and the mule to come get it. I wasn't shocked to see that Noah came alone to pull the car back.

The heat inside the car, even with the sun full gone behind the mountains, was suffocating, and I'd been in there for far too long. So while Noah hooked the car up, I killed the engine and jerked off my helmet. Sweat plastered my hair to my face and fading adrenaline pumped my heart against my ribcage.

Noah caught my gaze as he straightened in front of the car. When I was a kid we'd gone to the beach a few times. Every trip I'd gone deep sea fishing with Dad and Aiden. Getting caught staring into Noah McKay's eyes was like leaning over the rail of the boat and peering off into the deep blue depths of the Gulf.

I felt like I could get swallowed up and no one would be able to find me.

Trembling, I jerked my gaze away and slipped the gearshift into neutral. Focusing on the steady methodical motions of removing my gloves kept me from glancing at him through the windshield. How did I deal with the emotions churning inside me when he wouldn't let me in?

The slight jerk as the ATV started to pull the car forced out the breath I hadn't realized I'd been holding. I'd never been so off kilter, so unable to process my feelings. Noah made everything blurry, took the wheel from my hands. There was no control here—nor was there any going back.

Qualifying first was a high that quickly pushed away everything else. The entire team rode the wave of exhilaration and suddenly Ed wasn't angry with me for agreeing to attend the banquet with al-Nazir.

I was in the trailer with Noah and the diminutive car chief Pete when Ed came in. I hung my race suit on the rack against the wall and turned to face him as he came up the steps.

"You got a dress, kid?"

Something dark and dangerous flashed in the ocean-like depths of Noah's eyes.

"Yes, sir." I was amazed at the strength in my

voice.

"Good, the banquet hall of the hotel is on the main floor, past the bar. Starts at seven. I'll meet you in the lobby."

I swallowed despite the dryness in my mouth and nodded once.

"Marcus and I will both be there. You don't talk to anyone without one of us, got it?"

Like the dutiful mockingbird, I repeated my response. "Yes, sir."

With a curt nod, Ed disappeared out of the trailer.

Like he could see the storm brewing in Noah, Pete was quick to follow, shouting over his shoulder. "Lock up and give Bree a ride back to the hotel, McKay. Take the white truck."

Then we were alone. My heart thundered manically in my chest and my left eye twitched. I fumbled in my pocket for a piece of candy, ripped the gold wrapper off a disk, and tossed my butterscotch savior into my mouth.

All lean muscle, tense jaw, and angry eyes, Noah watched me. I wanted to simultaneously strip naked and run away.

"Got a date?" He leaned back against a toolbox and crossed his arms over his chest. "Didn't you think that was something you should have told me?"

"It's not a date." I knelt and busied myself tying my Chucks. "It's just some sponsor thing."

"Sure it is. I take it al-Nazir will be there?" When I didn't readily respond he snorted in the derisive way that was all too Noah. "A man like that, Breanna? He'd break the part of you that makes you special, he'd crush your spirit." He took a deep breath, scratched at the phantom itch on his arm. "I'll meet you in the truck."

The keys to the trailer landed with a clang on the corrugated metal in front of me when I didn't stand.

"You ass." I snatched them up and chased after him, like I always did, stopping long enough to slam the trailer doors and lock them.

"You don't get to do that," I growled when I climbed into the passenger seat of the truck.

"What's that, Casey?"

"Treat me like that, like I'm a piece of shit you can bark orders at."

He cranked the truck and tilted his head, the muscle in his jaw clenched. Which was my undoing, I kept on.

"You don't get to act like you have some say in what I do and what I don't do, when you come and go in my life on whatever whim suits you. Your judgment? Can go to hell."

The problem with telling someone off when sitting in the cab of a truck with them, was that you couldn't stalk off in a self-righteous huff. I settled for thrusting myself against the seat and glowered out the window as Noah wheeled us from the track.

I was further infuriated by the fact that he said absolutely nothing in response. It was always going to be like this. We'd never find common ground—we were the crash and burn sort of couple.

"I've never judged you," he said quietly.

"Really? Sure as hell seems like you do that a lot." And it stung every time he did. No matter how many times I told myself it didn't, Noah's opinion of me really mattered. I crunched down on what was left of the buttery candy.

He rolled down the window, pulled out a cigarette, and lit it. I couldn't help but watch his nimble fingers and remember for an uncomfortable moment how capable they could be.

He spoke through a long drag, "I worry about you. Rick wanted me to keep you safe, and you make it damn hard to do."

I laughed without humor. "Keep me safe? You mean bang me senseless?"

"Jesus!" He spat the word and thumped ash from his cigarette with force.

"What? It's true. You're all worried about me, right up until I screw a perfect stranger."

I got a lot of side-eye for that one.

"I'm not a stranger, Breanna. And when we're together, it's more than that."

"Aren't you? Is it? You haven't told me shit about yourself, we barely have conversations. This is the most you've talked to me since the flight here. And if we aren't having sex—you're making me feel like…" My voice trailed off and I effectively gave up. There was no use. I couldn't make him understand or change who he was.

"I've told you things." The end of the cigarette flashed red as he eased the truck onto the interstate on ramp toward the hotel.

He had. He'd told me a few important things. Then…nothing. "But I don't know anything about you. I didn't know you had a mom."

"Of course I have a mom, everyone does, Breanna."

"I didn't know she did cool things for the guys you served with, like send them care packages"—which sounded pretty June Cleaver to me—"or that you told her I was your girlfriend."

The cigarette was flicked with efficiency out the window. "She wanted to know why doing this was important to me"—he broke off and lit another cigarette—"the crowd, the people, she worried it would be too much. I had to tell her something."

I didn't know what to say to that. I'd seen what being here did to him. In truth, I'd wondered often why he did it at all. Whatever anger I'd had ebbed away until I collapsed into silence for a long time. Noah was exhausting.

"If I'm not your girlfriend, you can't keep shaming me for the decisions I make for my career or getting angry because I don't tell you things." I turned to him and gave a watery smile, which cost me a lot. "This is *my* life, Noah. You don't have to be here. I know what it costs you, and I don't want that on my hands, ya know?"

When his only response was to kill the engine and shut the driver's door in my face, I got out and went inside. Whatever issues Noah McKay had, couldn't be mine. Not when life for me was changing at a drastic pace.

It was time to put on a dress and go to work.

Chapter Twenty-Four

The dress was the classic little black number and showed off entirely too much leg. Let's face it, as tall as I was *everything* showed too much leg.

Not blessed with my sister's curves, I'd learned how to accentuate what I had. The sleeveless, low-cut top with sparkling trim, could only be worn by someone with small, pert breasts. With enough sparkle, I didn't look like I had the body of a prepubescent boy.

The gossamer fabric brushed across the tops of my thighs with each step I took, taunting me about how far out of my element I was. I would have been far more comfortable in a race suit.

I smirked and slipped into a pair of high heels. Al-Nazir wasn't a short man, but I doubt he'd appreciate having to look up at me.

On a pause, I took a brief turn in the mirror before strutting out of my hotel room. I looked damn good all dressed up, it was a shame I couldn't show off for Noah. Quite a bit of time had passed since the Rooster bathroom and the tiny gold dress he'd nearly peeled off me.

The large banquet room was attached to the bar, so that people from our party could slip easily in and out, and wait staff didn't have far to go to the kitchens. Emotion slammed against my chest. Noah and his friends would be through those doors. So close and yet…

To quench my sudden need for sugar, I perused the large, buffet style tables of hors d'oeuvres. Tiny brownies coated with icing and butter-cream dinner mints would have to suffice. I shoved a round, chocolaty morsel into my mouth and barely chewed before forcing it down. Snakes of nervous energy twisted around themselves in my belly. I couldn't eat. I should never have agreed to this. I chucked the rest of the plate into the trash—not even sugar could save me.

The blame for my lack of appetite and overabundance of apprehension lay with Noah. I wasn't scared of al-Nazir, I was worried of what Noah might think. Never in my life had I cared so much for one person's opinion of me. Which just pissed me off. We weren't together, not really. I couldn't be my own woman and *his* at the same time.

With a quick swipe of the back of my hand over my mouth, I wiped away the scowl and replaced it with the most fake smile I could muster. Al-Nazir and his entourage of handsome, dark-skinned, suit wearing lackeys had arrived.

"Breanna, I'm so glad you could join us." He took my hand, brought it to his lips, then leaned in to brush them across my cheek.

I deserved an award for not openly gagging on his cologne. "Thank you, Mister al-Nazir."

"Again, call me Rasheed." He winked and released my hand.

"Rasheed."

Across the room Marcus and Ed had entered. The elder Calloway was making a beeline straight for us, his brow furrowed and his lips tight.

One of the suited men lifted a brow and searched the crowd. Something passed between him and al-Nazir, though whatever it was dissipated as the Calloways approached.

"Glad to see the gang's all here." Ed leaned close so that only I heard him. "You were supposed to wait on us before coming in."

With a hitch of my shoulder I grabbed a glass of champagne from a passing tray. Nobody was there to card me and as the men began their roundabout way of discussing sponsorship I found Kaliq al-Nazir at my side.

"It's like watching two stags pair off, seconds away from getting hung up in each other's antlers." His voice was tinted with amusement. Though, his comparison was off.

"More like a tiger and a rhinoceros." I chugged the rest of my champagne.

He all out laughed at my correction and took my empty glass, replacing it with a full one.

"So you know that my brother is looking to start his own set of teams, a driver and car for each class. With only a limited schedule, he assumes you are not fully bound to Calloway with a contract."

I figured as much and I wasn't. I took another sip of champagne and cast a glance toward the bar, hoping for a glimpse of Noah. "Then why's he entertaining Calloway?"

"It's not Calloway he's entertaining." Kaliq was younger, more attractive, and didn't leave me feeling like I needed a shower. So, I took his words to heart. "Be careful with my brother, Breanna Casey. He has more than one idea for the purposes you'd serve."

And with that, he turned to a group of gentleman I'd not met and continued about his evening as if he hadn't just dumped a truckload of truth all over me. Not that I'd be telling Noah he was right. Nope. Not today.

"Finally." Rasheed detached himself from Ed and turned his wolfish smile on me.

Kaliq's words and Noah's reservations haunted me. My skin crawled with thousands of tiny fear spiders, their legs pricking and prodding, and my mouth went dry.

My exit was only a few feet away, through the open doorway into the bar. If I craned my neck at the right angle, I could almost see Noah. I imagined him throwing back beers and laughing about old times. Which, is what I'd rather be doing now that I'd had that lovely conversation with Kaliq al-Nazir.

"Your boss thinks to convince me to finance his car—with you as the driver—for next season." Rasheed gestured toward Ed with his glass.

I grunted and took another sip of bubbly to wash away the snark infused comment about my conversation with his brother.

Rasheed eyed me like I was the meal now and lowered his voice as Marcus moved to us. "I have no interest in paying Ed Calloway to do things I can do myself."

It was my turn to raise a brow and feign surprise. For some reason, I'd developed a touch of loyalty to the younger al-Nazir brother.

"I could make you a superstar. Your face on billboards, take you to Europe and the Middle East. Make more money than Calloway Racing could dream of."

Several of Rasheed's employees—they were far too classy to be called goons—intercepted Marcus who cast me an anxious glance. Not worried enough, though, because he'd left me with them in the first place.

The entire room began to shrink, the air grew oppressive.

For arguments, Rasheed had made a good one. If I had been in this for fame or money, it would be a dream come true. And maybe, had Noah not been right all along, I might have contemplated doing it. But the thought of betrayal and judgment swimming in his dark blue eyes left me sick to my stomach.

I'd spent my entire life wanting to race, to live in my very own fast lane. I didn't care if I was famous, not really, no matter what anyone said. The attention wasn't what drove me—winning was.

"And if I didn't want to go overseas?" I drew to a halt the second I realized al-Nazir had been slowly moving me toward the main door.

He laughed, a rich sound. "Of course you would want to, there is so much more to this world than the bubble you live in. I can show you."

Noah's words haunted me. Working for a man like al-Nazir would stifle me, I'd break under that sort of pressure. He was right.

I opened my mouth to say something but couldn't.

Searching for a lifeline, I spotted Marcus in the growing crowd. Al-Nazir replacing my empty glass for a full one, much as his brother had. Only when Kaliq had done it the move had seemed almost chivalrous. This was not.

"Car is held up in tech." Marcus came up,

annoyance creasing his handsome face. “Dad said for you to go on back to your room, get rested up for tomorrow.” He peered at the glass in my hand. “You can’t be caught drinking, Breanna, the DRAA will pull your license for that until you’re twenty-one.”

I pursed my lips more because Rasheed laughed with amusement than because Marcus had chided me. Being treated like a child by everyone around me was getting old—fast.

With a sweet smile, I handed the glass to Rasheed and inclined my head to Marcus. “Sure thing, I’ll head right up.”

The hell I would, I was ditching this party and going to see what Noah was up to.

Al-Nazir misinterpreted my intentions when I’d lied to Marcus. “Nicely done, Breanna. I ensured there would be a snag to ensure we get time to talk.”

I swallowed hard as he gave a gentle tug on my elbow. Now, I was in a precarious position. I could scream and send everyone into a panic. Make an ass out of myself and Calloway racing. Or I could go with al-Nazir—and then what?

If I’d been driving the ’Vette this would never have been an issue.

“I think I need a stronger drink,” I mumbled under my breath.

Again, al-Nazir’s laugh rolled through the room. Heads turned as he leaned in, close. “Come upstairs with me, I’ll pour you a stronger drink and we can talk contracts.”

Old Breanna wouldn’t have hesitated, even when his nefarious intentions were written all over his face.

New Breanna needed time to plan her escape.

"Excuse me, I need to use the lady's room."

On a smooth pivot I darted into the bar and headlong into disaster.

The bar was swanky, all dark wood and low lights, and smelled of expensive liquor and bad intentions. I flagged the bartender down with a wave of my clutch. Male laughter floated over and washed off the seedy amusement that clung to me from my run in with Rasheed al-Nazir.

"Tequila, two shots," I said and prayed silently the bartender didn't ask for my ID.

He didn't and dropped two glasses on the counter and filled them with gold liquid.

"That bad, huh?" Noah leaned against the bar between two stools.

Why did one guy look so hot in a simple black T-shirt? It had to be those sexy blue eyes or the sarcastic curve of his lip. I downed the first shot immediately, the burning liquor coating my dry throat.

I sighed.

"Something like that"—I fired back the other shot and gestured for two more—"You were right, he wants me to drive for him."

Noah stole one of the glasses and downed it with a grim smile. "Told ya."

No further rubbing it in was necessary.

"How's it going with your buddies?"

He shrugged and closed up like a vault—like he always did. Shutting me out when I needed him to let me in.

"Al-Nazir wants me to come to his room, I'm pretty sure he doesn't want to discuss contracts," I blurted in desperation for a reaction.

Noah's face changed, something dangerous and unnameable flashed in his eyes. I wasn't afraid, instead, I had to physically restrain myself from climbing all over him like a cat in heat.

His head slowly tilted to the side and his grip on the glass turned white. "And?"

I couldn't stop myself, I wanted to see that flash again—taste the heat behind it. This time, I was the one shutting down and keeping my secrets.

He didn't get a chance to put words to the violence that swarmed him, as a drunken Jerry came swaggering up and dropped an arm around his shoulders. "Another one for *this guy*!"

Then, he pointed at me with the tip of his beer bottle. "He's a god-damned hero, driver lady, I hope you know that."

"Easy, Jerry." Noah held him steady as several other guys approached.

"Did he tell you?" Jerry focused his bloodshot eyes on me.

When my response was to blink with curiosity, he cursed under his breath and shook his head. "He never does."

"Let's not relive that shit, bud. Once was more than enough for a lifetime." Noah tried to steer him away from me and the current topic of conversation, but Jerry took a seat on the stool to my right and spoke sincerely.

"Outside Jalalabad, took some heavy fire from insurgents lost half the unit or more. Noah was medic, trying to save everyone he could. But we were done for, gonna die. Every…damn…one of us. Only like six still alive as the bastards took the building we were holed up in."

Behind him Noah shoved a hand through his hair and backed away. The anger was gone, replaced by disgust and something else—shame? I wanted to go to him, but the emotion in Jerry's drunken voice kept me rooted to the spot.

This was the secret Noah had fought so hard to keep to himself, this was the reason for medication and the panic attacks. It wasn't morbid curiosity that had me hanging on to Jerry's every word. No, this was more than that. To love the man, I had to truly know him.

I cast a glance at Noah, willed him to believe that no matter what Jerry was about to say—I'd still see him just as I did every other day.

Chapter Twenty-Five

Noah was tense but lost in his own head as Jerry kept talking. I could see it in the way his eyes took on the dark sheen the sky does just before the storm clouds roll in. He wasn't here anymore, he was there. I rubbed my arms for warmth and signaled for another shot.

Jerry had gone somewhere else too, his eyes were wide despite the alcohol in his system. "Noah covered us up, with bodies, man, our brothers. We lay there, days, covered in the stench of rotted corpse while those bastards carried on around us—the things they did to the bodies, man." His entire body seemed to heave with one giant shudder and he swiped a palm across his face, like he could wipe away the tainted memory.

I stopped short of gasping. Every word he said played in high definition in my mind, to the point my stomach rolled with nausea.

"One night he crawled from under the pile. Recon, he said. Then he comes back, pulls us out and screams for us to run. We were all hurt, save for him and one more guy. We weren't moving real fast—couldn't, needed a head start, a diversion."

"He gave us one of those, all right." A blond, stout guy, his hair still cropped short like most Marines, sidled up beside Noah and tipped his bottle in salute.

Jerry snickered. "He blew the whole god-damned block up. Our *medic*, blew it all to shit. After laying under the dead bodies of our brothers, I couldn't think much less try to get out. I'd given up. But not McKay, he just kept going. Got us out. We'd be dead if not for him. Got to a place we could communicate, called a bird in—

"A fucking hero." He saluted stiffly.

I was fighting tears. Too many emotions, too much going on for me to process. I needed to breathe.

"I'll drink to that." My voice stayed even as I clinked another shot glass to Jerry's bottle.

I hadn't realized it had been so gruesome or so—sweat prickled at my brow as I looked for Noah, he'd moved from our group. He was in a corner, beer in hand, still staring straight ahead but not seeing anything.

I left my perch at the bar and went to Noah.

"Hey."

He didn't look at me but spoke with a chilling quiet. "Are you going with him tonight?"

"Are you seriously asking me that after what Jerry just told me?" Of course I wasn't going up to al-Nazir's room. He knew me better than that, yet right then I couldn't be angry at him. Not after what I'd just been told.

Everything had changed. When I saw him now, I saw so much more than the jerk of a mechanic at my dad's shop or the man whose touch drove me wild. The layers to Noah were far more complex than I'd ever imagined.

"I live with that every day, Breanna. It's not a thing for me"—he gestured between us—"this, *is.* Are you going?"

There were times, like now, when dealing with

Noah was exasperating. "I can't figure it out, Noah. I get whiplash every time I'm alone with you."

Save for the twitching of the muscle in his jaw, he was stone.

"You know what, never mind. Nothing I'm going to ever do will make you happy anyway. It's never good enough. Half of me wants to tell you yes, just to see if I get a reaction and the other half—can only tell the truth. No, I don't want to go to that creep's room—contract or not."

I spun on a spiked heel and stormed away. How dare he mix me all up, confuse my emotions, and then just check out? It wasn't fair.

Al-Nazir caught me right as I rounded the corner into the banquet hall. I'd been hoping to just storm through and avoid him altogether. I *never* got that lucky.

"There she is! Come, Breanna, I was telling my brother of your interest in my proposal. Perhaps we should go upstairs now, I can put some ideas on paper for you to go over."

Kaliq raised his brow in a high class *I told you so.*

Rasheed placed his hand on the small of my back, causing me to shiver but not from desire or warmth. I sidestepped and tried to pull away. He held tight, moved his grip to my hip, and ushered me to the door.

His brother watched with interest, as if waiting for the next shoe to drop. It was like the guy knew I'd make a scene or something. Amazing, I'd met the guy a handful of times and Kaliq al-Nazir seemed to know me better than anyone at Calloway. He sort of reminded me of Isaac.

I shoved al-Nazir's hand off my hip with force and

sidestepped him with my mouth twisted in disgust. “If you have an offer to sponsor me through Calloway Racing, Rasheed, put it on paper and bring it to me tomorrow. But right now, I need to go.”

He brushed off the hand his brother had placed on his arm. With a warning glance to the younger man he stepped closer. Annoyance and several other emotions waged war inside me. I never intended to go to Rasheed’s room. I wasn’t stupid. To him I was a commodity, not a driver.

He snatched for me again, and I jerked away. Anger won the battle for my reaction and *the* Breanna Casey came out to play. “This is me saying I wouldn’t drive for a man who’d stab someone in the back and ask why they’re bleeding. I get the feeling you’ve done that a time or two.”

Incredulous, he spun me. “Are you—”

Whatever he was saying was swallowed up by a loud, incessant wailing. I blinked a few times as I was blinded by the flash of bright lights that gave us a second’s warning before water rained from the ceiling.

“Fire!” someone shouted above the earsplitting scream of the alarm. The droplets of water splattered across the dark patterned carpet and stained the white tablecloths. All around me people did their best to dodge the water and escape.

My reflexes were slowed by the champagne and tequila, and I was whisked away by al-Nazir’s goons toward the nearest exit. Putrid smoke was creeping into the ballroom, floating up to the ceiling, despite the sprinklers. It was pandemonium.

Something crashed and someone screamed, yet all I could think was how al-Nazir would think I owed him something.

He rescued me from a hotel fire.

The door loomed closer, al-Nazir's people pushing bodies out of the way and trampling them. I fought then, kicking and wriggling free.

Familiar, calloused fingers gripped my arm and with force pulled me away from al-Nazir and his flunkies. None of which looked back to see where I'd gone. *Oh yeah, totally safe signing with those guys.* I was nothing to him, after all, exiting the building and saving his own ass was far more important.

I landed against a wall of lean, corded muscle, and was spun onto my feet. Noah easily guided me away from where the crowd rushed toward the exit.

"What about the fire?" I am usually all for doing my own thing, but if the place was burning down I saw no reason to go back inside.

He leaned close, his breath warm against me. "The hotel *isn't* on fire."

I could smell the smoke, the acrid scent burned my eyes and my nose. When I opened my mouth to argue, he held a finger to my lips, pulled me through a now empty kitchen, and out a back door where staff had gathered.

"It was a paper fire in a garbage can in the kitchen off the bar."

I shivered at the brush of his lips against my ear.

Then burst out laughing as what had just happened dawned on me.

"Seriously?"

The corner of his mouth twitched and mischief twinkled in his eyes.

"Impressive, McKay. I'll be more impressed if you

manage to get Calloway to bail you out when they find out one of the guests set a garbage can on fire."

"They won't find out." He shoved his fingers into his front pockets and rocked back on his heels.

There was a finality to the way he said it that I didn't question.

"I had to do something to get you away from him, pretty sure smashing my fist through his face wouldn't end well for either of us."

I tossed my hands in the air. "I *wasn't* going to his room, Noah."

"I couldn't take the chance. When he touched you—like I said, I had to do something."

"When he touched me?" I glared in disbelief.

"I followed you, saw him corner you when you went back in. I didn't want to ruin a shot you had at a sponsorship."

The emotion that tightened in my chest, that wrapped around my heart and squeezed, wasn't one I could verbalize. Not yet. I raked water from my skin, where it had gathered in small droplets.

"You started a fire for me," I whispered, in awe.

"I'd burn down the whole damn town for you."

He grabbed my face and kissed me. It was the kiss of the damned. The meeting of two souls that were made for each other, despite all the faults that piled up between them.

****

I spent the night with Noah, never questioning who I was to him or all the things that he kept from me. I *knew* him, truly knew him and he me, and that's all that mattered.

Noah drove us to the track that morning and my

world was perfect. If al-Nazir didn't want to sponsor us now? Who cared. There were other sponsors. I was making my mark on this industry and I was here to stay.

But one thing was missing—my family. I missed them. Text messages and video chats about Raelynn's pregnancy cravings and my baby nephew Devin saying his first words wasn't the same as being there. No matter how crazy they drove me, they were mine.

If it weren't for the light, tickling sensation in my center that Noah McKay caused, I'd have been a blubbering wreck when we pulled through the gates at the track. It was now, as everything fell into place, that I needed my family the most.

There was only one way I could think of other things, forget about the gaping hole in my chest that was Arkadia, Texas and all I'd left behind. My right toes twitched, the desire to shove my foot through the throttle so ingrained it had become involuntary.

I was too much of a Casey to get race day jitters. Instead, saliva pooled in my mouth and my muscles tensed in anticipation of the crush of adrenaline.

Stepping out of the truck and into our pit, I had my game face on.

Ed Calloway did too. His eyes were narrow and his jaw tight. I'd spent the night with Noah, which always seemed to encase me in a sort of lust thickened fog. Nothing else mattered when we were alone like that, the outside world ceased to exist the moment he touched me.

That was more addicting than any drug or any race. But it left me on uneven footing, standing face to face with a man who was visibly perturbed.

"What's up, Ed?" I tried to smile, but as awkward

and forced as it felt I'm sure it looked worse.

"There wasn't a god-damned thing wrong with my car at tech. Just conveniently wouldn't pass when that bastard wanted a chance to proposition you to drive for him." Lit up and ready for a fight, he jabbed a time gnarled finger in my face.

Marcus jogged up his face twisted and chagrined.

"So?" He snatched his hat from his head, twisted it a few times, and shook it in my face.

My gaze darted back and forth, searching frantically for an escape.

"So, what? Chill, Ed. I have no interest in driving for Sheik Creep-face."

Marcus threw his hands in the air before elbowing his dad. "See, told you."

"One of these days I'm going to shove a car straight up his—"

"How about you let me do that?" Noah's voice cut through the conversation like a sharp blade.

Over Ed's shoulder, Noah knelt by the race car. The knowing smile he gave me, was all the incentive I needed to shove my race car right up Team al-Nazir's ass.

****

I'm not a morning person. Unless morning happens after ten or so. So when the bed sank beneath Noah's weight and I realized the space beside me he'd occupied all night had gone cold, I cracked open one eye and scowled.

"Get in bed or go away," I grumbled and tried to jerk the sheet up over my face.

Noah snatched it from my grasp and pulled it down. Sunlight streamed in from the window where he'd pulled the curtain open. I closed my eyes against it, though my vision was filled with a bright orange glow.

"Wake up. I brought you something."

His voice was easy, happy. Not something I was particularly used to from him. That sound coaxed me to open my eyes again.

"You're too damn pretty." I scowled and sat up. It was the God's honest truth. From the sharp angle of his jaw to the dark blue of his eyes and the way his bottom lip was slightly bigger than the top—even the scar didn't deter from that.

"You ain't too bad yourself." He leaned down and placed a gentle kiss on my lips; the scent of coffee laced with something far sweeter beckoned me.

I pulled away and scrambled to my knees. "Do I smell mocha."

With a laugh he handed me a to-go cup with one of those cardboard coffee shop sleeves on it and cast his chin toward the tiny table in the corner. "And beignets."

In nothing but my panties and one of Noah's white T-shirts I shot from the bed and across the small hotel room. The first sip of chocolate and sugar laden coffee scalded my tongue, but it was worth it. The scent from the white paper bag was even better.

I didn't bother sitting down. Placing powdered sugar on dough and putting it anywhere near me was a dangerous situation. Within seconds I was chewing my way to confectionery heaven and the table looked like it had snowed.

Noah's laugh echoed in the empty room. He'd sat down on the bed, stretched out his legs, and leaned against the headboard. The way he watched me turned something inside me to a self-conscious ball of fluff. Like cotton candy that was wrapped around my middle. The sort of thing that reminded me of my brother and his fiancée and how they made goo-goo eyes at each other.

I popped another piece in my mouth and carried the bag and coffee back to the bed, where I straddled Noah's middle and sat on top of him. "Remember that time you bet me a hundred bucks my brother and Hadley were fooling around?"

His blue eyes were warm and crinkled a bit at the corners. Could he be any sexier? "Yeah."

I shook a little donut piece at him, showering his shirt with powdered sugar. "This *almost* makes up for that."

"I'll remember that. Sugar makes you sweeter."

Legitimate.

The part of me inside that missed home, that longed for Arkadia, could usually be quieted with the gentle curve of Noah's lips. Not this time. Everything with al-Nazir had left me off kilter for the first time since Devin had died. The thought of my friend jerked the homesickness back so that the powdered sugar soured on my tongue.

"What is it?" Noah straightened and anchored me to him with his fingers on my hips. Concern showed in his sharp features, casting his eyes in haunting shadow.

I shivered. Most times I'd toss my ponytail and make a flippant remark to distract the attention focused solely on me. Not now, not with Noah. It mattered that I didn't, that I be honest.

"Every once in a while it gets too much and"—I swallowed hard while his thumbs massaged my hips—

"I miss them. Especially after last night."

He kissed me. Had he held me, attempted to wrap me in his arms to soothe me, the calm I was suspended in would have broken. I'd have pushed it all back down then, the fear and the sadness. The anger.

Instead his lips caressed mine, easing the tension and the wash of loneliness. Nimble fingers slid up my sides to my back and down again. A rhythmic, gentle persuasion that chased away the melancholy.

When he pulled away, my heart was beating fast and my lips swollen. I looked down to keep from getting lost in the emotion I saw in his gaze. When I plucked at his shirt, the sugary snow poofed between us.

"Here." He chuckled and pulled the shirt off and tossed it.

Shirtless Noah did little to slow my heart rate.

"Better?"

My laugh rang out despite the heaviness that still hung in the air. "I mean yeah. That ain't so bad."

He bit my bottom lip and settled back on the bed. "Good. Last night was a lot. The past few months have been a lot for anyone to handle. You're young, Bre—"

"Oh no," I interjected and moved to climb from him. Though, Noah's hands snaked back to my hips to hold me in place. "Not you too."

He shook his head emphatically. "I don't see why you don't just drive the 'Vette for your dad. Aiden would tune it for you, hell he'd love that shit."

Pain gave a heavy lurch in my chest and I slid from atop Noah. Unable to just disappear in my silent grief, I dropped the bag of beignets with a papery crunch onto the nightstand and paced the room.

Noah leaned forward and wrapped his arm around bent, denim clad knees. “What did I say this time?”

There was a prickly, tingling sensation in my eyes. It took several laps of the hotel room before I realized I was on the cusp of crying. Very few people could weasel their way into my heart in such a way to make me *feel* like this. My family occupied most of those spots.

I thought I’d let the wound scab over, that thinking of my father’s decision to not let me drive wouldn’t hurt so much. And maybe it wouldn’t, had Noah not mentioned Aiden’s desire to be a part of it.

“You said Aiden would love to tune a race car for me?”

Noah’s voice was soft in a way I’d never heard it before, like he cared about how I reacted to every syllable. “Yeah. We talked about it, before you left. He said your dad didn’t think you were ready, but he did. And that would be awesome if he could tune a car for you and race his own on the street.

“They love you, why wouldn’t they want to see you happy?”

I snorted before smashing my palms against my eyes to fend off the tears. Saying the words out loud, admitting that I wasn’t good enough for my own father—was harder than I’d ever imagined.

“It’s not that he thinks I’m not ready, Dad doesn’t want me to ever drive the car. He said that I shouldn’t be a race car driver. End of discussion. And that’s how I ended up here.”

My heart hammered off a rapid staccato in my chest. When Noah didn’t say anything, I dropped my hands and opened my eyes to hazard a glance in his direction.

He watched me with thoughtful, sad eyes. “C’mere, Breanna.”

I went to him, unsure of what came next. It might be silly to most, but for me I’d just exposed myself to Noah in a way that left me more vulnerable than I’d ever been with anyone.

With the gentle persuasion of his fingers, he guided me back onto the bed and against his chest. I wasn’t weak for seeking the comfort I found there. At least, that’s what I told myself.

His voice rumbled through me as he spoke. “Everyone here wants something from you. They’ve all got dollar signs in their eyes. Even your friends. You’ve handled it better than Aiden would have, hell better than drivers twice your age.” He eased my face up to his with a nuzzle against my cheek. “I’m damn proud of you for that. But more, you’re one hell of a driver, Breanna. He’s an idiot if he can’t see that.”

With a nip to my lips he rolled us onto the bed and kissed me, with feeling. “Let’s see if we can’t bring back that smile.”

Chapter Twenty-Six

Skipping a few days with my family helped me keep the homesickness at bay. What was the point in going home if my dad would barely look at me? Without his support, the rest didn't matter much. Especially not after I got a win under my belt.

I rode with the crew to the track in Louisiana, only a few miles outside of Arkadia. My last race before Grand Nationals and my last chance to secure a full ride sponsorship. *No pressure or anything.*

As terrifying as it was—I had a boyfriend. Someone whose opinion of me mattered more than anyone else's and who grounded me. Not just companionship or sex but a real relationship.

There was a connection I'd never felt with someone before. Noah understood me, knew when to step back and give me space. And he knew when to step closer. I'd just been too afraid to let him in, and he hadn't known how to explain himself to me. Weren't we a complicated mess?

We were figuring this out in the most thrilling way imaginable. For the first time in my life, everything was falling into place. I didn't miss the things I shouldn't have, pine for a life that had never been meant for me. I was blazing my own trails—which was the sort of adventure my soul craved.

A guy like Noah was the sort to hang on and enjoy

the ride. Thank God for that.

And really, with him around, missing home was less of a big deal. There wasn't any sneaking off and making out. Didn't really need that when we were sharing a hotel room.

Heh, I'm already shacking up with my boyfriend.

The track wasn't as busy as some of the others had been, the race itself not as big of a deal with less of a payout to the winner. But, there were points to be had so we were racing.

Noah was more relaxed here with the smaller crowds. The constant tension seemed to loosen, and he moved with more grace than he had before. Or maybe I just watched him closer, without fear of repercussion.

He was mine, wasn't he?

The thought both thrilled me *and* freaked me out. Because if he was mine then I was *his*. And I didn't belong to anyone. The juxtaposition I placed myself in made my head spin.

Too much was happening too fast. Not just with Noah but with me. I had a career, a complicated relationship, a life. I was living for the first time. I'd always known leaving Arkadia in the dust would be the best thing to happen to me. This just proved it.

I sat on the steps on the side of the trailer, cleaning my helmet, when a familiar voice called my name.

My chest lightened, unadulterated happiness bubbling up as Isaac practically loped across the parking lot. I'd only been lying to myself—I missed my family. Not that I would tell anyone. "Oh my God, you guys!"

Behind him, Cara beamed and Vic laughed as he took a drag off a cigarette.

I screeched and launched myself from the steps and straight at Isaac.

He caught me in strong, well-muscled arms and pulled me up so that my legs wrapped around him. When had my best friend put on so much muscle?

I hugged him tight, before releasing one arm to pull Vic in as well.

"See, I told y'all she'd freak out." Cara was laughing, freckles dancing across her nose in the sunshine.

I hopped from the guys and scooped my friend up and swung her around. I'd only thought everything was falling into place. Having my friends here was like putting the final piece of the puzzle in its place. Hell, the only thing that could be better would be—

"Hey, Breezy." My brother's hair was down, the dimple in his cheek winked as he grinned.

Family.

"Aiden!" I moved from Cara to immediately punch my brother playfully in the shoulder. Then slap him in his other shoulder, all the while fighting back the burning tears that stung my eyes.

I trembled a bit as he hugged me. Memories flooded in, pushing away everything else. He smelled of home, of life, of nights after scary movies when he'd let Raelynn and I sleep in his bed. My brother.

I released him when I saw Hadley bashfully brushing at her eyes with the backs of her hand before sliding her sunglasses back on. "Raelynn and Jordan were going to come too…but she woke up puking her head off this morning and he wouldn't leave her."

I was too happy to be upset that she hadn't made it, hell being a newlywed and pregnant she'd more than earned a few get out of jail free cards with me.

With a shake of my head, I took them all in. The presence of some of the most important people in my life filled a void inside me. Sure, leaving Arkadia had always been my dream. But family was family.

"You guys are really here, wow!"

Noah and Marcus approached our motley crew. My guy was wiping off his hands on a shop rag, his face a mask of guarded solitude.

I wanted to reach out to touch him, so I grabbed Hadley's hands as everyone else greeted each other. "Where are the kids?"

"With your parents. Your mom was more than happy to watch them while we came down here."

Ed Calloway was pulling Aiden away from the group of us. He and Marcus showing him the car, wanting his opinion, the real racer's opinion. I swallowed back the bile in my throat.

I couldn't hate Aiden for it, even if it pissed me off.

"You're ready for tonight, right?" Isaac was jittery with nerves beside me, jumping up and down as if there was too much pent-up energy in his larger body.

With two fingers, I pinched a bicep. "Where'd this come from?"

But he wasn't listening to me. Shadows had crossed my best friend's face, changing his expression.

Something was wrong, I knew him well enough to see that. Vic was the one that was hard to read. He was sneaky as shit when he needed to be. One of the reasons I loved him so much. Vic Morales was the most honest, loyal snake in the grass I'd ever met.

Vic was with my brother now, and Isaac was looking right at Noah, as if something was about to snap.

My heart pummeled down to my feet. Cara caught my worried gaze, her face twisted in an angry, bitter expression. She didn't know, none of them did. Noah and I…what had happened before we left—

My stomach dropped to my knees. "No," I said, though no sound left my mouth.

The fire had been lit, and it blazed in her eyes. She'd told Isaac what I'd told her about Noah before I left, about the night we'd spent together.

I was too late, the ball was already rolling and Isaac already moving. Vic wasn't the only Morales that was loyal to a fault.

Confusion swarmed over the small group of us. It was then I noticed Cara hadn't come alone, but was gripping tightly to Brody's—Isaac's dildo of a friend—hand. There wasn't time to be angry or judgmental about that, not when my best friend was about to rip the face off my boyfriend.

Isaac nearly knocked Hadley to the ground in his effort to get to Noah. I could grab him or her. I chose to keep my future sister-in-law from face planting on the ground.

"What the he—"

Noah wasn't confused in the least. He'd read Isaac's anger and his body had grown rigid in the way of a Marine—of a man trained for combat.

"You told him?" I barked at Cara, betrayal skittering across my skin, as I ran after Isaac.

"Told who, what?" Hadley's voice was barely audible over the pounding of my pulse in my ears.

Sprinting past Isaac, I did the only thing I could do, I stepped in front of Noah.

His hand instinctively went to my hip. To push me away or hold me close, I had no idea, but his fingers dug into my skin through my shorts.

"Isaac, whatever honor you think you're defending. You're *wrong*." Everything had changed. What had happened between Noah and I before I left—wasn't where things stood now. It was some awful, horrible misunderstanding, and I couldn't let two of the people I loved most in the world come to blows over it.

I'd once accused my sister of enjoying this sort of thing. I really regretted that now.

Isaac snarled angrily. "So, I hear you like to sleep with girls then tell them to get lost? Use them and toss them away, bro? That how you roll?"

Behind me, Noah's laugh was void of humor. I could almost see his sneer. "You don't want to do this, Isaac."

"You don't know shit, homie."

"Isaac!" I shouted, my voice tight and shrill. "This is ridiculous, whatever you were told wasn't the entire story. So whatever honor you think you're protecting, doesn't really matter."

"Oh it matters, you're better than this piece of shit."

"Think so?" Noah's snarl rumbled in his chest and against my back.

Isaac moved—quicker than I'd ever seen him do so. In his rush, he shoved me to the side and to my knees.

"Aiden!" I screamed for my brother, putting all my trust in the wild-eyed boy that I'd grown up with. He could stop this.

When I turned to Noah, his face was tense with the

same sort of anger I'd seen that night in the Rooster parking lot. They were fighting over me. Isaac because he thought Noah hurt me, Noah because Isaac had knocked me to my knees.

Sickness and bile tumbled in my stomach as I fought to stand.

Even with the muscle he'd put on, Isaac never had a chance. All his self-righteous indignation he'd pumped himself up with wasn't going to help either.

Noah snatched him up before Isaac threw a punch, fingers twisted in the front of my best friend's shirt. He tossed him to the ground, Noah landing on top of him. Isaac's face twisted in surprise as Noah's fists rained down. Once. Twice. Three times.

Blood splattered against the concrete.

Everything happened so fast, it stole my ability to move. I stood still, cold despite the heat of the sun against my skin. The easy happiness of the previous days ripped away—karma's way of laughing at me.

Out of nowhere, a vicious dark blur tackled Noah around the middle. The scrappy move proved that Vic was unlike his younger brother. This Morales brother could hold his own. He'd grown up fighting with a man that was as much myth as legend in Jordan Slater.

My brother pulled Isaac to his feet and pushed him away from the group as I struggled to force my body to move. My arms were held in place by feminine hands, on either side of me Hadley and Cara gripped tight.

Stronger than either of the other women, I jerked free, tossed myself into the fray, and took an elbow to the side of the face for my efforts.

Security rushed across the pavement as I screamed incoherently at both men—my friend and my lover.

Vic backed off first. His chest heaved visibly, his nostrils flared, his dark eyes flashed with anger and violence.

I was on the ground now, sprawled on top of a trembling Noah. He didn't move, other than the gentle convulsions he was stark still.

"Noah?"

Tenderly, his thumb traced across my lip. He would have walked away from Isaac, I could see it in his eyes. But hadn't, because of me—whatever he'd done was to protect me. Because Noah was that guy, he was the one that would take the punches just to keep those he cared about safe.

Like he'd stepped in front of a gun for me at the Rooster.

Before I could say anything, I was ripped away from him by unfamiliar hands as bright lights flashed on all around us. When I cast my gaze around, became coherent of the situation, all around us people were live feeding and taking pictures.

Oh shit.

Chapter Twenty-Seven

The sun was so bright I was forced to stare at the tops of my feet. The lace of my left sneaker was untied. I made no move to tie it.

Stillness overtook me, as the fight replayed over and over again in my mind. Vic and Isaac had been escorted off the property immediately. Being a crew member on a race team, Noah was taken into the offices behind me with Ed and Marcus.

I'd followed. Not that I'd be allowed in that meeting. Noah was done, that's the way things happened here. Even if the DRAA gave him a pass with a fine, Ed Calloway wouldn't. Not after the way everything had gone down with al-Nazir. You couldn't piss off one of the deep pockets and not have it come back to haunt you when something happened. Collectively we'd all done just that.

The concrete block at my back was warm, though the rest of me was cold with guilt. The fight was my fault, just like Noah had said so many times with so many things before. I couldn't keep my mouth shut when it counted. I shouldn't have ever told Cara anything.

Or maybe if I'd spoken to her since so much had changed—explained the full story to her.

I hadn't. Now two people I cared about were hurt.

The decrepit bench creaked with the weight of

someone taking the seat beside me. The shadow on the pavement was as familiar as my own. The scent of him, caught on the gentle evening breeze, was the same soap he'd used for as long as I could remember.

"You didn't do this, Breanna." Aiden's voice was soft. Here he was, same as always, trying to smooth over the hurts. He was always the one picking up his baby sister when she fell. He'd do the same for his children.

I loved my brother. But, in this he was wrong.

"Yeah, *I* did. I should have never told Cara. I should have known I can't trust anyone but myself."

He raised a brow. "So, now we're mad at Cara?"

"Yes. No." I blew back a chunk of hair from my face. "I don't know."

Aiden cringed and rubbed his thumb across the throbbing ache on my jaw. It was definitely going to be bruised as bad as my ego.

I was mad at myself, at Cara, at Isaac, at the whole damn world. And to think not long ago I'd been thinking about home and how much I'd missed these people—that part of my life. "Everything was going so good until you guys showed up."

I knew the words were hurtful as soon as they left my mouth. It didn't matter, I'd say them again. I'd never been the one to tiptoe around my feelings. "My life was perfect, then *bam* you guys show up and it all goes to shit."

I stood and shook my head, hot angry tears streaming down my face. "I just got him figured out—was so damn close to having everything I'd ever wanted. But people I trusted, put my faith in, fucked it all up."

Aiden sighed, wearily. "They meant well, Breezy. They love you. We all do."

I shoved my hands in my pants. "Do me a favor. You love me?"

He nodded.

"Give Noah a ride back to Arkadia. Ed'll fire him for this. And tell Rick not to send another keeper. I've got this. I'm better off alone anyhow."

I didn't make it three steps before the door opened and Noah and Ed walked out. The older man's face was still red with anger, his motions jerky as he stormed off without sparing me a backward glance.

Noah stood, watching me with a guarded expression. I started to go to him but stopped when he tensed.

"Hey." I stood with nervous energy prickling my skin. I'd meant to be away when he came out so there wouldn't be this big dramatic confrontation.

So I wouldn't have to look at him when he broke up with me.

He raised his brow but said nothing. Shimmering anger brimmed under the surface, his skin slick with the thin sheen of sweat it left behind. I'd seen it before—before everything had changed between us.

My brother kept his distance, choosing wisely to let me fight my own battles.

After several long moments of silence, Noah tossed the Calloway crew shirt at my feet and turned away. It was more of a swagger than a stalk, but the intent was clear. He chose to walk away from me. We'd been through so much, he'd gone to such great lengths to keep me from the likes of al-Nazir that the shock of his decision to leave me overrode the dagger to my heart.

I chased after him, something I'd sworn I'd never do.

"Go back to your pit, Breanna," he growled when I jumped in front of him.

Here, the only nosy people wore track personnel shirts. It was as close to alone as we'd get at the track—short of locking ourselves in a car hauler.

"No. Not until you talk to me." I was scared. That realization was a harder hit than the elbow I'd taken to the face during the fracas. My body throbbed with the emotional pain, swaying a bit.

"I tried that, more than a few times. Turns out, you just turn it around on me, use it to get your way, to start shit." He made a fist, bit his knuckles, then snorted. "Hell, you can't be happy, can you? Not unless you're making life harder on everyone else. I'd heard you tried it with your sister, then with Hadley and Aiden. Now us?"

It was a miracle I didn't fall to my knees. Something inside me broke. Yes, I'd made mistakes, but never from a place of malice and never to us. "N…no…that's no—"

"That's *exactly* what you do, Breanna. You aren't happy unless someone else has problems. You took my words, my feelings, turned them around on me—told your friend some bullshit and next thing I know, I'm fighting my boss's best friend! For what, Breanna? For what?"

He cast his gaze toward the sky, then to the ground, anywhere but on me. My heart shattered.

Up until that point, I'd only cried when I was angry. Now, tears streamed down my face leaving desolate tracks filled with devastation. I opened my mouth, but no sound came out. When I lifted my hands I immediately dropped them. He'd never let me touch him, not now.

"Go do you, Breanna. Maybe one day you'll grow the fuck up. Until then, I'm out."

He left me standing there, staring but not seeing.

Nothing else mattered.

I was numb. My entire body stiff, my feet moving like lead, thudding on the ground with each step I took toward the Calloway Racing pit. People called after me, occasionally blocked my path, but I moved ever onward, and ignored them all. None of it mattered. I'd thought it would, that I could do everything on my own—but that was before Noah.

My face was covered with the mask worn by the brokenhearted. Each breath I took was deliberate and slow, to hold the crippled sobs at bay.

In the pit, Ed turned to me, still so angry I worried briefly for his blood pressure. He took one look at me, though, and softened, biting back whatever acrid insult he'd had at the ready. You couldn't dress down the beaten—it didn't do much good.

"When this race is over, you and I need to have a conversation about your future with us. Certain behaviors won't be tolerated, this is not some juvenile street race in Arkadia."

I nodded. He was right. I never thought losing my ride was a possibility and suddenly it was. I'd had it all, or so it seemed, now I ran the risk of losing literally everything I'd ever dreamed of.

All because I couldn't keep my big mouth shut.

The rest of the afternoon was wrapped in a fog. I sat inside the trailer, waiting on the other classes to finish and watching the crew ready the car. None of them spoke to me. I couldn't figure out if that was out of fear of me—or Ed. Probably a healthy dose of both.

My limbs were heavy, making them difficult to fold through the roll cage of the car. I cursed the metal bars. They claimed the network of welded metal tubes served a purpose, but I begged to differ. A damn roll cage hadn't done a damn thing for Devin.

As everything fell apart around me, I missed him all the more. Devin kept my secrets, had I told him about Noah, not Cara, none of this would have ever happened.

For the first time in a long time, a deep ache formed at the pit of my stomach. I'd been so wrapped up in my life, the constant forward progress of life in general, I'd not thought much about him.

I knew now that I hadn't been in love with him, not like I'd thought. My brief relationship with Noah had shown me that much. But I had *loved* Devin. And here I'd gone and almost forgotten.

With a deep breath, I wrapped my trembling fingers around the steering wheel and settled in the driver's seat. If I tried hard enough I could still smell him, still hear his laugh. But if I strayed too long in memories, Noah came to the forefront. Watching him walk away had been one of the most difficult things I'd ever done aside from burying Devin.

I banged my head on the steering wheel, the helmet hitting it with a thump. I had to stop comparing the two. What I had with Noah I'd never had with anyone else. I understood why it could have never been Devin for my sister, why she chose Jordan. My friendship with Devin had been irreplaceable, and special in its own right. But it wasn't anything like what I'd had with Noah.

Love wasn't something you could just ignore for the sake of someone else's happiness. It's all consuming, life altering. I understood that now, and when I saw Raelynn again, I'd tell her as much.

"Fire her up." Ed's voice crackled in my ear.

No more lamenting over all the things I should have done differently, it was time to get to work. I flipped the ignition switch and tapped the gas as the car roared to life. The seat beneath me rumbled, stealing the breath from my chest.

By now, I'd usually be race ready. The adrenaline would be pumping and my chest tingling with anticipation and excitement.

Not today. Losing this race didn't mean much when Noah had walked out on me. I tried to find anger, defiance, anything to get the blood humming through my veins. But, nothing. I was cold. Because Noah was right—all of this was on me. No one to blame or be angry at but myself and I was too emotionally exhausted for any of that.

Suck it up, buttercup.

No. I was not going to blame myself for this. My one true love was and would always be racing, not even Noah could take that away from me. I inched the race car forward, allowing the anger to seep into my soul and replace the angst. How dare he. This was my life, I wasn't going to let some self-righteous asshole come in and steal it all away from me. I'd worked too hard for this.

Pete and Marcus lined me up and my gaze narrowed on the Christmas tree start light. It didn't matter who was in the lane beside me. I was winning this, if nothing else, to keep my ride with Calloway and to prove I was more than just some punk, piece of shit street racer.

At yellow, I let go of the button, and by the time the green light flashed the car tore off down the track, full tilt boogie and hell bent for leather. By the time the eighth of a mile marker blew by me I was at over three digits and the racer's tunnel closed in around me—a vision of the finish line with everything on either side just a blur.

There were moments in time that happened so very fast that it seemed like everything had stopped. Some sort of mind trickery to constantly remind us of how badly we'd screwed up. As my tires spun on the track, everything slowed violently.

During a hit, your reaction times had to be at the millisecond level, faster than your brain could process movement. Mostly, they had to be instinctive and mine were. I lifted my foot off the gas at the same time my brain registered the spin of the tires against the surface. Only, the spinning didn't stop as it should have and smoked filled the car.

The wheel jerked in my hand and my heart stopped. I knew, even as I reached for the emergency shut off, that I was fucked.

My throttle's stuck.

There wasn't a thing I could do. My breath caught and my fingers wrapped around the emergency shut off as the concrete barrier wall sheared off the nose of my race car in a grinding, metal ripping cacophony. Then my entire world turned upside down, literally, as the car jerked into a barrel roll.

The engine died and the only sound was the *rush,*

rush, rush of the car spinning. Was this the last thing Devin heard and felt? Was his stomach ripped to his knees, his bladder screaming for sudden release?

Asphalt then sky, asphalt then sky, I couldn't count how many times I saw either. I wasn't scared, I didn't have time to be. Within seconds it was all over in an explosion of fiberglass and ambition.

In the distance, sirens wailed. Or perhaps they were memories of another crash, of a lost friend.

Then nothing as it all faded to black.

Chapter Twenty-Eight

"He said it could take up to an hour." A soft, familiar voice spoke over an incessant beeping. The pain was evident in the slight crack after each word. I wanted to focus on that voice, on the memories that tugged at the foggy corners of my mind.

Beep. Beep. Beep.

What was that sound? Someone needed to make it stop before I lost my shit. Over and over again, in time with the beat of my heart. So, annoying, keeping me from slipping back into the warm embrace of the fog that lay over me.

"I know, I can't help it, baby. She's never been so quiet for so long in her entire life."

Mom. I knew that voice as well as my own. It wasn't changed despite the almost frantic edge to it. She needed some of this fog too.

The other one, the broken sounding voice was Raelynn. Maybe. Sounded like her.

Beep. Beep. Beep.

"And we only get fifteen more minutes. After that, we can't see her until next visiting hours. I don't want her to wake up alone."

Who are they visiting without me? I was missing out, apparently. But I was so tired. They could go, I didn't want to make them late. I just needed to sleep some more, snuggle deeper into this heavy feeling.

Besides, I didn't want to deal with a pregnant and emotional Raelynn.

Beep. Beep. Beep.

Ugh! Irritation pushed the cocoon of comfort away, leaving me slowly aware of the throbbing pain that gripped my entire body. I tried to smack the alarm clock but couldn't quite get my arm to move. Too sleepy. But that relentless noise was making it hard to hear them. They needed to go, before they were late. Only fifteen minutes, probably less now—time was weird here.

Beep. Beep. Beep. Faster now, as my pulse increased. I didn't know which was worse, that damn beeping or the pain. It hurt so badly, every time I tried to move it was like being shot with a bolt of razor-laced lightning.

The heart monitor continued its faster pace. I'd heard that sound before, I recognized it now that the fiery agony coursing through me pulled away the warm heaviness I'd been trapped under. My grandpa had been attached to one before he died. I'd gone with Mom to see him in the hospital when I was thirteen.

Wait.

I sniffed. The astringent scent of a hospital assaulted me, singeing my nostrils. I gagged and almost screamed as my throat burned like someone had poured race fuel down it.

Struggling, battling against the inability to move, I finally managed to crack my eyes open. The lights were dim, but the sterile white of a hospital room was easy to make out.

The crash. *Oh God.* I'd wrecked the Calloway's car—did I cross, was anyone else hurt?

"Hey, Breezy." Raelynn came into view as she leaned over the bed. Fuzzy at first, but my vision of her slowly started to clear. Her face was swollen from crying, her eyes bloodshot and still filled with tears.

I opened my mouth to speak, to tell her to stop crying—I wasn't dead. But I couldn't so much as squeak.

But more, the thirst overwhelmed even the pain. Every part of my mouth was achingly dry. I wanted to tell them how thirsty I was, feeling like a fish plucked from the sea and dropped into the desert. My cracked lips throbbed, dry skin pulling and tearing as I fought to push my parched tongue against them.

"Here, let me help." My mom stood from her perch beside me and produced a tube of chapstick.

My hero.

The soothing, waxy substance was heaven sent. I groaned, though the sound was more like a dying animal's than a human's.

My mouth was still on fire, this time it was Raelynn to the rescue. She pulled out a stick with a little sponge on the end of it.

"This is all they'll let you have right now."

I parted my lips as she pressed a sponge into my mouth. The absorbent material was soaked with the very breath of life. Lemony cool liquid seeped into my tongue and mouth, momentarily rejuvenating me. At least until I swallowed, when the water turned to shards of glass that ripped their way down my esophagus.

I cringed but opened my lips again when she repeated the process with a new stick-sponge contraption.

"Glycerin swabs." Raelynn smiled and gave my

head a few tender caresses.

It's amazing how much pain hides behind a dry mouth. Groggy, I'd only known my mouth and throat were on fire. Now, sharp pangs impaled my chest with each breath, ripping and burning their way through my being, and my hip and leg throbbed with an intense, breathtaking vigor.

My eyes watered with it. I must have whimpered, because Mom hit the button for the nurse.

"Get some rest." She smiled down at me as the nurse pressed something into my IV. "We'll be here when you wake up."

****

Despite my mother's promise, I woke up alone. Though, the beeping had been silenced and the lights were still dim. I couldn't move much without pain ricocheting all over, so I kept time on the analog clock on the wall. Seconds ticked off and then minutes; I lost count after a while.

On the hour, every hour, a nurse came in to check my vitals. After two, she came back and shot another dose of the heavy blanket into my IV drip and even watching the clock was too difficult after that.

Being alone didn't bother me. Especially when I was so weak and drugged I could barely do more than turn my head without needing to doze for half an hour.

There were several days like that. My nights watching the minutes tick by between nurse's visits. The days spent waiting on my mom and sister during visiting hours, where they'd push glycerine swabs in my mouth and apply chapstick to my lips. Both would fill me in on mindless chatter, spending the entire time looking as if they might cry.

Day three or maybe four of half-hearted consciousness brought a new visitor.

With his face pale and pulled gaunt, my brother looked haunted. His dark hair hung loose around his face as if he were hiding behind it—too much a man to let me see him afraid. I wanted to jump up and scream that I was fine. Other than the pain, I was.

"Dad came last night when we got here, but you slept the whole time. The nurses took pity on him, let him stay past time. I fell asleep waiting on him.

"Everyone else is here too, but they're only letting immediate family in to see you."

I wasn't sad I'd missed Dad's visit—if he'd gloated I hadn't been around to hear it. That was a small miracle, considering this was the perfect opportunity for a dad lecture. I'd ended up right where he'd said I would, just like he said I would.

A tear trickled down my cheek and Aiden gave me a weak smile, no doubt misunderstanding my emotion. Or, maybe not. My brother was a smart guy.

He settled into the vinyl chair by my bed that our sister usually occupied when she was here.

"Yeah, Jordan was *pissed*." He grinned. "He's out there with Rae and Mom and some other people now. Mom is waiting to come in with Rae—so she doesn't come alone."

What'd they think, that she'd pop a squat and drop out the baby in my intensive care room? And if she did, pretty sure the nurses would be better suited to care for her and the crotch fruit than my mom.

I must have made a face, because my brother chuckled. "I think they're more worried about her emotional state. You saw her when Devin died—this is worse."

Wait, worse? Raelynn's emotional meltdown after Devin's crash was bad. Enough that I'd actually felt guilty for being angry with her. I was alive, breathing, and would be just fine. It was silly if she was that worried about me.

"S'okay," I croaked and grimaced. The pain in my chest was growing steadily more tolerable, but my throat still burned.

"Oh yeah." Aiden stood and swabbed my mouth with surprising gentleness. "Rae told me to do this."

" 'Sanks."

"You're messed up kid but still pretty." He thumbed my nose, like he'd done often my entire life. I tried to smile and this time, my lips didn't crack and burn.

The real question was, just how messed up was I?

"How?" I tried to ask how messed up I was. In all this time, nobody had told me a damn thing. Not the assorted doctors who checked me out at dawn every morning, the nurses who constantly changed shifts, or even my own mother. I wanted to scream, *What the fuck is wrong with me?*

"Broken collar bone, from the belts. Mild concussion. Fucked up your hip pretty good, fractured your left fibula. Got some swelling, you've definitely looked better." He cracked a grin and laughed under his breath, pushing his hand through his hair in a way that left it parting in different directions. "Considering you smashed into a wall at more than two-hundred miles an hour, I'd say you're pretty good. But you'll be here a while."

He wasn't telling me something. Sure, the pain in

my chest was bad. But…I'd been exercising my eyes for several days. I cut him the hardest glare I could muster. Which wasn't a lot.

Aiden's breath released on a sigh. "Lungs are bruised, they did kidney surgery. You lost your spleen, not sure what you would have used that for anyway."

A friend in middle school had a splenectomy. He told us all about it, even proudly showed the scar that ran all the way down his torso. He didn't have a belly button. Look, I didn't have a lot going for me in the body department. My sister had the body of a curvy back road and me, I was left with the drag strip. But a flat stomach? I could show that off all day.

I panicked, my breaths quickening. Which hurt like hell. I must have made a face, because Aiden swooped in—smoothing my hair back and kissing my temple.

Sue me, the idea of never wearing another bikini was painful on its own.

"Easy, Breezy. You're all right, you're going to be okay. You'll just be in here a while."

The softness of his face was just like Dad's. Enough so, that the twinge in my chest wasn't from the broken collarbone. Too many emotions waged war inside me and there was nowhere to run. I was stuck here, with myself, weak and feeble.

I hated every moment of it. I swallowed and tried to speak. The words were swallowed up by pain and emotion. Major surgery—I'd had a tube down my throat. "Wanna go home."

"Soon. Mom said the doctor told her they'd move you to a regular room in another day or so. After that, things will only get better."

Said the guy who could walk around the room and

didn't sound like a crippled frog when he said shit.

****

By the end of the week, I could talk, and I'd been upgraded to munching on ice chips. The most surprising part came when it was Dad's turn to babysit me during ICU hours. He never bothered to shove it in my face that he'd been right and I'd been wrong.

Instead, he'd sat quietly in a chair by my bed, stared into nothing, and silently cried.

In my entire life, I'd never seen him cry. Sure, he'd tried to hide it, but not before I'd seen the silent tears roll down his cheeks. I'd done a lot of messed up shit in my life but never made either of my parents cry. This was a tough pill to swallow.

It took the next week to recover from the emotional fallout from that one. Neither of us spoke of it, just like we said nothing about the crash.

I was in Texas, apparently the closest trauma ER hadn't been in Louisiana. It wasn't home, but close enough to it that even my extended family was making the drive every day. Isaac and Vic both had the ICU nurses eating out of their hands by the time the doctor lifted the immediate family only order.

I could sit up on my own, eat solid food, and make a trek (wheelchair and all) to the bathroom by the end of two weeks of consciousness. According to one of the surgeons, my age made it easier for my body to heal quickly.

Not that I'd heard him. He'd lost me back at *private room*. Ready for a room where all my family could come and go as they pleased. Under most circumstances I'd have snarled at the idea. Now? I almost cried with relief.

"Hey, Rae." I sat on the edge of the bed, my leg throbbing and my chest burning like kindling in hell. "Can you help me get out of this ugly ass thing?"

I motioned to the hospital gown. The garment was beyond hideous with its green and cream checkered pattern. Not that it mattered what I wore—I was grasping at any excuse to see my scar. Sure, I was a tomboy, but splitting me right down the middle like a Christmas Goose would leave a big, puffy, gross scar.

"Sure."

With little fanfare, she pulled the curtain that blocked my bed from the door, then gently untied the gown.

Fear clenched my eyes shut as the fabric fell away. This was stupid. I knew it was. A scar was a scar, I was *alive*. That's what mattered the most, not some superficial anxiety.

Cool air left chills across my chest. My fingers trembled across my skin, moving tentatively to the spot just between my breasts. I'm sure Raelynn thought I'd lost my mind.

My breath caught. Beneath the pads of my fingers, was just chilled skin. I traced the line to my throat and back down.

A giggle interrupted my thoughts. "You'd accuse me of touching myself inappropriately."

Raelynn gestured at the lower left side of my chest, beneath my boob. "The surgeon said you wouldn't have a huge scar. Another one on your back from the kidney stuff. That's it. Save for the ones where the pins are in your leg." Explanations weren't needed, she'd understood almost immediately. Yet another reason why I had the best sister ever.

I laughed, then wheezed, then cut myself off to keep the pain in my chest and side minimal. Relief so warm and heavenly it could have been a blanket slipped over me. Shallow wasn't a word I'd have ever used to describe myself and yet here I'd been worried about a navel when I should have been glad I was alive.

How would Noah have looked at me without a belly button? All the happiness and warmth chased after the thought of him as it rushed from the room. There was no Noah, not anymore, not after what had happened.

Raelynn pulled a white tank top over my head, gingerly lifting one arm and then the other. I obeyed like a flesh and blood puppet, unable to think about anything else other than how fucked up my life was.

By the time she helped me wiggle into panties and stretchy shorts I'd managed to crawl mostly from my pit of despair and self-pity. Sisters—even pregnant ones—were helpful.

"So, who do you think will be my well wishers on this fine day—" With a groan I hefted myself back onto my bed all the way—"in my new abode."

"Probably Noah." She was big enough in the middle, that her back was swaying and she waddled. I wasn't up to speed on pregnancy one-oh-one, but from the looks of things she'd be birthing crotch fruit any day now.

I blinked back the brand new dose of jilted anguish. "Noah?" He'd made it perfectly clear what he thought about me. So why in the fuck would he want to see me?

"Yeah, he's been here every morning—stays here right up until Mom and Dad leave. It's a little tense between he and Isaac, but I don't think even Jordan could have made the guy leave."

I held the shocked retort on my tongue.

"What's going on with you two?" There was no condescension in her voice. The question was the easy sort that passed between close friends—sisters.

"Too much." I snorted.

After opening the curtain, Raelynn managed to curl her swollen, pregnant form into the reclining chair. I envied that she could look so comfortable—even with the round, protruding tummy. Which, when I thought of it, was sort of cute.

"You know, you can talk to me, Breanna?"

My body throbbed from the excessive movement in changing and getting situated on the bed. Not to mention the trek before to pee and brush my teeth. This was my perfect excuse to lay back and leave her question hanging in the air between us. "There's nothing really to talk about. It was a thing, now it isn't. End of story."

She chewed on her bottom lip in the way she did when she wasn't going to let a subject lie. "He definitely cares a lot about you."

I sighed. "Yeah, well, he should have thought about that before he dumped me and walked away."

"Ouch. Been there, done that. It hurts."

I gestured to encompass my entire body. "Some things hurt a fuck of a lot worse."

The agony of old wounds ripped wide open flashed in her eyes. "Yeah."

A gentle two-tone rap on the door stole my chance to apologize for bringing up Devin's accident like that. But I'd heard that knock dozens of times over the past few months. My breath caught, my mouth went dry, and emotion clogged in my throat.

Raelynn made a warbled dash across the floor mistaking the wave of my arm as an apology, instead of recognizing it as me asking her to stop.

Too late, as she opened the door and Noah filled the empty space.

Damn him.

Chapter Twenty-Nine

My response to Noah McKay was staggering. Or maybe that was the pain meds talking. But even angry, hurt, and with everything else going on, my pulse quickened and my heart raced. It shouldn't be this easy for him. Frantically I searched for that part of me that hated him.

Ugh.

Hell, who was I kidding? He was by far the hottest guy I'd ever laid eyes on. Knowing what was beneath the gray fitted T-shirt and faded jeans worsened the punch of attraction.

Self-preservation paired with my innate ability to be a complete asshole fueled my anger. I nearly told him to march his tight ass right out of the room. To walk until his boots wore off. Or maybe tell him off and remind him of how he'd used me then dropped me like a bad habit. What I'd told Cara had been the truth. Noah said hateful, ugly things to me after the first time we'd had sex.

But wasn't I partly to blame for that? I'd manipulated the situation and Noah to gain an end result that was purely for my benefit. No, I couldn't rage at him for that comedy of errors—we'd both been at fault.

Being angry at me for having feelings was stupid. Treating me like an insolent child was worse. None of that had been my fault, I still wasn't deserving of any of it. Since I was taking the high road in this instance, I couldn't spew forth the ball of self-righteous indignation that formed in my chest. I bit my tongue and twisted the bedsheets into my fingers.

I pursed my lips and waited. For what, I had no idea.

When Noah stood unmoving in the doorway, at such an angle I couldn't see his face, my sister cleared her throat. "I'm going downstairs to find Mom and Dad, see if they want to get breakfast. Text me if you need anything."

She wiggled her fingers at Noah as she did a toddling scamper from the room.

Just like that, we were alone with the uncomfortable silence stretching out before us like a never ending train wreck. This metaphor for our entire relationship was ironic.

"You look good."

Damn. His voice was thick with something I couldn't name. In the sterile hospital, with the scent of stale breakfast from the cart near the door, he'd made me think of sex with three words. And they had nothing to do with the horizontal boogie. Not that I could do *that*, even if I wanted to do it with him.

I turned away, cursing him mentally for all the things I wanted to say but couldn't—because I was trying valiantly to be a lady. Or something.

He stepped into the room with stiff, almost robotic movements and shut the door behind him. The gentle click echoed with resounding fanfare.

Caught in the bright morning sunlight that washed through the windows, he looked like a ghost of the man who'd read me the riot act several weeks before. He was pale and gaunt, with dark circles under his eyes. I bet he hadn't eaten or slept since my crash.

"I probably look better than you. Considering I'm missing internal organs and haven't showered in more than a week—that's saying a lot."

His lip curled, but there was no good humor there.

"I'll be fine, Noah."

"Indestructible?"

"I prefer resilient."

"Yeah, that you are." He moved around the room. Guarded, jaded even. Like a caged animal preparing for a fight.

"I'm not going to argue with you, Noah." Or at least, I was going to *try* not to.

Good for him, they put me on the good drugs.

"That would be a first." He peered out the window, as if it hurt to look at me.

Which was a blow to my pride. I chewed on my bottom lip in an effort not to scream, *Why the hell are you even here?*

"Thank you, for being here. For staying while I was in the ICU." A *herculean* effort.

I was captivated momentarily by the muscles in his neck working as he swallowed. I waited too, for the apology he owed me. He'd humiliated me in front of far too many people for me to count. Made me look like an asshole. Then? I'd crashed Ed Calloway's car.

The gossipy whispers were so loud I could hear them all the way at the hospital. *"She's too young, too emotional. Dangerous to be behind the wheel of a race car."*

"But, you shouldn't feel obligated to be here." He

should go.

The idea that some misplaced feeling of responsibility was what had kept him here all those days was—well, it was something I didn't want to think about. Turned out, Noah made me start to think about a lot of things I didn't want. And while this was probably his fault—somewhere—I didn't want to live with the nasty, bitterness that was churning inside me.

"Is that why you think I'm here?" He turned to me and I was caught with the full, onslaught of emotion that his gaze brought. Thick lashes curtained, haunted blue eyes. *Beautiful.*

So, there's only so much tongue biting Breanna Casey can do in a single encounter. "Considering our last conversation, I can't think of a single other reason for you to be here." Bitterness thy old friend. No matter how much I wanted to rid myself of it, there it was.

"Really?" His brow shot up and he pivoted to face me fully.

"It's not rocket science." My chest and hip throbbed, but I ignored them and fought to look much stronger than I felt. I couldn't be weak, not in front of him, not after he'd left me.

"You nearly died, Breanna. You think it would put things in a better perspective for you."

I clenched and unclenched my fingers and gave up with the sheets, leaving my hands in fists at my sides. "Oh, I've got plenty of perspective, McKay. I can start with your arrogance. Coming in here, talking to me like that, after you threw me away like old trash and humiliated me?"

He swore and pressed his knuckles to his temples. "I didn't throw you away and you aren't trash."

"Then what would call what you did when you told me you were done and walked away?"

"Saving myself."

That was like getting throat punched.

"I didn't mean it like that, Breanna." He stepped forward and dropped his hands to the side.

"You should just go." The lid to *Mount I'm Pissed* was about to blow. There wasn't enough Percocet to stop it.

He exhaled before speaking. "We wouldn't be here, like this, if you hadn't said anything."

"We wouldn't be here, like this, if you hadn't told me I wasn't worth having sex with."

"That's not what I meant, Breanna, and you know it."

"I'm really damn sick and tired of what you *meant* or *didn't mean*—you're so damn caught up in all your own bullshit, that you won't see what's right in front of your face." Pain was rocketing through me, tears stung at my eyes. I would *not* cry in front of him again.

A nurse ducked her head in the door. "Is everything okay?"

"It's fine," I muttered.

"Then could you take it down a notch?" She disappeared where she'd come from.

"Sure," I assured her with a trembling wave of my hand. "Noah, you should go."

"I never should have come."

"Fair point."

The moment the door shut behind him, the tears came. The sobs hurt worse than shouting at Noah. Reliving the breakup, was an unexpected road bump to my recovery. God, I just wanted to be free of whatever it was about him that kept reeling me back in. It mattered more to me what he thought than I cared to admit—more than what all the drag race gossip mongers would have to say.

How did you get over someone when you couldn't even admit to yourself you were in love with them?

****

Three weeks in a hospital was enough to drive anybody insane. Considering I had a difficult time sitting still, even on my worst days—I was like a crackhead looking for a fix.

Turns out, my fix was the one place I'd spent most of my life trying to get away from. *Home.*

I sat in the back of my father's large SUV watching as familiar landscape stretched out before me. Armed with pain medicine and the best of intentions, I was going home. Not to the life I'd imagined, what I'd wanted for myself, but to something altogether different.

Failure.

I'd crashed and burned, literally. With each flip of the ProMod my dream had slipped through my fingers. All the flashbulbs, endorsement offers, everything—gone. I was, at the core, the scumbag street racer they'd all accused me of being.

Worse still, I hadn't been able to make a relationship with Noah work either. I hadn't saved him or myself. I hadn't been able to do anything right. Instead, I'd be stuck running parts for my brother the rest of my life.

My stomach churned, a mix of regret and grief for what could have been.

I must have turned green, because Dad caught my

gaze in the rearview mirror. "You okay, kid? Need me to pull over?"

"Nah, just a little carsick." I looked away. Who cared if he bought the lie. Even with meds, I *hurt*. The two surgeries on my leg sort of trumped everything else. I could distinctly feel where the pins were exposed through the skin. The bone deep ache resonated all the way up to my chest, which wasn't giving me as much grief.

We passed the shop, my favorite little store that belonged to Hunter East's parents, the car wash that my brother still took all his cars to, and then…home.

A very pregnant Raelynn was rocking in the chair on the back porch. Her husband, Jordan, was leaning against the rail and looking very *not* scumbagish. I sneered a little when I thought about it. The reigning King of the Streets was the farthest thing from a piece of trash I'd ever met. Rasheed al-Nazir beat him by a country mile.

Jordan would be a great father. I had zero doubt in my mind about that. Together, their family would be as amazing as Hadley and Aiden's. And just like that, a little chunk of my self pity rolled away.

Mom opened my door, but Dad took off up the steps with an armload of hospital stuff, balloons trailing behind him, instead of retrieving the wheelchair from the back. Not that there was a wheelchair ramp anywhere.

I didn't come around to what was going on until Jordan walked to my door.

I laughed outright. "Are you serious right now?" Then muttered, "This can't be happening."

"Yup." He unhooked my seatbelt and hefted me

gingerly from the backseat. He was warm, strong, vibrant—and he was cradling me like a small child.

I was beyond embarrassed as he carried me up the steps. “If we speak of this again, I will murder people. The ones you tell go first. Then you last, so you have to suffer alone.”

My sister laughed and held the door open as Jordan toted me into the house. “I liked it when he carried me.”

“Yeah, but you’re married to the big galoot.”

“Easy.” He cut his gaze, but laughter twinkled in his dark eyes.

The same love I had for my brother, for Raelynn, welled inside of me. Jordan was family, had been before he’d ever married my sister. “I love you.”

“Me too, kid.” He set me, with painstaking care, on my bed. “But stop with the sappy shit, they’ll start taking you to a shrink if you keep that up.”

“Fair point.” I socked him in the shoulder. “Thanks for the lift.”

“Any time.”

“Now, go home and take care of preggo.”

He shook his head with a smile. He moved through the small crowd that gathered at my bedside.

“Oh my God, y’all, I’m not on death’s doorstep! Shoo, all of you, go!”

With a grin, the two men immediately did as asked. Mom scowled as Raelynn, with effort, climbed onto the bed beside me.

“Mom, we’re both right here and okay. You can fret over us both later. I promise.” My sister was practically glowing.

This time my nausea was directly related to *her* pregnancy.

"You even make being fat look cute."

Her eyes grew wide. "You did *not* just call a pregnant woman fat?"

Smugly, I settled into my pillows. "Yup, because you can't hit me. I'm injured."

Raelynn's eyes went glossy two seconds before waterfalls crested her eyelids and torrented down her cheeks.

"Whoa, damn. I'm sorry." I made an awkward effort to reach for her, but dropped my arm when I realized how weird the situation was. One time, I'd called her the worst of the worst insults and she hadn't cried. Now…"I won't call you fat again."

"No, it's not that." She blew her nose with a loud, resounding honking sound. "We—I—almost lost you, Breanna. Losing Devin was horrible for me. Losing you, I don't know what I would have done. My baby wouldn't have an aunt, I wouldn't have a sister, like—"

She burst into sobs again and all I could do was stare at her. Crashing had been less terrifying than this. "Jordan!"

He rushed in, a wall of terrified muscle. "Rae? What is it?"

The haunting melody that played in his voice almost broke me. Apparently, this wasn't an unusual occurrence.

"Oh baby." He sat gingerly on the bed and pulled her to him.

"I'm sorry," her response was muffled against his chest. "I do this a lot."

"No, it's cool. You're fine, baby." But he caught my gaze over her head and gave a strained, scared smile.

The entire scenario, the little pregnant woman and the terrified big guy who regularly drove a race car down a dark street at stupid fast speeds, that they were both in my room and all of this was over me—or hell it might have been the pain meds. I laughed.

And laughed.

Until tears were streaming down my face instead of Raelynn's. Complete hysterics, with no care to the pain that erupted down my abdomen. The release of all that pent-up emotion was breathtaking.

When I stopped, she'd pulled from his arms with her eyes swollen and nose red. Both were staring at me as if I'd lost my mind. Maybe I had.

"I'm sorry, this is just too much. I've missed too much. Y'all are freaking hilarious."

My sister's mouth screwed up. "Yeah, we're a regular comedy duo."

"More like a freak show, but whatever." I laughed some more.

She hit me upside the head with a pillow at the same time Mom walked back in. What transpired was a moment I'd dreamed of since I'd been a child. The golden girl, Raelynn, was scolded.

"Raelynn!" Mom's voice was all high pitched and scary, like the time I almost burned down the entire backyard.

"But, Mom—"

But our feisty mother was not going to budge. Her next step was the dual hand on hip action. "She has a concussion."

Gleefully, I threw a glance at Jordan who was rather bemused. "This is great."

"You both need rest," Mom softened on a sigh.

"She's right, Raelynn." This from Jordan.

My sister leaned over and pressed her lips to my cheek.

"Aiden said he'd come over when he gets off, Noah's back at work and picking up the slack for him and Dad. So, Aiden said he'd try to get off early so you don't have to put up with the babies too long during the day."

Though my niece and nephews weren't that big of a deal. I'd probably spent more of my time in a drug-induced slumber. The bigger issue was Noah.

I'd really thought he'd leave, go back to wherever he'd come from. But he'd stayed, not only that he'd gone back to my family's shop to work. Why? It was obvious what brought him here wasn't what he'd really wanted after all. Turns out, for Noah that delivery girl might have been more trouble than she was worth.

Well, screw him.

Outrage flowed through me, but I tempered it long enough to yawn and rub my eyes. "Mom's right, I'm tired."

The three of them filed out, my mom quietly shutting the door behind her.

I lay back and made a face at the wall. I could fix this. Tell my dad and brother how I felt about Noah, what had really happened between us. I could make a big fuss, pitch a fit, and by doing so cost him his job.

A year ago, I'd have done just that. Hell, I'd successfully pushed my own sister from her home and job, why not some asshole who'd broken my heart?

Because, in the long run, it would hurt my family. I could do a lot of shit to myself, but I couldn't put them through anything more than I already had.

And maybe, I knew I didn't really want him to leave.

****

The screech of tires spinning relentlessly against concrete was a sound you didn't forget. Not the loud, drawn out bark of a teenager learning how to pop the clutch for the first time, or a burnout inducing donut. But the thunderous roar when rubber meets the road and howl of the tires spinning.

In street racing, that cry is what you hear when a throttle gets stuck. Plumes of smoke trail behind a race car like a pissed off dragon and that dragon *screams* with fury. Probably a wild, terrifying ride. The driver praying not to get taken out by a utility pole before the motor shut down.

I didn't have time for that sort of fear when I crashed. When tires spin relentlessly against the treated concrete of a drag strip the noise and smoke are momentary. There's an abrupt moment of panic before the wheel is jerked out of your hand, the front end turns toward the concrete barrier, and—impact.

Fiberglass didn't stand up too well to that sort of thing, it's sheared off pretty quick. The chassis bent and if you're lucky the roll-cage held.

Mine did, mostly. The side caved just enough for my leg to slam against it and break in two places. Every other injury was from the sheer violence of the impact.

I startled awake each time I fell asleep. Didn't matter what sort of pain meds I took or didn't take; or if I was alone in my room or on the couch watching car restoration shows with Dad. Each time I closed my eyes I was hit with a phantom force that shocked my system almost as fiercely as the first time.

The crash itself was like a vacuum. I knew, logically, that it was loud and violent. But my memories—even those that forced me awake like a falling nightmare—had no sound at all. I was sucked up in deafening silence as my life and what it could have been held on an imaginary trapeze wire, flipping end over end.

The pain came later, thanks to the medically induced coma they put me in.

Each time I jerked upright, eyes wide, chest pumping with rapid breaths, my dad would pale. Grief stricken almost, similar to how I imagined he'd look standing over my coffin.

Sure, it sucked. But I was *alive*. I could deal with quasi-nightmares and the rest of the bullshit. It was nothing compared to what Noah—and soldiers like him—went through.

The thought of him made my head ache, right behind the left eye. It beat the soul crushing weight of disappointment that memories of him brought the day before. Each day I woke up a little stronger—on all fronts.

I focused my attention on Dad and his guilty glances so that I didn't have to think about Noah. My love life was not something I was capable—maybe never would be—of fixing at the moment. Rick Casey, I could.

"I'm not dead, Dad."

He grunted, confusion twisting his features, before he shook his head. "No shit?"

See, I'm not the only person in the family with snark.

"Ha! I'm just saying, you don't have to constantly

look like you're at my funeral."

He cut his gaze in a way that was far too reminiscent of my sister. "You'd be a lot quieter if I was."

I chucked a pillow at him and stuck out my tongue. "I was being serious."

"Yeah, you have been lately. It's freaking us all out." Aiden came through from the kitchen, his youngest, Devin, perched on his hip. "How do I wire money to the alien that abducted the real Breanna—that way they don't send her back."

"Shut up, ass—" The side eye from my father cut me off mid-insult.

I huffed with a shrug. "Of all the things you do and my being nice is freaky? Hadley needs to step up her game."

He snickered and sat beside me. "She doesn't need to step up anything. She knows ex—"

"Aiden! You hush your mouth." The aforementioned Hadley entered holding Molly's hand, my nephew Luke trailed behind her pushing a small collectible car on the hardwood.

My soon to be sister-in-law was blushing scarlet, her blond hair swinging from a high ponytail. So pretty, even more so in love. I was glad—for both of them—that they'd worked everything out. All five of them as a family, made my heart swell.

"Are you okay?" Instantly she was on me, releasing Molly's hand to perch on the arm of the couch.

"Jesus, yes, I'm fine. Calm down, y'all." I sat up and pulled my knee scooter closer. The effort made my entire torso scream in protest. "Maybe not, I was getting all mushy. I think it's time for a nap."

"Mushy?" Aiden cocked a brow.

"Yup, I was thinking about how happy I am for all of you. Starting to get the feels and shit."

"Oh God." He paled. "Between you and your Percocet and Raelynn and the pregnancy, I can't handle any more of this. It's worse than puberty."

I flicked him off. Luke, ever watchful, mimicked me, and Hadley yelped her disapproval.

It was good to be home.

That feeling was the biggest shock of all.

Chapter Thirty

Cabin fever was real. My entire body grew itchy and after a few days I was pretty sure that the world outside my parents' home was dwindling to nonexistent. An alien invasion could have happened and I'd never have known. And my room was depressing. It hadn't been painted in my entire lifetime, from what I could remember, and if I stared hard enough I could still see the outlines of swimsuit model posters from Aiden's time here.

To say I was thankful for the little knee scooter that allowed me to move about the house was an understatement. After a few weeks of recovery, I managed to wheel myself across the street to my sister's house. It was like an adventure or some sort of dysfunctional pilgrim's journey.

Calling it my sister's house was weird, even if she'd lived there more than a year. It was Old Man Slater's house to me. Not Raelynn's. But slowly her touches were appearing everywhere. A picture of the two of us when we were kids hung near the television, there were more mirrors now, and a soft throw blanket lay on the back of the couch.

The inside wasn't as cold, masculine as it had been before. It felt homey, comfortable, in a way it never had. I liked it.

Also, they'd built a nursery where Devin's room

had once been. It seemed like all reminders of him were slowly being wiped away. Even his car, had become something else in my mind—Aiden's. I wasn't sure how to feel about that. Sure, we all had to keep living, but…

"You okay?" With a hand planted firmly on her back, Raelynn rolled her shoulders.

"Yeah, it's just—" I couldn't tell her. How could I say that I hated her making this room the baby's? That I hated the way we were all moving on, changing.

Or maybe everyone else was and I *wasn't*. I'd tried, of course, but failed in epic fashion.

"I know." She sighed and went back to folding gender neutral baby clothes and stuffing them into a drawer.

At one point I might have argued with her. Told her how there was no way she knew what I was feeling, no way she would understand *me*. I didn't. Because—I'd spent far too much time flaunting my bitterness in her face. Rae and Jordan had lost as much, if not more, than I had.

I didn't like this new me, she wasn't flattering. Or maybe she was and that was the problem.

"Why not find out what the baby is?"

She shrugged. "It was Jordan's call."

"Really?" I figured the big guy would want to know so he could prepare or something. Not that I saw him walking around with a baby harness strapped to his chest.

"I think he wanted to make sure that no matter what the gender, the baby knew we loved him or her anyway."

I covered my mouth in an attempt to hide the snort

and failed. “You know how ridiculous that sounds, right?”

She gave me some serious side eye. “If you’re just here to criticize, Breanna, I’m really not in the mood.”

Gone was the delicate flower, crying on my bed. In her place was an angry midget filled with tenacious hormones.

“I’m always here to toss around criticism. Sort of my go to.”

“You can shove your go to up your ass.” She all but growled.

“Ouch.” I rubbed the threatened aspect.

She bit her lip and closed her eyes. “Sorry, moody, tired, just—”

“Ready for it to be over?”

“Yeah, ready to hold my baby. See what she looks like.”

The wistful tone of her words made me smile and wheel my scooter fully into the room. “You said she, Raelynn.”

“Huh?” Confused and befuddled she blinked at me.

“It’s a girl. I’m ordering frilly little dresses when I get home.”

She giggled.

“You laugh, but all I have going right now is an online shopping addiction. It fills the void between slouching in bed and loafing on the couch.”

“Oh, I believe it. I was laughing at you being superstitious.”

“All racers are superstitious.” I shrugged. “Or maybe I just believe in you.”

She got quiet, turned her back, then brushed at her cheeks with the backs of her hands.

"Oh no, not again."

In mock panic, I backed slowly out of the room and called for Jordan. "Slater! She sprang a leak again!"

I was socked in the face with a blanket sleeper. I only knew what they were because Aiden's kids had used them. "Shut up, Breanna!"

Jordan walked by, took a look around the room, and carried on down the hall as if he'd rather be anywhere but in a room alone with the two of us.

By the time I wheeled myself back home, hopped up the steps dragging my scooter behind me, I was exhausted and in pain.

Of course everything hurt. A month before I'd nearly died.

It was a fact that stuck with me during my entire visit with my sister. Maybe I wasn't meant to race, to drive. Maybe Arkadia was all there was for me, all there ever would be. How bad was that, really, in the grand scheme of things?

Devin was gone. So completely that we'd started the process of moving past his loss, the pain left behind. I could have easily been the same, one day someone redoing the very room I lay in, staring at the ceiling, to make a play space for the grandkids.

I'd be a memory. Let's face it, not always a fond one.

So, now what?

****

Several days later I'd gone pure and total stir crazy when Dad popped into my room and asked if I wanted to go for a ride. At this point, even scooting over to Raelynn's wasn't keeping the walls from closing in.

Without much fanfare, Dad helped me out of the

house and into his truck.

The good thing about dads? They don't care if you haven't washed your hair in a week, that it's a hot mess piled atop your head. Nor do they care if you're wearing faded flannel pajama pants that had once belonged to your older brother, or that your knee scooter had developed an annoying squeak.

Nope. None of that mattered to them.

Dads hefted you into their truck and took you for ice cream in forty degree weather. Because, dads.

I'd finally stopped thinking about Noah every second of the day. Though, mostly because I was so consumed by self-pity I didn't have room to think about anyone else. At least I was woman enough to admit it. So I managed the ride in the cab of Dad's truck as if it were the biggest, happiest adventure I'd ever been on. Every piece of scenery was brighter, newer, more special to me.

New Breanna was making my eye twitch.

Dad and I sat in a booth, my scooter standing silent guard beside us. Early afternoon on a weekday meant that the place was empty save for a frazzled mom and her small children.

I munched happily on my chocolate dip cone while Dad worked up to whatever it was he needed to say. Much like Raelynn, he couldn't just come out with it the way Aiden and I could. Rick Casey had to pick the right moment to broach the topic at hand.

Judging by the amount of thought he was putting into this, it would be a big one. Hopefully, not another argument. Our last one had been epic, and my inner rage monster couldn't muster any more energy for the foreseeable future. Between Dad and Noah, I was plum out of animosity.

"I'm sorry."

Two words. So quietly spoken that I don't think I'd have heard them had I not been waiting on him to say something.

I froze, unable to move or so much as comprehend what was going on. One of the little kids was crying, sad that they were leaving. I remembered those days, always upset because Mom and Dad were rushing us here or there for something Aiden or Raelynn had going on.

Raelynn had taken dance, played soccer for a while. I hated going with Mom to that crap, so I'd go with Dad. Aiden raced for as long as I could remember, Junior Dragsters and such. God, how I wanted to do that too.

But no dad allowed such a dangerous pastime for his baby girl.

Now he was apologizing. But for what?

"Huh?" Not my most bombastic response.

His eyes were watery, the lines on his face deepening with what looked like guilt. "I'm sorry that I wasn't there. I should have been, I should have done something."

I snorted and bit into my cone. "Like what? Watched in horror as my throttle got stuck and I flipped down the track? Keep me from racing altogether? Leave me stuck here in Arkadia, my entire life, watching other people do the things I want to do instead of me doing them?" Wow, where did all that come from? I hadn't realized I'd bottled so much up until it came tumbling out.

"No, I—" He pressed his fingers to his eye, like I

did when mine twitched. "I never meant to hold you back. I just worried about what racing would do to my baby."

I hitched a shoulder and licked the dripping ice cream from the cone. "It broke my leg, took a swing at my pride, and left me with a squeaky wheel."

"This isn't funny, Breanna."

"Sure it is, because if it isn't funny it's damn depressing." I contemplated the remnants of my crumbling cone. The sugary, crispy dough a metaphor for what was left of my racing career and my relationship with Noah, which I'd come to rely on more than I cared to admit. "At the end of the day, I was stuck right back where I started with nothing to show for it.

"You were right all along."

I finished off my cone and avoided looking at him.

"I should have been there, you should never have been racing for someone else. I could have—"

"You can't blame yourself. Calloway is a world class operation." And Dad didn't want to be there, he'd made that perfectly clear. His guilt about it wasn't working for me.

"Yeah, but they aren't me or your brother."

"Yeah well…" I finally caught his gaze and gave a sad smile. "Nobody is, really. But, it doesn't matter anyhow. Ed isn't going to keep me and I pissed off my only other viable option, so I'm out. You've got your delivery girl back."

I stood and placed my knee on the scooter. "Well, at least you will once I get rid of this thing."

"It's not the delivery driver I wanted back." He squeezed my shoulders and kissed my head as he stood.

"It's my daughter."

"I'm here, Dad, and I'm sorry too." I smiled up at him. "We'll be all right."

I meant that. I wasn't angry anymore. I loved my dad, I understood him better now. Hell, I was hobbling validation of his worst fear. Either way, I'd just have to learn how to be happy with the hand I was dealt, with my family, and this shithole of a town.

The door whooshed shut behind me, leaving me wheeling myself into the cool air with the sun finally high enough in the sky to warm my skin.

Across the street, parked at a gas pump, stood Noah McKay. There was that all too familiar twinge of regret and sadness in my chest, the sickness in my gut, and a weakness of muscle I couldn't explain. I'd be a lot happier, probably, if he stopped showing up. Because even at a distance, he turned me inside out.

****

I had Dad do me one last favor. I had him drive me into the city limits of Arkadia, a few blocks away from downtown to a small, white house that had become as synonymous with *home* as my own.

"Thanks, Dad." I kissed his cheek and hobbled from the truck at the same time Isaac stepped out his front door and raised an eyebrow.

He was on the small front porch, watching me with a quizzical expression when I squeaked my way to the steps.

"Help me out, you ass."

He crossed the porch grinning in that devil may care way he and his brother had. My heart warmed and the weirdness of seeing Noah at the gas station disappeared. With ease I'd not expected out of my scrawny best friend, he lifted me up the steps and set me down in front of the swing. Of course I'd noticed he'd put on some weight, but now he was *strong*. I wouldn't be winning any more wrestling matches against him, and I wasn't too sure how I felt about that.

Had I been gone and then locked away in my own head for so long, that he'd changed on me overnight? Always tall and thin—sinewy muscle now tightened his clothes and left his baby face more masculine.

"Why are you looking at me that way?" He twisted his lips and crinkled his nose, like he smelled something funny.

"Because you're ugly?"

He chuckled and took his seat on the swing. "No, like you don't know who I am or something."

"Maybe I don't." I shrugged and eased down beside him. "You look different. More manly. Time for you to trade in that tiny car for a real one."

He snorted. "I've always been manly."

"That's why you dressed like a girl and let her drive your car?"

He stretched an arm out on the back of the swing. "It's not my fault you look like a boy in the dark. It's why I've never hit on you."

"You're ugly, I look like a boy, we'd make quite the pair."

He laughed and pulled me to him. For the first time since his fight with Noah, since my wreck, I hugged my best friend. For a long time, I held tight.

"Hey now—" He pulled back and examined me with dark eyes fringed with thick lashes.

"I'm sorry, Isaac."

"For what?"

"That shit with Noah, starting so much drama that didn't matter. I'm surprised you aren't mad at me."

He shook his head. "I was, then you crashed. After that, I was so damn scared it didn't matter."

"Well, I'll take what I can get. For what it's worth, thanks."

"What's the deal with that guy, anyway?"

I laid my head on his shoulder as the swing creaked rhythmically back and forth.

"I love him." I knew before I said it, that I was saying the worst part of the entire thing. But only with Isaac could I share such a humiliation. "He doesn't love me."

Isaac kissed the top of my head. "Then he's not good enough for you, mama."

"You're supposed to say that, though."

"Yeah, but it's true. If he was good enough, he'd show up and show out. No way he lets you walk away. Nah, not if he sees what he's missing out—he'd never do better than you." The emotion in his voice was a stark reminder of why we were best friends and why I loved him so much.

Though my time away hadn't really been long, life in Arkadia had moved on without me. While I'd been living my so called dream, the people I loved the most had changed. Not the least of which, was Isaac. He wasn't just physically different, he was more mature, different. Or maybe I was changed and just saw him for who he really was.

I fought back tears. I'd wanted so much to leave this place and now I was wishing I never had. Especially after the way my relationship with Noah had crumbled.

"I'm glad you're back." The steady creak of the swing lulled me into a false sense of security.

"Me too."

The screen door slammed with a bang.

"Isaac, who the crap is this?" An attractive, young, and highly pissed off woman stood on the porch in her panties and a tank top.

Chapter Thirty-One

I wasn't trying to laugh. It wasn't my fault the amused snort slipped past my brick wall of self-control. When Isaac's—visitor, friend, whatever she was—nostrils flared with anger, I completely lost it. I was cackling on the swing, holding my belly as laughter rolled out. Let's face it, my wall was missing more than its fair share of bricks.

In an attempt to head her rage off at the pass, Isaac leaped from the swing and crossed the porch. Even with a gimp leg, I had no fear of the small Latina. Not when she was flanked by the Morales brothers. Isaac took the pretty, cussing, storm of a woman in his arms as Vic edged past them out the door.

"Keep your conquests off the front porch, *hermanito*." Vic's eyes flashed with humor. "The neighbors are gonna complain."

Isaac's reply was swallowed up in the tenacious screeches from the girl as he managed to finagle her back into the house like a pissed off cat. Her demanding questions were audible through the exterior walls. I could make out enough to know that if Isaac didn't tell her exactly who I was and do it quickly, he might find himself missing a very important appendage.

"I don't think she likes me."

Vic dropped a kiss to my head before taking a seat beside me on the swing. "What gave it away?"

"Dunno, somewhere between all the name calling I sort of figured it out."

He laughed, rich and vibrant, as his full lips twisted into a sly grin. Older, slicker than Isaac, it was easy to see why there was a steady crowd of women in and out of the Morales residence. "So you weren't gonna, ya know, hobble over there and start swinging on her?"

I snorted. "Nah. I've got better things to do."

"Now see, that's what I like to hear. Good decision making. I'd hate to see that hellcat mess up such a pretty face." He stretched his arm around my shoulders.

It felt good to laugh. For the first time in weeks my chest and belly didn't burn with pain. Leaning my head against Vic's shoulder something let go inside me I hadn't realized was holding me back.

"Well, I don't always make the best decisions," I mumbled and wiped the laughing tear from the corner of my eye.

Vic kissed the top of my head. "Mama, you're smarter than most. Everyone makes mistakes, that's a part of life. But not everyone knows who they are and where they are supposed to be. You do."

At that moment in my life, I didn't know the answer to either of those. I doubted I ever really had.

When my only response was to sigh, he set the swing in an easy motion and continued. "You're one of the best drivers I've seen. Which is the only reason I kept Devin's little secret and Isaac's too."

I bolted upright. "You knew D let me drive?"

The sparkle of mischief in his eyes, paired with the knowing upturn of his lips was proof he had, the whole time.

Inside the house, the angry tirade had shifted to

flirtatious giggles in record time. Looked like Isaac had learned a thing or two from his brother.

"Jordan and Aiden would have skinned both of you, if they found out. But damn, Breezy, your reaction time is on point. Doesn't matter who is working the light or doing the arm drop, you're leaving that line first—every time."

Vic's praise was a big deal, not the sort of thing for me to take lightly. He was Race Master, after all. From Grudge Night to Street Kings—it began and ended with Vic.

"Well, I wasn't fast enough last time."

He leaned forward and rested his elbows on his knees. "You know, shit happens. You can't always control everything. But it'd be a damn shame if you stopped driving."

****

"You know, I don't need a babysitter." I pulled the brush through my wet hair, jerking through the tangles in a small fit of annoyance. I'd spent the entire night before, wide awake and staring at my ceiling, thinking about what Vic had said.

Would I ever drive again? Could I? I'd wallowed so deep in my self-pity I hadn't considered having a career in racing after this. Did I want to?

"I don't know if I'm babysitting you or you're babysitting me." Raelynn sighed as she rubbed her swollen belly.

Entirely possible as she looked like she was about to pop. My conversation with Vic left me itchy, ready to do something—anything. "Eh, either way, I was looking forward to having some time to myself."

She rolled her eyes. "Gee, I love you too."

"No, I don't mean it like that. I just, it'd be nice to not have someone breathing down my neck asking if I'm okay. Hell, I get this cast off in a few days and get a walking boot."

I turned and cast a longing gaze out the window. "Sweet freedom."

When Raelynn didn't at least chuckle, it worried me. Her face contorted as she struggled to lift herself from the seated position on my bed.

I dropped the brush. "You okay?"

"Yeah." Her breaths were shorter than she was.

Anxiety wasn't something I was used to in life, in truth. But it was suddenly clawing at my chest with undeniable urgency. "Are you sure, Rae?" I hobbled to standing.

"Yup." But her voice was too high pitched. "I just need to text Jordan right quick."

I grabbed my scooter, followed her from the room, and pulled up short when she stopped in the middle of the hall.

"Rae?"

"Shut up, Breanna!" She growled through clenched teeth, standing stark still for several terrifying seconds before moving again.

Raelynn wasn't a yeller. I couldn't think of the last time she'd screamed at me. Before Devin died we'd gotten into a huge fight and Rae didn't yell, not even when I was hateful and said horrible things about her.

Anxiety slipped right into full blown fear. "Dude, are you in labor?"

She turned to me in the living room, clutching her phone in one hand and staring down at her middle, her eyes wide and her bottom lip sucked between her teeth.

My gaze followed hers to where it looked as if she'd peed herself.

"Yeah." I over-enunciated the word.

"My water broke," she said softly, before dropping her phone to clutch her sides, her face twisted in pain.

"Oh my God, whoa…whoa…" The hospital was twenty miles away or more, Arkadia being the rural small town it was. "We gotta go, you're having a baby."

Nothing else mattered but getting my sister and her baby to the hospital. I snatched my keys from the table beside the front door. Technically I wasn't supposed to drive until my leg had healed completely. And I was on a damn knee scooter, but none of that mattered. We were having a baby.

"Two, maybe three more weeks…" Raelynn muttered, as I pulled her by her arm to the front door. She balked, stared at me, and shook her head as if to clear it. "I need to change. I can't leave like this."

"Ugh!" I wheeled my scooter, squeaking the entire way, back to my room to retrieve a pair of sweatpants I'd left lying on the bed.

When she entered the room, I tossed them at her. "Strip, put these on, meet me at the door."

I wheeled past her, grabbed her phone, a Tasmanian devil with a squeaky wheel, and tugged on my jacket. Everything was happening fast, but I felt like I was trudging along in quicksand. The baby would need a doctor, a nice clean hospital room—what if something went wrong?

"Let's go, Rae!"

"Coming." She leaned against the doorway, in my sweats now, and made the pain face again. For some reason, I counted. Fourteen-second-long contraction. I checked her phone to see the time, to see how far apart they were.

My heart pounded the entire time, three or four beats a second.

When she straightened, I flung open the door. I caught myself before I started rushing her again. My panic would only make hers worse. That couldn't be good for the baby. I took a deep, patient breath, and waited as she waddled with extra material from the pants legs bunched at the ankles, out of the house and toward my truck.

Holy crap, my sister was having a baby.

I followed on my scooter. Who cared if the wheel squeaked the entire way?

Creak, Creak. Creak.

Not me.

"That's going to drive me insane." She flinched again, grabbing her sides like she was trying to grab her back and her belly all at once.

Okay, so Rae cared. I boosted her into the vehicle by her arm as the contraction subsided. "Good thing the truck doesn't squeak."

In my head I counted, this time to eighteen before her face softened.

One minute apart, eighteen seconds long.

There was a metal clang as I tossed the scooter into the bed of the truck. The muscles in my arms sang out when I used them to lift myself fully into the cab. Doing so avoided putting unnecessary pressure on my leg. A throbbing appendage, near anxiety attack, *and* a sister in labor? I could only take so much. Hell, I was already breathing heavy.

Not as much as Raelynn, though, who was pink cheeked and panting now—despite the chill in the air.

I cranked the engine, turned up the heat, and counted as another contraction hit. Twenty-five seconds this time.

"They're getting longer," I told her. My fingers trembled as I put the truck in gear. Logically, I knew enough from the birth of my oldest niece and nephew that babies didn't just pop out super quick. Yet, I couldn't help think that this one might be different. I could barely take care of myself, much less my sister giving birth in my truck and a newborn.

"Ya think?" She gritted out between clenched teeth.

But I could drive—fast. Pieces of gravel rattled against the wheel wells and slung all over the driveway as I tore off down the road. It was the first time I'd been behind the wheel of a vehicle since my crash. I didn't have *time* to be nervous about that. The contractions were coming steadily, at increasingly shorter intervals, and lasting longer.

Arkadia was a blur in my rear-view as I headed toward County Hospital. Raelynn had prattled on and on about her *delivery plan* during my recovery. I knew where the suitcase and all her things were—at her house. Someone else could go back and get them. Maybe Jordan or my brother.

"Oh!" I fished her almost forgotten phone from my jacket pocket and called him. "Jordan, the baby's coming. We're—"

He ended the call before I could finish.

Yeah, buddy, me too.

****

I'd played the waiting-room game during the birth of my brother's two older children. Aiden hadn't even made it for the birth of the third—or known about it, for that matter. But those were different, regardless, because I despised his ex-wife.

Thankfully I really liked his fiancée, Hadley was great. She was also *late*.

With the back of my hand, I wiped at a bead of sweat on my brow. "When is she going to be here?"

Aiden glanced away from the hanging television in the waiting room, his lips twisting in an amused fashion.

"Ugh." I trembled. I needed to do something but I couldn't pace. I'd tried and my squeaky wheel had annoyed everyone so they'd made me stop.

I couldn't just sit there playing on my phone, waiting for Jordan or Mom to magically appear and beckon us to see the baby. The last time I'd seen my sister, just before they'd started this whole delivery thing, she'd been wracked with pain and on the verge of tears.

I needed a distraction. Hadley would be that, if she ever got there.

It felt like an eternity before she rounded the corner, blond ponytail swinging in her wake.

Immediately my brother stood and kissed her. "The kids?"

"Cara. I left her with my car, her truck is tore up. Noah brought her to the house for me. He closed up the shop, too, when everyone freaked out and left."

At the sound of his name, I looked past her to the tall, handsome guy with the unruly wisp of hair on his forehead. All he needed was a black jacket that said T-

Bird's and he'd be ready for Grease.

"Thanks, man." Aiden shook his hand.

I swallowed a knot that formed in my throat. It rolled down my chest, settled in my stomach, and turned everything cold. I couldn't move. I'd stood and rolled my knee scooter just a fraction of an inch forward when Hadley rounded the corner. Any farther and the dreaded squeak. Which, after being chucked into the back of my truck and bouncing around during the ride here, was more like the squawk of a pissed off mockingbird.

Melting into the drab gray tile of the waiting room, to avoid being noticed by Noah, seemed a far better option than any other I had. Why did he worry me so much? We weren't together—that was definitely over. Yet here I was, all anxious and jittery.

Then, he saw me.

The ball of cold dread at my center spun wildly, tendrils of self doubt whipping out to strike me all over. I couldn't do this, not today when my nerves were already shot.

I gripped my scooter to the point that the grips flattened beneath the force. And still, I stayed caught in his gaze.

Noah spoke first with a nod of his head. "Breanna."

"Hi," I croaked before backing up the squeaky wheel express and seeking an exit. "I'm getting a drink." I rolled away, squawking squeak and all, before anyone could stop me.

I'd already been through almost the entire candy collection in the tiny refreshment area. I had a pocket full of wrappers to prove it. Still, I grabbed a soda and a pack of oatmeal cookies. The hard kind, with the icing on top.

I was halfway through the bag, eating them so quickly I barely had time to taste them, when Noah ducked around the corner.

I didn't quite choke on my cookie but stopped chewing and glared at him. Fortified with sugar, it was easier to be annoyed with his presence.

"Your mom came out, the baby is here—everyone is going back."

I spit the cookie out in the open wastebasket and thrust my purchases at his chest. "I gotta go."

"Yeah." He chuckled.

My scooter noisily heralded my escape. I didn't have time to worry about Noah McKay, I had a baby to meet.

Chapter Thirty-Two

She was beautiful.

I sat on the side of my sister's hospital bed, cradling her newborn daughter. Raelynn beamed and Jordan loomed nervously over me. Though, neither gaze was on me.

Everyone was staring at the gorgeous, pink faced, black haired beauty in my arms. None of Aiden's kids had hair like this, I couldn't resist leaning down to kiss the soft locks, nuzzle her head and inhale the powdery scent of new baby and whatever it was they cleaned all the goop off them with.

"I can't believe you bathed her." I grinned up at Jordan. "She's not much bigger than your hand."

"I'm going to have to hold her on a pillow until she gets bigger." His voice was filled with more awe than I'd ever heard.

I kissed her again and passed her off to Mom.

"She's beautiful," I whispered to Raelynn as if I couldn't quite believe it. Maybe I couldn't. "What are you going to name her?"

That had been a great debate for quite some time. With Jordan, it was bound to be something race related.

Raelynn's face lit up. "You don't know?"

I shook my head.

"Chevy Rae."

I hiccupped a laugh before slapping a hand over

my mouth.

Only Jordan would name his kid after a car.

As if she could read my mind, Raelynn grinned impishly. "It was my idea. He liked it."

"Of course he did."

I couldn't tease, not really. Chevy Rae was by far one of the more amazing things I'd seen.

I held her again before I left the hospital. This time sitting in the rocking chair Mom forced me into, while she and Hadley got everything ready for my brother to bring Luke to meet the baby. My oldest nephew was quite excited over the new arrival.

Around me, the room was bustling enough I could whisper to Chevy without anyone hearing me.

"You're special to me. I tell your cousins that too, when no one is looking. I'll pretend like I don't like you sometimes or maybe even yell if you get into my stuff. But you are always special."

I kissed her hair and once again inhaled the sweet scent of new baby. "You have great parents and you'll have an amazing life. But always remember how special you are and that I love you, very much."

She was back in her mother's arms when I scooted my squeaky wheel out the door.

Raelynn is a mother.

Talk about a culture shock.

Noah leaned against the wall outside the waiting room, his ankles crossed, head back, and eyes closed. A normal person wouldn't be standing, much less sleeping.

Then again, from the tight grip he had on my half empty soda bottle and the tension that was evident through his shoulders, he was awake. And probably knew I was coming.

Hell, with the noisy ass scooter, a deaf man wouldn't need his hearing aid to hear me coming.

He cracked an eye open but made no effort to move when I stopped in front of him.

"Thanks for holding my stuff, you didn't have to. You could have cut out, nobody would have blamed you." I was feeling generous, so my tone was light and easy. There was a new, healthy, beautiful baby girl in my life. My sister was fine, Jordan was properly nervous and happy—all was right in my world. Not even Noah McKay could mess that up.

He arched one eyebrow in that way that made his forehead wrinkle, and my mouth went dry. It really wasn't fair that one man should make me so—crazy—on so many levels. And yet, here he was, doing just that. Even if I'd avoided him for weeks, the potency of my attraction to him was great.

"Actually, I'm your ride home."

I blinked. So maybe he could screw everything up. "Uh, I drove here. *I'm* my ride home."

"Nope, not while you still have metal poking out of your leg." My dad's voice didn't quite thunder down the hall, but it might as well have.

The two men in my life I'd argue against with the most ferocity were both glaring at me. My dad was tired but happily so. And Noah, well, I didn't want to spend too much time thinking about what he looked like. Especially not while he was public enemy number one on my personal shit list.

I handed Dad my keys without complaint, kissed him, and nodded toward the elevator. I was not causing a scene and ruining the high my family was operating on. We deserved this chunk of happiness. "Let's go, Noah. I'll see you later, Dad."

The small compartment for six floors was filled with awkward silence. Even with the elation of Chevy's birth—it was an almost painful ride. How would being in the shop truck for the trip to Arkadia feel?

I swallowed hard and gripped tight to my scooter handles.

As I'd predicted being stuck in the cab of the truck with Noah wasn't much better. I tried to think of happy things to let the anxiety from earlier in the day slowly fade away.

Then again, I could only withstand the silence for maybe five miles before I opened my mouth. "I'm sorry you got roped into this."

He shrugged but said nothing.

His brooding silence was infuriating. I plowed through what was left of my cookies, crunching with as much noise and fanfare as possible, checked my phone to find out it was dead, and twisted the cap on my soda off and on, off and on.

When Noah chuckled, I almost jumped—startled.

"Does being close to me affect you that much, Breanna?"

I thought about it for a long moment. My first answer was to tell him no, that was idiotic. But I'd be lying, and he seemed to be one of the rare few who could see right through me when I tried that.

So I stated simply, "Yes and it makes me hate myself."

"I'm sorry," he said after several long minutes.

"It is what it is. The best I can do is move on."

"Are you moving on?"

"You know, Noah, I'm trying. But it's not just a broken heart I have to move past. Everything I'd ever wanted, all my dreams, just got smacked with reality and are in a downhill tumble to God knows where. I take it a day at a time, enjoy the good things—like today. Am I moving on? No. I'm healing. Or trying to."

"I never meant to hurt you." The low sound of his voice was so achingly haunting that I wanted to reach out and stroke his face.

Instead, I balled my fingers into a fist at my side.

"I can't—process things the way you do. I can't look through the same rose-colored glasses you wear. The world, life, it's not so simple for me." The same sincerity laced his words.

Familiar anger boiled in my gut. I didn't see things the way he thought I did, I wasn't the person he thought I was—yet no matter how hard I tried, I couldn't make him see past that.

"I'm never going to be who or what you want me to be, Noah. I have nothing to say to that. I could argue with you, pitch a fit, but would that matter?"

He pulled into my driveway and I reached for the handle of the door.

I spoke quickly, before he slid from the driver's seat, "You already made your mind up about me a long time ago. I keep trying to show you that I understand or that I've grown. I just, I don't know what to do anymore."

I hopped out before he could open my door, and eyed him, willing him to see the *real* me. For whatever reason, it was important he do so. When he didn't respond, I grabbed my scooter from the back of the truck and waved him off when he started to get out.

"I'm not the one with rose colored glasses, Noah."

****

"The boot is ridiculous." I didn't groan, but I did sneer down at the offensive navy, plastic, nylon, and velcro contraption. It was by far the ugliest thing I'd ever seen. I'd been wearing it now for several weeks. No more metal rods or craziness, the last surgery behind me. Life was, for the first time, feeling normal again. I was healing.

My other foot was shoved into a rather cute black, leather wedge boot.

"I'm going to ditch it."

"No!" Cara swung around from the mirror where she applied makeup. The first race night of spring. I couldn't drive, I couldn't race. And I couldn't blow off steam in any *other* way—being a spectator on a dark street was the best I could do.

Sort of.

Since Raelynn and Jordan had gotten together, then Hadley and Aiden paired off, Cara had become my constant race night companion.

I'd shoved a pair of charcoal colored leggings into both types of boot and topped that with a tight black sweater dress.

"You'll still look like Mrs. Buxton from third grade, with or without the boot."

Not race-night ready. The outfit screamed "trying too hard."

"Ugh." I'd been trying to downplay the contraption wrapped around the lower portion of my leg. My aim had been early spring, dress casual. Anything really other than jeans and pajama pants. I hadn't been out of the house in ages it felt like.

I peeled off the teacher dress and flung it into the pile on my bed.

"Admit it, this is less about the boot and more about a guy who might be racing tonight."

I cocked my head sideways. I hadn't spoken to Noah since the night Chevy was born. And because I was still living off my earnings from race season—made easier by living at home—I hadn't gone back to work yet. Yeah, I was having some avoidance issues. Who cared? It's not like I could shake off being in love with someone.

Not everyone could be all mushy like my brother and his fiancée or as smitten as my sister and her husband. Nope. Sometimes, love just flat out sucked.

I stalked, nude from the waist up, to my closet and snatched a white tank and a black fitted hoodie. I pulled them both on, ditched *both* boots and shoved my feet into a pair of Converse.

When Cara eyed my left leg, I picked the boot up and tossed it by my purse. "If it starts swelling or hurting, I'll put that stupid thing back on."

I looked like a clean, attractive, yoga instructor. Nothing to see here, not trying to impress any-damn-body. Cara, on the other hand, was dressed to impress. Tall black boots with heels, short black skirt, and a cropped scoop neck shirt.

She was race and party ready. If she'd painted on a few extra layers of makeup and padded her bra, she'd have made a great pit bunny.

"Let's go, hop along."

I snickered, as she had no idea what I'd mentally been comparing her to. "Oh, the irony."

It felt good to be on even footing with Cara. Had it

not been for the crash, I might have stayed angry with her for who knew how long. However, I'd had enough time to think and understood her desire to protect me. Girls like us had to stick together.

We both knew what it was like to lose.

****

The desolate strip of country road on the back side of Cara's family farm was blocked off by a row of big trucks with bigger mud tires. The only vehicles allowed past that point were the rigs and race cars.

If the cops showed up, spectators would have to scatter across the recently plowed fields to the various designated parking areas. Not us, of course, we were bustled around in the cab as Cara maneuvered her uncle's old truck across the field from her house.

In a few weeks they'd plow it for planting, so we'd have to walk.

Lights had been set up beside Jordan and Aiden's trailers. Hunter East had his setup there too.

Until I stepped out of Rascal's truck, I hadn't realized how much I'd missed this. There was an eager crackling tension that came with street racing. That anxiety built from the danger of being caught that was absent from track racing.

Prickles of excitement skittered across my skin as I ambled down the street.

My brother leaned against his car, Hadley pulled against his chest, and his tongue stuck down her throat. Okay, maybe not that far, but they were locked like seal-tight at the lips.

"I'm gonna barf."

Cara giggled behind me, and Hadley pulled away. I didn't need light to know her face had turned bright pink.

"Where's the remainder of your leg, cyborg?" My brother separated from his woman and tightened the hood down on the glistening, black Camaro. It still stung to look at that car, but slowly it was becoming more Aiden's in my mind than it had ever been Devin's.

I rolled a shoulder as if the question didn't matter. Any response I would have made was drowned out by the throbbing blare of rap music from Jordan's rig, parked in front of Aiden's.

The two lane road was lined on both sides with trucks and trailers, and street raced cars. The race cars here didn't bling with sponsor stickers. Hell, some of them weren't painted at all. These were blue collar guys, the sort that sank every spare dime they had to their names into their cars.

My type of people.

This was home. So why had I wanted to leave so badly, why was I constantly running away? In a year I'd learned more about myself than I'd ever thought possible. I wouldn't run again, I knew now where I belonged.

Not all the race cars were on trailers. A familiar primer gray third-gen Camaro rolled through the line of rigs and slid into the space in front of my brother's car.

Unready to deal with Noah, I spun on my heel and went in search of someone—anyone—else. Wasn't hard to find a crowd to lose myself in.

For the next twenty minutes—after I parked my rear end on the side of Jordan's open trailer—I was assaulted with well wishers. I listened to Vic, who had weaseled his way back in that day, describe my crash and how expertly I'd handled a stuck throttle.

There was no handling it, I just held on for the ride.

Being back though, Vic's arm draped around my shoulder, the smell of tire prep, hyped up race fuel, cigarette smoke, cheap perfume ala pit-bunny, and hip-hop bass throbbing in my chest, was the first time I'd been truly happy since my last race.

Then I saw *him*.

He was leaning against the fender of his car, wearing faded jeans and a long sleeve black shirt. His hair brushed back from his face. Cleaner than the last time, smoother, slicked back. A cigarette dangled rebelliously from his lip. The light of the full moon did little to deter from his appeal, only made him look wilder—sexier.

Sure, I'd stopped by the shop a few times but avoiding him had been easy enough if I stayed in the front or Dad's office. He'd made the effort too, which was a blessing. As much as I hated to admit it, seeing him still hurt. Not as bad maybe, but there was a twinge in my chest, like plucking the spring on a doorstop each time he was close.

If I closed my eyes I could smell him, feel his fingers drag up my sides.

I jerked my gaze away, my buzz of happiness evaporating.

He stood no more than fifteen feet from Vic and Isaac. It took balls, immense ones to still associate with the same people who you'd fought with months before.

Then again, that was the way in Arkadia. Jordan and Hunter East had beaten each other to a pulp, right out in Felt's parking lot…and Hunter had been at Jordan's wedding. Hell, he was leaning against the trailer right now talking to Vic.

Guys were weird.

I slipped from the trailer and went in search of my brother-in-law. My sister was home with the baby so he could probably use my help. Mostly, I needed to distract myself from thoughts of Noah McKay.

"Hey, are you all right?" Cara ran up, flushed so that the freckles across her nose shone in the moonlight.

"Yeah."

She had that look on her face. Years of friendship told me something was wrong. What, I had no idea.

I dug a water out of Jordan's cooler, twisted off the cap and took a swig, waiting for her to explain herself. She didn't, merely bounced from one foot to the other with the frantic look of a startled cat.

"Why wouldn't I be, Cara?"

"Noah's here—on a date," she blurted.

I choked, sputtered, and spit water across the corrugated metal floor.

Isaac, who was standing behind us, turned around and patted my back. "You good, Breezy?"

"Don't—" I coughed. "Call me that."

He snorted and went back to checking Jordan's tires.

"What do you mean a date?" I shouted over the din as the next song played.

Cara stretched on tiptoes so she could half shout in my ear. "Like, he's here with Andrea Flynn. She used to date Eric, Vic's friend? But they broke up a few months go."

Leave it to Cara to know all the gossip. "She's a PB."

Noah with a pit bunny? That seriously wasn't his

style.

I looked over her shoulder, and sure enough a dolled up redhead with more makeup than class and more cleavage than ass was all but crawling all over him. A small group of the out of town racers, sizing him up.

"What a douche."

How dare he come to my place, with my friends, with some slut.

"Hey, Vic!" I gestured him over with nod.

"What's up, baby?"

"Noah gonna race?"

"Think so, why what's up?"

"Can I flag it?"

He thought about it for a while, before his slick grin spread. "If that's what you want, Breezy, that's what you got."

I spun on my heel, Cara following like shit was about to get real.

Good thing for Andrea Flynn I had enough class for both of us.

Chapter Thirty-Three

I had no intention of flagging Noah's race in a giant hoodie. I hid in my brother's trailer to change, my left leg throbbing now. Adrenaline had kept me on my feet longer than I should have been. Hell, the night was still young. I was going to pay for this in the morning—in more ways than one.

I jerked my hair down from its ponytail, finger combed it, and tossed the sweatshirt. One of Aiden's flannel shirts hung on a peg inside the trailer. I ditched the tank and donned the flannel; tying it so that my flat midriff was bare. I left it unbuttoned, and tore my bra off through my shirtsleeve.

I'd winged it toward the large toolbox as my brother stepped in. Black lacy material flew right by his nose.

"The bra is Breanna's, Hadley, I swear it." He called over his shoulder and made a face caught somewhere between disgust and confusion.

Hadley, following close behind, merely raised her brow and shoved the piece of black silk into the drawer. "You look—"

"I've got a plan."

I hopped out of the trailer, my brother's voice chasing after me. "I don't like the sound of that!"

Yeah well, I wasn't going to stand around while Noah paraded another chick in front of me. He wasn't interested in her, if he was he wouldn't have been watching me for a reaction while she climbed him like a randy stud horse.

"Oh my God, Breanna, I'm going to have to put a leash on you." Cara chased after me at a good clip. "And what plan, what are you talking about? Holy shit, stop for two seconds!"

She gripped my elbow, bringing me up short. Her eyes were wide with questions, her lips parted as she caught her breath.

"He doesn't get to do this." I scowled.

"Do what?"

"Show up here, to my world, with that tramp." I trembled with a rage I hadn't felt since Devin told me that my sister had betrayed him with Jordan.

"Oh." Her lips popped shut.

"My plan, starts with"—I made a circle and pointed at my target—"him."

Cara followed my finger to Hunter's stripped down truck he raced, where Matt Foster knelt, tightening lugs on the wheels.

I sauntered up, Cara in tow, and leaned against the side of the trailer. "Hey, Matt."

"Hey, Breanna."

"Remember that night you were going to race but blew your battery cables? Had like a grand on the line in a bet and I got out of bed, swung by the shop, and brought you some?"

He unfolded from the ground and smiled. "Yeah, sure do. You're a saint."

"I need a favor."

He nodded. "Anything."

"For the next hour, pretend like we're leaving here

to have the best sex of your life."

Hunter, who had walked up, whistled. "This is going to end badly."

Matt laughed. "I won that race." He turned to me. "You're on. But if I'm cutting off all my other romantic possibilities for the night, you at least owe me a kiss."

So, he was cute. And a good kisser.

I placed my finger against his lips and grinned. "We'll see."

****

Ignoring the sharp, searing pain radiating up my leg was much easier when I was focused on Noah. Then, my leg was eclipsed by the desolation of heartbreak. It started in my chest, wrapped around my heart, and burned all the way to my soul.

Vic's steady presence beside me was some comfort. There was a time when I'd felt as if I were all alone in this small town. It had taken me years to realize how strong my ties were, how many people had my back.

"You sure about this, mama?" Vic eyed me with concern.

"Yup." Sure. Maybe. Probably not. I wasn't going to tell *him* that.

My competitive streak was so violent I wasn't above using my family and my friends to make sure that Andrea Flynn wasn't at the center of Noah's attention.

For the rest of the night he was going to be looking at me.

"Yo guys, Breezy here's gonna be flagging this party. I'll let her walk through how she's going to do it, then she'll handle the coin flip. Any questions?"

"Yeah, who the fuck is she?" The other driver, a white guy with a buzzed head and a tattoo on the side of his face.

I sneered. "The chick standing here, not pretending to be hard like some wanna be gangster."

He stood taller and stepped forward as if to challenge me. I didn't back down, didn't need to. Not when Vic had my back. Then again, it wasn't Vic whose face morphed with rage.

Noah all but growled. "She's faster than you, bitch."

"Scared, Rogers?" Vic added.

Noah's body was tense in a way that made me think of things that had nothing to do with fighting. His date, however, had taken a step back and her eyes were wide. She wasn't going to last very long in this crowd.

"She'll do." Noah jerked his chin at me. "Got a coin?"

I palmed the coin and gestured to both drivers as I began my spiel. This wasn't my first time, Vic had trained me well.

As soon as they rolled up I'd bring them in. "Don't pull up until you're ready, I won't tolerate any whining about not having boost or not being ready."

One lane, then the other. I'd look over my shoulder to check the road, just like Vic taught me, then jog back a few feet. I was tall, I'd usually bring the light to my chest before hitting the button.

When Andrea slid up to Noah's side, I altered course and raised the flashlight above my head. "I'll bring it here before I hit it."

The evening breeze hit my stomach and flirted with the underside of my breasts.

Noah couldn't tear his eyes away.

"Now—" I grinned and pointed at the out of town guy "—call it in the air."

"Tails."

I flipped the quarter in the air; end over end it tumbled until the jangling slap of metal on pavement. The coin rolled to a stop at the scuffed, white toe of my sneaker.

"Heads."

I caught Noah's gaze and for a long minute, nobody else existed.

The sharp, cracking smack to my butt broke the reverie. Matt's goatee tickled the side of my face. "You about ready, baby?"

Foster's act was good enough to make Noah's nostril's flare and the little vein protrude from his neck. Oh yeah, I could own him at this little game.

"Your lane, McKay?"

His grin was a slow, angry challenge. Damn the man if it didn't make him ten times sexier. "Left." He spat at my feet and sauntered away on a lazy pivot.

"He is *not* happy," Matt commented in my ear.

"You're playing with fire, here, Bree." Vic pushed a hand through his jet black hair. "This ain't gonna end well."

"He started it, I'll finish it." I turned and laid one on Matt. A big, long, tongue stroking kiss. There was a rush, I hadn't expected, that sizzled right down to all the girly parts of me.

"Whoa." I shook my head clear when I pulled away.

"Burned, kid, just watch!" Vic called out, several feet away, half laughing-half serious.

"It's a good thing, I like things hot," Matt mumbled and shook his head. "Do that again, and I don't care who he is. I'll run him over for one night with you, Casey."

"Shut up, Matt. Let's get Hunter ready to race."

This *was* all for show, wasn't it?

****

Noah's date was piling on the flirting, hard. What made it worse was she wasn't just a pit bunny. She was one of those prissy, girly-girl types. Like Hadley, only not as cute. The sort of woman the Noah I knew wouldn't go for. That he would even entertain the idea of dating someone like her, pitched my respect for him right out the window.

"It's going to be difficult to pull this off, if you don't stop glaring daggers at the poor girl." Matt pulled me to him as we waited on the start line for my brother to roll through his burn out.

I'd be the one walking in his headlights, backing him up to the line.

I made a pointed attempt to not stare at Noah. When Matt raised an eyebrow, I rolled my shoulders and worked to loosen my tense muscles. Pretending to be attracted to Matt wasn't hard. Not when he could kiss like the devil. He had a goatee now, he hadn't before. It didn't hide the full lips, rather brought attention to them. I could kiss him again and wouldn't consider it a chore.

Neither was flirting with him.

I set about doing just that, laughing and teasing. When his hands roamed all over me I feigned annoyance, then made sure to lean in and inhale the scent of his cologne as I brushed my lips across his neck.

Noah watched, I could see him in my peripheral, all but ignoring his date. Judging by the white knuckled grip he held on his water bottle—I was right on the money.

So, I moved closer to Matt, got more touchy.

Noah put his arm around Andrea.

I trailed my fingers up and down Matt's back while he nuzzled my neck.

Noah pretended to be incredibly attentive to his date.

I hugged Matt a little too close.

Noah flirted and made her laugh.

"Jesus, Foster. If you're waxing the finish, get a room. She's my sister for fuck's sake." Jordan grumbled, low and deep before disappearing into a cloud of rubber smoke and the roar of my brother's engine.

Three racers from the track had showed up, thinking they had something for the Kings of the Street. They didn't, of course, but tonight Jordan, Aiden, and Hunter would put on a clinic.

We lined Aiden up and the Camaro screamed through the eighth of a mile to an easy win.

When it was over, I sought out my brother's enclosed trailer, and languished in my own company for several minutes. The entire night was a downward spiral of anger and jealousy. I was so close to imploding, I could feel it. Not to mention my leg was dying.

I sat on the floor by one of the toolboxes and propped my leg up on a box of shop rags. There I contemplated who I'd murder first. Noah or his petite, made up, completely oblivious—

She walked right into the trailer and I all but swallowed my tongue.

The tiny redhead jumped when she saw me. “Oh! Wow. Sorry, I didn’t know anyone was in here. Aiden said I could grab a water, and Hadley said there was a mirror I could use to touch up my makeup.”

I stared at her, dumbfounded, before utter betrayal swept in and pushed out all other emotion. My brother and his fiancée had sold me down river in favor of this bitch? *Oh hell no.*

I could try to drown her in a bucket of race fuel, but her humongous tits would save her—flotation devices. Though, she might choke on the mascara that would run. Her perfume was probably more toxic than the fuel anyway.

“This is so cool, I haven’t been to an actual street race before.” It was apparent, quickly, she had zero clue about my relationship with Noah or the pure loathing I felt toward her.

That didn’t make me hate her any less.

I gave her the most epic, Breanna Casey side-eye on the planet. When her smile didn’t falter, I added a good dose of stank on it.

She giggled nervously. “When you’re with a hot guy, you gotta make sure you look good. Am I right?” She smeared on an unneeded layer of lipstick.

I snorted. “Sure, if you say so.”

When she pulled out her makeup bag, I snarled. “Go easy, Picasso. Your hot guy isn’t a fan of all the warpaint.”

“Huh?”

“The guy you’re with, Noah?” I stood from my

spot and moved to the door. If I stayed in the trailer any longer I'd do something we'd all regret. "Doesn't like all the makeup. I know, because one night not long ago, right after he screwed me—he mentioned how much he liked the natural look."

I left her in my brother's trailer, staring after me as if I'd just slapped her.

I wished I had.

****

Noah's race was between Aiden's and Hunter's. Jordan had pulled the card to run last. The true street cars, like Noah's ran in between the behemoths like Jordan's Malibu.

My jaw was set tight, flashlight with new batteries palmed in my hand, as I waited at the start line.

"What did you do?" Cara ran up, face flushed. She might be in a tiny skirt and boots, but she still didn't look near as out of place as the Andrea chick.

For the span of several seconds I was confused. Then I saw my brother crossing the sparsely lit road and heading toward me; his shoulders squared off in annoyance.

"Nothing." I shrugged. "Just told that little bitch with Noah, that I'd had sex with him."

Cara barked a laugh. "Seriously? She's over there at Noah's car crying like you slapped her."

I totally should have.

"Nope." I sighed.

I threw my hand up in my brother's face before he said a word. "I called her Picasso, told her not to wear so much makeup, and that I had boned Noah. All true. Anything else is bullshit. If you're all pissed because I told the truth, I needn't tell you what I think about that." I popped a fist on my hip. "Nor what I think of *you* for letting that trash into your trailer."

"Jesus, Breanna." Aiden shook his head so that hair fell from its tie. "You'd think you were the big bad wolf or something."

"Nope. But next time I'm sulking, don't send the reason for said mood right to me."

"Didn't realize you were in there or I wouldn't have."

Cars fired up down the street. "Too late to straighten Noah out about it."

"Fuck him." My upper lip curled.

Cara laughed again. "Who needs those real housewives shows when you have pit bunnies."

And then I was all alone on the start line. Rogers' crew ran through his burnout. Noah's crew, much to my infuriation, was *mine*. Or at least, half of my crew. My brother, headed it up. Jordan helping here and there as well.

I could throttle every damn one of them.

My jaw was clenched so tight my teeth ground, the sound barely audible over the engines of the souped up daily drivers. Behind the car, Little Miss Not So Sunshine glared at me, the crocodile tears in her eyes more from the burnout smoke than anything else.

I didn't spare a glance through Noah's windshield until I pulled him to the line. I'd expected to find him as angry as I was. Yet, he stared right past me—all cold confidence.

A check over my shoulder, three steps back, light over my head, and they were off.

The wind sucked around me, pushing me in all directions as it rushed off both cars in an acrid wind tunnel of speed and fortitude.

I didn't watch the race, instead found Vic and waited on Rascal's call. When it came, I was done.

Matt tried to stop me, but I waved him off. I'd walk back across that damn field, climb into my truck, and go the hell home. Throbbing leg and all. I didn't care anymore.

Done.

The angry, telltale sound of a high revving motor, followed by the harsh screech of tires braking behind me brought my head around. Noah flung the Camaro in gear and left it parked sideways across the make-shift pits.

He hopped out and took several long strides toward me, his face contorted with rage. "Where the hell are you going?"

I looked around me, searching for someone else. There was no way in hell he was speaking to me that way.

"Nah, I'm talking to you, Casey."

My laughter was mocking. "Wherever I decide to go, is none of your business."

"It is, when I have something to say to you."

When he reached for me, I dodged, stumbling a bit on a leg that had been through too much for one night. I bit back the curse of pain and growled at him through clenched teeth. "Don't you dare touch me."

"Oh, I can't, but everyone else can?"

My eyes widened and my pulse raced. Suddenly, the pain in my leg didn't matter so much.

"Excuse me?"

He rolled back on his heels and raised his brow. "Wanna do this right here, in front of everyone?"

A crowd had gathered around us like we were the main attraction. "You're the one who has the fire up his ass. I don't have an issue with you."

He grinned, without humor and pointed to where Andrea Flynn stood, watching with a defiant and antagonistic gaze.

"Then why are you starting shit with her? You don't get to shit all over people, just because you're unhappy." His nostrils flared and the vein throbbed in his neck. I wanted to karate chop him right there, then maybe shove my medical boot right up his—

"All I did was tell the truth. Does that embarrass you, Noah?"

I threw my arms out wide, did a little shimmy, and couldn't keep the high pitch from my voice. "Hey everybody, Noah and I had sex. A lot of it. He's seriously pissed off because I told little Miss Lipstick and Cheap Perfume *all* about it!"

I'd jumped straight past out of control and full on into self-destruct. I had everyone's attention now. "Or how about that time he told me I wasn't good enough for him to have sex with, or when he fought my best friend, or called me a horrible person because I confided my feelings to someone!"

"You can't just hurt people, to make yourself feel better, Breanna! That's not the way any of this works. Lashing out, playing games, when all I ever did was exactly what you asked me to do!" Noah was angry, trembling, and starting to get that look in his eye that came just before he checked out.

I backed up three steps. My brother and Jordan stood not far away, confused and anxious.

Noah wasn't the only one trembling. Now, I fought

back emotion and tears. “Or better yet, why don’t *we* just tell everyone how I tried everything I could to make you love me and it was never enough. I was never good enough!”

I whispered the last bit, just for him, hot tears streaming down my face. “Fuck you, Noah McKay. All you’ve ever done is stomp all over my heart and humiliate me. Now everyone knows how awful a person I am. Happy now?”

Chapter Thirty-Four

The best thing about Cara as a friend, was even when she's not there—she's there. Like the fight with Noah. I hadn't seen her—not until she'd pulled up at the side of the road in the old farm truck. Ready for me, ride or die.

"I'm so glad I have friends like you." I wasn't sniffling. I could admit to crying, but I would not admit to turning into a sniveling girl.

"Isaac came and got me." Her lips twisted in a soft smile. "I was just flirting with some guy anyway. You're more important."

I choked on a phantom sob. *Nope. Not gonna cry anymore, no matter how amazing my friends are.*

"Where do you want to go? I'll go with you, just need a bag from my house." She peered at me from the driver's seat with a sad smile. "I figured you wouldn't want to go home."

She was right, I had no desire to answer anyone's questions. Notorious for my disappearing acts anyway, I stated quite simply, "Raelynn's."

Sometimes, home was the best option. That had taken me more than two decades to learn. But it didn't have to be the four walls of my parents' house. Sometimes a girl just needed her sister.

****

The baby was asleep by the time Cara dropped me

off. Raelynn, however, was nervously cleaning when I walked into the door. She was Mom, only younger and with less attitude. Or maybe more, depending on the day or the situation.

"Hey, Aiden sent me a text. You okay?" Blue eyes bright with worry, her gaze darted frantically from the top of my head to the tips of my toes.

Well, as high up on my head as she could see anyway.

I dropped onto the leather sofa and shrugged. "Just Aiden? Not like, half of Arkadia?"

My leg was screaming in violent revolt. I snatched the boot from my oversized purse and gingerly toed off my sneaker.

"Why did you take that off?" She ignored my question and fished an oversized T-shirt from a laundry basket.

Which told me that Aiden hadn't been the only text or call she'd gotten. The disadvantage of living in a small town. Everyone knew everything as soon as it happened.

"It wasn't stylish?"

"Breanna, do you want more pins in your leg? What happens when that bone doesn't heal the right way?"

I cocked my head sideways. "You know, you have a kid and a husband now. Save the mom bit for them, mmk?"

"I also have my house, that you're in, so watch it before I send you across the street to listen to Mom's bitching."

I balked. I'd said some serious shit to my sister over the years and never had her snap at me like that.

Especially not over snark and sarcasm.

"Yeesh."

"Sorry." When she pressed her finger to her eye, much like me, I couldn't help but grin. "I haven't slept much this week. I was worried. My hormones are shot."

"Well, the baby is asleep so why don't you crash? I'm fine, I can lay here and go to sleep until the morning." There, I could have the emotional security of my sister, but not have to *talk* about any of this Noah stuff. Or worse, about myself and all the damn mistakes I'd made.

"No." She tossed me the shirt.

I let out a long sigh. It had been worth a shot.

With compact movements, she crawled onto the couch beside me and tucked her legs beneath her. "The last time you lost your shit like this, the fallout lasted for months. I know you, whatever happened is going to eat at you from the inside out."

She was probably right. But at least that was a slow process that I could fortify myself against.

"It's like the wreck, Rae. The throttle got stuck and I didn't have time to make the right decision if there was one at all. Now I'm rolling down the track. Only instead of seeing track and the sky, track and the sky, I'm seeing Noah loving me and Noah not loving me."

I didn't cry. The thickness in my throat was evidence I could have, easily, but I didn't. So much had changed in such a short amount of time. I'd never imagined being in love could hurt so much. Or that the person you loved could be the one who broke your heart.

"I mean, he brought a fucking date. *My* world. *My* family. And he brought this little pit bunny bitch." I fisted and unfisted my hands, imagining I was punching the cheap lipstick right off her face. "Why would he do it, if not to make a point, to hurt me in some way?"

To keep from pacing on my already throbbing leg, I changed into the shirt Rae had given me. "So, I gave it right back to him."

She pointed at my would-be cleavage. "So that's the reason for the girly-gun show?"

"I'm not as well armed as you, but I tried. There's a bra in Aiden's trailer, he made sure Hadley knew it was mine."

Raelynn shook her head with a grin, wisps of hair tumbling from the messy bun at the top.

"It's like, I'd decided I loved Noah or something—wanted to give him a chance, see if we could figure something out. But, he'd just moved right on past that into shoving his new sex life in my face."

"Whoa." She sucked in a breath. "Like, love him, love him?"

"Yeah. Even after everything. It's like no matter what happened we kept leading with the wrong foot. And then—we weren't even dancing to the same song."

"You know it's deep when Breanna Casey spends the entire conversation speaking in metaphors."

"Go get some sleep, Raelynn. I'll just lay here." I pulled the throw blanket from the back and wrapped it around me.

I'd thought I'd been in love with Devin. But no, knowing he loved my sister had never broken my heart the way seeing Noah with someone else had.

****

I wasn't asleep when Jordan came home. A gentle rain started to fall right after that, the clouds fending off the bright rays of dawn and the hum of precipitation lulled me to sleep.

I'm not normally a heavy sleeper, so I was surprised that I hadn't heard the commotion that had my sister leaning over me, who knew how long later.

"Wake up, Breanna. Jordan's out back with Noah."

"What?" I blinked to make sure I was present, not dreaming.

"Yeah, do you want to talk him?"

"Jordan?"

"Noah."

Wow. Yes. No. Not really, not now. I was tired, I was hurt, and I couldn't think of a single good thing that could come from a conversation with Noah at this point. It was done, finally and truly.

I fumbled for my phone to check the time and pressed my finger to the twitching tingle in my left eyelid. "No, not now. Whatever he has to say, he should have already said."

"Agreed. Got it, we'll let him know."

I rolled to my side and bent my arm beneath my head, anything to find a comfortable position to go back to sleep. Not that I would, knowing Noah was right outside. He wanted to talk to me, to start this vicious cycle of will he or won't he all over again. I couldn't keep doing it, not like this.

Not when I'd finally begun to figure out who I wanted to be. He changed things, made me crazy—well crazier than I already was.

I strained to hear what was being said through the door and waited for Raelynn to come back inside. The urge to ask her how he looked and what he was saying forced me to sitting.

Muffled sounds grew to muffled voices, which grew to distinct voices and a sound I was all too familiar. Guys in my life, often spoke with their fists.

I jerked the door open, barely realizing I'd moved from the couch.

Noah was sprawled on his back in the wet grass, rain pelting him. He stood, swayed on his feet, and made a run at Jordan that stole my breath. My brother-in-law was a big guy, the sort with shoulders you could build a tree house on. Noah, though as tall, didn't have the bulk of muscle.

He hit Jordan full on, shoulder down, and all his force behind it, right in the middle. It would have laid out a mere mortal of a man. But nah, Jordan only staggered back with a grunt, cursing under his breath, his ball cap toppling to the grass.

The storm cloud darkened sky made it hard to judge the time of day. Midmorning, maybe? Not that it mattered, my heart hammered in my chest, a mimicking tremble vibrated up my throat to my parted lips. I opened my mouth, but there was no sound, save for the buzz in my ears.

Beside me, Raelynn gripped the porch rail. Her compact form tight, as if frozen with nervous energy. I'd never seen her afraid to throw herself in the middle of a fight. Not when Jordan was one of the offending parties.

But, normal Arkadia fights came with a good dose of entertainment value. Not like this. Noah's eyes were glazed over, unseeing, in a way I'd experienced with him before. Noah had checked out, lost himself to a place where things moved in a different way.

It wasn't particularly cold out and the awning over

the porch blocked my sister and I from the rain pelting the brawling males, yet I shivered with a chill.

"Jordan—" I croaked out, unable to make my mouth work.

It was enough, though, for Noah to hear.

"Breanna!" He jerked away from Jordan and spun on a pivot that would make any fight instructor proud.

His voice though, was cracking and full of an emotion that shot right through me. Unable to take that sort of emotional punch, I took a trembling step back.

That was all the reaction Jordan's protective instincts needed. With a steady grip, he horse-collared Noah, swinging him backward.

"I told you, she doesn't want to talk." It was his fist, this time, that sent Noah to the ground.

Noah, recovered quickly and stood up, swiping at the blood from his nose with the back of his hand. He charged toward the porch again, never swinging at Jordan, barely seeing the other man.

Jordan hit him again, the sickening crack of bone to flesh contact. Noah stumbled but didn't stop, and again Jordan swung his massive fists.

"Breanna, do something," Raelynn whispered.

"Stop!" I shouted, finally finding my voice, and hobbled in my boot down the rain slick steps.

Not hearing me, Jordan punched him again. This time, two shots to the stomach that sent Noah back to the ground. The blood and dirt stained white T-shirt clung to him in the rain.

"Jesus, Jordan, stop it with the Hulk-Smash already!" I fell to my knees in front of Noah and cupped his face as he struggled to sitting.

Jordan hovered, his face twisted somewhere

between confusion and anger. “Bree—”

“It’s fine!” I spat, wiping at the blood that was running down Noah’s face, watered down by the storm dumping buckets on our heads.

The world around us grew lighter but still gray.

“Go inside”—and when he didn’t budge I shot him a softer look—“He won’t hurt me.”

“He ain’t right.” Jordan shook his head.

“No, probably not. But, it’ll be okay.”

Slowly, dark blue eyes that had been out of focus and wild, latched on to me. Noah’s face softened, and his fingers wrapped around my wrists.

“You make one hell of an entrance, McKay.”

He dropped his forehead to mine. The metallic scent of blood wasn’t as strong as it should have been, masked now by the cleansing of spring rain.

“I needed—*need* to talk to you.”

I was distinctly aware of Jordan walking away.

“So, talk.”

He didn’t say a word, instead, he pulled away and tugged his shirt over his head. He used it to mop the blood from his face.

I watched him, because I had nowhere to go. I’d taken those steps, come this far, but for what? My hands fell to my sides, this wasn’t a problem I could drive myself out of.

Who were we? Whatever the answer to that question, it couldn’t be this painful, emotional tug of war that our relationship had been.

He kissed me, before I could fully wrap my head around the moment. His lips, demanding something I didn’t think I could give. He kissed me in the rain until I’d forgotten why we were there in the first place.

"I'm sorry." Noah was breathing heavy as he pulled away.

He laughed, the laugh of a man half-crazed with love and the weight of the entire world strapped to his chest. He stood and pulled me to standing with him, my leggings and sister's T-shirt clinging to me uncomfortably.

"I love you, Breanna Casey."

I was so dizzy in that moment that I squeezed my knees together in an effort to keep from toppling over. "You're drunk."

"No. Yeah, but no—" He let go of my arm to push his hair from his face. Shirtless, he seemed to pay no attention to the chill of the rain that pelted us. "I run away from everything I love. Because love, it doesn't last, not for real. Death, violence, those things last. Not love."

He shook his head, as if shaking away ghosts that haunted him. "I could run for a thousand lifetimes and always run right into you. I tried tonight, to forget you existed and there you were. I've tried a hundred times to leave this place, and I can't leave you."

Before he'd come here, I'd been so over it. We'd made a mess of things, hell I'd made a mess of my entire life. Now…

"You said all you'd done was try to make me love you. But, Breanna, I've loved you since the very first day I saw you."

I blinked in the rain. He could have slapped me in the face with rotten fish and I'd have expected that more.

When I didn't say anything, he pulled me close, the tip of one finger tracing my lips. "I stopped at a store, just off the interstate. Needed gas. Speed Shop truck pulled into the parking lot and caught my attention."

I'd heard this story before and couldn't help but smile.

"The delivery girl was this hot chick with legs for days. I took one look and knew I had to have her. So, I followed her back to the shop and got a job."

I laughed. "You hated me, Noah."

"No." He nuzzled his face to mine. "You were everything I thought I didn't want and everything I needed all wrapped up in one snarky package. I've loved you every day since, and I'll love you until I take my last breath."

"Noah." I couldn't respond to that. For the first time in my life I was completely speechless. Even in my head, I drew a blank. It was a good thing my heart knew exactly what to do. I kissed him, softly at first. My lips slipped against his in the rain. I kissed him with all the feelings I could give voice to, I kissed him the way I should have from the very beginning.

Chapter Thirty-Five

"Come home with me," Noah murmured.

Four of the sexiest, most exciting words I'd ever heard in all my life. I was shivering, wet, and pretty sure some of the blood from the fight had dripped onto my borrowed shirt. Yet, at the core of me something warmed. It was far too easy to forget about all the hateful, hurtful things that had passed between us.

I went home with him. Not stopping to go in and tell my sister, she'd figure it out. The ride to his place was quiet, the only sound the rumble of the engine and the squeak of wipers on glass.

The apartment was dark, the only light filtering through the blackout curtain over the one window, a dim product of the grim morning that had dawned. I was shivering, in need of a shower, but couldn't turn away from the shirtless man who stood in the middle of the room, toeing off his sneakers.

We'd taken a long, painful route to get to where we were. Yet, I could think of nowhere else I'd want to be. I wondered what Picasso the Pit Bunny would think of how things had worked out now? It was petty, sure, but she deserved it.

A tingling rush started in my chest, moved to my stomach, and settled somewhere near my ovaries. Not that I was still, I shifted from one foot to the other and chewed on my bottom lip.

When he unsnapped his jeans and peeled them down his hips, I all but groaned. Noah's body was long and lean—except that one spot that wasn't very lean.

"You should warm up in the shower."

"*Well*, when you say it like that." It was hard to sound sexy, when you were pulling off your best impression of a drowned rat.

His upper lip curled and he stepped out of his pants. My gaze was increasingly drawn elsewhere. It was obvious that Noah wasn't nearly as cold as I was.

"When you flagged that race"—he pushed up the hem of my T-shirt, stopping at the underside of my breasts—"and your shirt rose up, my mouth watered, Breanna, I barely managed to keep the car straight."

He leaned down while I trembled with arousal. I was perpetually impatient, yet I couldn't move a muscle, not when he leaned down to brush his lips across the bottom of my breasts.

My stomach clenched and my body tightened almost painfully. The whoosh of inhaled breath only brought my chest higher, pushing the shirt up so that a nipple slipped out. Noah claimed it in his mouth, the heat a stark contrast to the chill of my flesh.

"Noah…" I gasped through a ragged breath.

He pulled away long enough to jerk the shirt from my body, tossing it with a wet thud somewhere behind me.

"I love this part of you." He caught the other nipple between his teeth and tugged lightly. I moaned outright and probably would have melted into a puddle on the floor had he not wrapped his arms around me.

"I always thought they were too small, that I looked like a boy," I squeaked. I'd never admitted that to anyone, ever. Not even my sister, who I constantly teased for her curves.

"Bullshit," he growled and kissed his way up my chest to my throat, before claiming my lips.

Somehow, as he kissed me, he managed to strip my leggings and panties to the floor, even gently slipping the Velcro boot from my leg.

"We aren't going to make it to the shower." He tumbled back onto the bed, pulling me with him. "But I can think of other ways to warm you up."

Which he did, his hands slipping over every inch of me, warming my skin as he kissed me stupid.

My legs parted for him, as if we hadn't just fought like crazy people in front of half of Arkadia. With confident, self-assured movements, Noah warmed me to boiling, hovering over me, his breaths warm against my face, as I clung to his sides.

My nails found purchase in his skin; the length of my legs wrapped around his hips. I didn't whimper but pleaded with the writhing of my body until he slid inside me, filled me until I cried out from the pleasure of it.

Like every other time, pleasure was an explosion of Noah and I, together, crashing against emotion and feeling.

Nothing else mattered, nothing else ever would.

****

Noah was asleep when I stepped from the shower. On his back, the covers tucked around his hips and his arms behind his head—like he had so many times when we'd shared hotel rooms. He'd fallen asleep with me on his chest and didn't so much as move when I'd gotten up to shower.

Never had he been so relaxed, in all the time I'd known him. Yet here he was, his expression soft with sleep, his muscles loose. He seemed almost innocent.

Wrapped in a white towel I sat on the edge of the bed and traced the lettering on his ribcage with the very tip of my index finger—*Semper Fidelis.*

His hand shot out and his fingers tightened on my wrist. There was a time I might have been frightened, even recoiled at such a startling grab. Not anymore, I'd spent too much time with Noah. I sat still and waited on the steady rise and fall of his chest to resume.

When it did, I spoke softly, "Good morning."

"Afternoon." He brought the back of my hand to his lips.

When he released his grip, I trailed my fingers down his chest, across the tattoos. "True story."

"Are we going to talk about any of it."

He sat up, wiped his face, and took his time replying. I didn't push, no matter how hard it was for me not to. I wasn't made to be patient. I was made to go at everything fast, with little thought. With Noah, that wasn't an option. Not when it came to this.

"Jerry told you most of it, I imagine. Otherwise you'd have been driving me nuts about it by now." He watched me through heavy lids and thick lashes. "So, just go with that."

"You're admitting to being a hero." I was only half teasing. I figured he was cocky enough to go with that.

With a finger, he pulled at my towel, but I caught it before it fell. When all I did was raise a brow, he sighed.

"I'm no hero, Breanna. I'm a survivor. Heroes step in when they can just walk away. Survivors do what they have to do to get out alive. What you did that night at the hotel, on the steps? That's heroic. I just got out alive, those who went with me would have done the same."

He bent his knees and leaned forward, nuzzling the soft spot behind my ear and whispering, "When you didn't keep walking up those steps, you saved me."

My skin was covered with chills, I closed my eyes to fend off the flood of love. Who had I been kidding, I'd never be able to live without Noah McKay.

"Whatever, I'm too messy to be a hero."

He kissed me, slowly, allowing me to commit the feel of his lips against mine to memory. When he pulled away, he was smiling. "My messy hero."

I snorted and stood. My wet leggings had hardened into a gross form on the floor. "Got any sweats I can borrow?"

"Yeah." He stood from the bed, naked, and crossed the small studio.

I'd forgotten the confidence he moved with. Paired with being completely naked, made me want to lick him from the tips of his toes all the way up—maybe spend a little extra time and attention on certain places.

My face burned with a touch of embarrassment when he turned and caught me appreciating.

I met his gaze and gave what I hope was my best predatory grin.

His response was to toss me a T-shirt and pair of basketball shorts with a draw string.

"I'm taking a shower, before I don't give you a chance to get dressed."

The ease in which he'd steered the conversation away from himself was not lost on me. "Is it difficult to talk about?"

He turned to me at the door to the bathroom. "It was, I don't know what it'll be like now."

I scrunched my nose. "Now?"

"It's different with you, more like I have a light in the dark now. I'm not alone anymore."

Well, damn.

****

We drove. Correction, I drove despite the nagging pain in my leg. The late afternoon sun had broken from the clouds. The scent of evaporation from rain soaked, sun baked asphalt was calming as it drifted through the open windows.

Noah, freshly showered and shaved was kicked back in the passenger seat, the sunlight glinting off his mirrored aviators. He was timeless in that moment, peaceful. Neither one of us talked about what had happened the night before at the street races or all the things that had passed between us.

At first, I thought it didn't matter. But, like with just about everything in life I tried to ignore, it started to fester. Somewhere along the way I'd learned to not leave the festering things too long, to get them out as soon as possible. Usually, they were there because I'd been wronged in some way.

Or someone I loved had.

Okay, who was I kidding? I couldn't let something fester for longer than twenty-four hours. It wasn't in me to leave the unsaid, unspoken. Nope. Couldn't do it.

"So, why Andrea Flynn and why the hell did you bring her to the races with you?"

I slowed the Camaro to a stop at the light near the Wash Out. Maybe I wasn't itching for a fight, but there were things that needed to be said when he didn't have his hands all over me. I couldn't think like that.

"You really want to do this?" he asked, correctly interpreting my quiet mood.

I shrugged and swung the car to the right, heading down to where the old highway bridge had washed away. The middle of the afternoon, the usual crowd of people that covered the gravel and broken pavement was gone. "Not really, to be honest. But, if I don't I'll always wonder."

He sucked his bottom lip between his teeth and let it roll out in a way that would drive any heterosexual woman completely insane. "She was the anti-you."

"You have no idea…"

He snorted. "Actually, I do. I figured if I had sex with her, spent time with her, I'd stop thinking about you."

"Did you?"

"Stop thinking about you? No. Never."

I stopped his car at the end of the road, the river stretching out in the distance. My stomach twisted itself into a sickening knot and I squeaked, "No, did you bang her?"

This time he laughed. His chuckling fit lasted so long I screwed my face into annoyance that he would mock me. "It's a serious question, Noah."

He got out of the car, shut the door, leaned into the passenger window, and peered over the rim of his shades. "No, Breanna, I didn't. I took her home, apologized for not being a better date, then went to the Rooster and tried my damnedest to drink you away."

He rose from the car and spun away, walking toward the end of the Wash Out that overlooked the water. "Turns out, the only way to get over you—is to not."

I was smiling when I caught up to where he sat, his legs dangling off the broken concrete. Yes, it was slightly petty to have been right about the pit bunny not being his type. I couldn't help myself.

"The Matt thing was just to make you jealous." I sat and stretched my legs out and crossed them at the ankles.

His arm slid lazily around my shoulders. "I knew that."

"You did?" My ego protested.

"Baby, you were laying it on pretty thick on the guy." He nipped my ear. "Which, oddly, turned me on."

"So, you're saying I need to throw myself all over a guy at the next street race?"

"If you want me to kill him, sure."

I laughed and some of the fear that had settled in my chest, broke free and floated away. "So, now what?"

His only response was a grin.

Chapter Thirty-Six

Being back at work wasn't as bad as I thought it would be. If only every customer wouldn't ask me to relive the crash or when I'd be back behind the wheel. Aiden and Jordan were getting ready to race for the top spot on the street and summer was in full swing. So, I saw a lot of customers.

My eye was twitching as I sauntered through the front door to the shop, metallic bells clanging behind me.

"That bad?" Hadley scrunched her nose.

I plopped on a stool, and massaged my eyelid with the ends of two fingers. "You'd think there were more important races happening, than that one time—"

"It was that way after Devin died," my sister interrupted on a sigh as she leaned across the counter in front of me. "It gets better, I promise."

Okay so, I'd thought coming back to the shop was better than answering ten thousand questions about the career I'd had go up in smoke. Nope. Not when two women were piling on the sappy faces and well wishes.

"Ugh." I hopped, sans boot finally, from the stool and escaped out the other door.

The buzz snap of air wrenches and the overpowering scent of motor oil beckoned to me from the bays. It was as close to a pit at a drag race as I'd get anytime soon. Not that it really mattered, over the hood of a Chevy truck I caught Noah's gaze.

In a red Casey's shop shirt and a pair of well worn jeans, he was the best looking thing I'd ever seen. And with him the past few months I'd been happy. Here, at home, in this little town in Texas. Could I be happier? Maybe, but I was content just like this.

I eased around the back of the truck and wrapped my arms around his middle. A few seconds to ground myself to the here and now, without all the bullshit and the old memories my sister had unwittingly dragged up. But of course, touching Noah, even with the best of intentions, never remained innocent for long.

The comfort he offered was a warm respite and I soaked it in, pressing my body against his. When his lips came down, how could I not kiss them?

"For the love of God, get a room!" Aiden slung a half empty box of shop rags at us and rolled his eyes. "Back to work, both of ya. Geez."

I pulled from Noah and stuck my tongue out at my brother. "Are we still swinging by to tour the love nest?"

"Stop calling it that, as that's not how I want to envision my sister using my trailer."

Noah laughed and ducked back under the hood of the truck.

"Get used to it. I had to put up with you sucking face with Wendy—things could be a lot worse."

The glare he shot me could have melted the finish off of every vehicle in the shop.

"Easy there, hoss. We'll be there after work."

****

Renting my brother's trailer until he sold the property had been Noah's idea. Why he'd been so adamant about it, I hadn't the foggiest. He pulled my truck up to the front door of the well-kept tin rectangle. Before they'd moved into the swanky old house downtown, Aiden and Hadley had lived here.

Hell, my brother had lived here with two different women. That was weird and one of the reasons I wasn't too thrilled about the idea.

I curled my nose. "I have to sleep in a room where my brother banged. That's creepy, Noah."

"We'll bang there too." He leaned over and nipped at my ear lobe.

I was shivering a bit and giggling when I climbed from the truck and fished the key from my pocket.

"And aren't you already sleeping in a room he banged people in?" Noah followed me up the steps.

"Yeah, no. None of us did the deed in Mom and Dad's house."

He watched me with a perplexed expression.

"Seriously! Aiden even said he hadn't."

With a shake of his head, Noah followed me into the trailer. "I call bullshit on that one. He snuck at least one girl in there."

I turned and wiggled my hips. "Would you have sneaked me into your room as a teenager, McKay?"

With a quickness that still surprised me, he snatched me by my waist and pulled me to him. "You're damn right I would have."

My blood was warming and my skin tingling when the sound of my brother's truck rolled past the trailer and toward the shop in the back. Dad's truck right behind it.

And just like that, my heart plummeted to my feet. In two weeks there was a big radial race. Huge cash payout, not to mention a big points deal. If you wanted to race all season, you had to be there. I'd seen Aiden and Dad with their heads together for days now.

It hurt, more than I cared to admit, that they'd be racing in it while I was stuck here in Arkadia. Even New Breanna, with her lighter attitude and frequent sex with the super hot guy, couldn't look past that.

I refused to cry, instead I pulled from Noah's embrace and moved to the window in time to see Aiden push open the large bay door.

"Let's go see what's up," Noah said from behind me.

"I know what's up, and I really can't happily go watch them do it."

Before I could storm from the trailer, he wrapped me up in his arms again. "For once in your life, Breanna, just trust me okay?"

The softness in his voice wasn't something I'd heard from him before and it gave me pause.

"Fine. Whatever." I stalked out the back door and across the yard, leaving Noah to chase after me.

The biggest surprise in months was what I saw when I stepped into the shop. The 'Vette was there, bright paint and scintillating sponsor stickers. Aiden and Dad watched me, eyes earnest and eager as my gaze landed on one sticker in particular.

This one wasn't a sponsor's and it wasn't on the body of the car itself. The italic lettering in the bottom rear corner of the driver's window simply read—*Breezy*. The annoying nickname Devin had given me years ago, that my brother and Vic still tossed around whenever they could.

But that particular sticker should have read Aiden

Casey, as it had for years.

"What's going on?" I wasn't stupid, I could see what was happening. I just couldn't quite comprehend it. It's way harder than most people realize to wrap your head around your greatest dream coming true.

Noah's fingertips were warm on the small of my back. "See, I told you to trust me. It's easier to work on the car after work, if we live here already."

Something annoying and wet rolled down one of my cheeks. I swiped at it with the back of my hand and searched my dad's proud, happy face for any sign that this was some horrible, mean spirited joke. I saw none.

"Are you serious, Dad?"

"Hell yes." This from Aiden who smacked my dad on the back with an open hand.

I'm not sure if I ran or leapt, but I cleared the space between my dad and I in the span of a blink of my eyes. I jumped on him, like a little girl at Christmas, and hugged him for everything I was worth. "You're letting me drive?"

"Looks that way, kiddo."

I was laughing and crying at the same time when I hopped from my dad's arms. "Oh wow, holy shit wow."

The largest sponsor sticker was bright silver and black. Kaliq al-Nazir Racing. "No way!"

Noah was grinning. "Turns out, he was as annoyed by his older brother as anyone else. Decided he needed his own circus to ringmaster."

Dad came around too, emotion thickening his voice. "You made quite the impression on him. He called me, right around the time Aiden and I decided to enter you and the car into the radial race."

"I'm all for being a trick pony."

Aiden grinned. “I figured you would be.”

And in that moment, I was living my very best life—full tilt boogie.

A word about the author...

Leslie Scott has been writing stories for as long as she can remember. Currently, she lives and writes amidst her own happily ever after with her soul mate, son, and domestic zoo.

http://lesliescottromance.com/

Thank you for purchasing
this publication of The Wild Rose Press, Inc.

For questions or more information
contact us at
info@thewildrosepress.com.

The Wild Rose Press, Inc.
www.thewildrosepress.com

Lightning Source UK Ltd.
Milton Keynes UK
UKHW021610230720
367047UK00009B/523